The Hair Princess
and the
Hog Temple Incident

by

KRISTAN RYAN

California
USA

Behler Publications
California

The Hair Princess and the Hog Temple Incident
A Behler Publications Book

Copyright © 2006 by Kristan Ryan
Cover design by Cathy Scott – www.mbcdesigns.com

All rights reserved. No part of this book may be reproduced or transmitted in any form or by any means, electronic or mechanical, including photocopying, recording, or by any information storage and retrieval system, without the written permission of the publisher, except where permitted by law.

> This is a work of fiction. Names, characters, places, and incidents either are the product of the author's imagination or are used fictitiously. Any resemblance to actual persons, living or dead, events, or locales is entirely coincidental.

Library of Congress Cataloging-in-Publication Data is available
Control Number: 2004094876

FIRST PRINTING

ISBN 978-1-933016-07-8
Published by Behler Publications, LLC
Lake Forest, California
www.behlerpublications.com

Manufactured in the United States of America

For my grandchildren
Summer, Sierra, Savana, Tyler, Emily, Delaney, and Cidella

For hairstylists everywhere:
You make the world a better place through touch.

Acknowledgements

Thanks to Karen Novak and Paul Chabrowe for their faith, generosity, and support.

Thanks to my mother Regina Francis Thomas Ryan, who taught me to read and to love and appreciate great literature. Thanks also goes to Nellie Garbee for teaching me that a woman in her seventies and eighties could be as vibrant and full of life as any twenty-five-year-old. Mom and Nellie, this book is for you, too, wherever you are in the world beyond this one.

And, finally, thanks to playwright Paddy Gillard-Bentley for reminding me that hairstylists play a crucial role in the human drama by providing the one thing that human beings need the most—touch.

"There was something awesome in the thought of the solitary mortal standing by the open window and summoning in from the gloom outside the spirits of the nether world."
— *Sir Arthur Conan Doyle*

"Everything is a part of the truth, but it is not the whole truth."
— *Avatar Meher Baba*

Prologue

When the toddler showed up, I had been stuck for half the night in a nursing home, two hours from where I lived in Brooklyn, with a broken left ankle that hadn't been set and a shattered right knee that needed surgery. The EMTs dumped me in a dirty room where the floors were covered in white dust, the television's channel changer was broken, and the curtains on the windows were as dry and cracked as the Dustbowl in the 1930s. To make matters worse, the TV was stuck on a station that played funeral service music, and all I could see from the window was a hint of light from the parking area on the street below, so I had nothing to take my mind off my unpleasant situation. While I wasn't ready for a visitor, toddler or not, I was ready for something.

I had just finished a screaming match with Nurse Mary, who was assigned to care for me, or so she said.

"I need something for pain, please," I had asked her. "My ankle is killing me and my knee is no picnic."

"Honey bunny, you don't need anything for pain," she said. "I looked at your paperwork and there's no prescription. I'm sure the doctor knew what she was doing."

"I'm sure there's been a mistake," I said. "Please give the doctor a call and have her prescribe me something."

"Oh, I can't do that," the fat little hag said. "There's a doctor coming on duty in about five hours and if he thinks you need something, he'll prescribe it."

"Surely you don't think I'm making this up," I said.

"This is New York. People tell all kinds of stories around here," she said, leaving.

"Come back," I screamed.

"I have to get my knitting," she yelled back.

I lifted the blankets off my ankle that the ER doctor had wrapped in an Ace bandage. She said she had to pull the bandage tight to keep my ankle stable until I could be taken to x-ray again and another doctor could set it. I stared at my foot. My toes were blue and so swollen they looked as if they were about to explode.

"Somebody come in here and loosen this bandage," I shrieked. Thanks to the ER idiot, I was probably going to lose my foot. Just as I was going to scream like a banshee to get someone's attention, my shattered knee began a rhythmic throb that made me want to perform surgery on myself just to make it stop. Instead, I howled and yipped, hoping that by sounding like a dog, I'd get attention.

Sure enough, Nurse Mary-Quite-Contrary returned, knitting in hand. "Do you need something?" she asked.

"Yes," I said. "I need this bandage loosened and some pain killer."

"Well, you're not getting either," she said. "The doctor said you didn't need anything for pain, so you can't be in pain."

"Are you insane?" I asked.

"Are you?" she asked.

I growled and bared my teeth.

"If you're really in so much pain, why don't you pray to make the pain go away?" she said. "Ask God to give you what you need." She smiled and fluttered her eyelids, her thick black lashes sweeping up and down in a way that made me want to kick her.

"You'd better pray I don't get out of this bed and choke the life out of you," I shouted. "That goes for the doctor, too."

"Go ahead and try," Nurse Wicked said, smiling. "I'll sit here and knit while we see how far you get." She then wiggled her fat ass into an armchair in front of the window and began to knit what looked like an oversized stocking cap out of a shimmering, translucent thread I'd never seen before. If I hadn't been in so much pain, I might have been curious about it.

"Would you like some water before you get started?" she asked, knitting and purling.

I wanted to wrap the thread around her neck a hundred times and yank. "No, thank you," I screeched.

"Water is the one thing we make sure we have more than enough of. A body can never have too much H-2-O."

I heaved my pillow, a gray lump of scratchy manmade fabric, bouncing it off her forehead. Any nurse with the IQ of a worm knew a person could drink enough water to drown the brain and die. Ask any frat boy. It had been done before, and I was sure if I sent Nurse Nitwit to search New York's prison records she'd find a few doing time for making some pledge do exactly that.

"Well, well," Nurse Mary said, snatching up her yarn and leaving, slamming the door behind her.

When you live in New York and you're single, alone, and can't take care of yourself because you've been seriously injured, the hospital social workers get to decide what to do with you, even if you are as bright and alert as a thousand-watt bulb and they aren't. They get to exercise some power when poor slugs like me land in their clutches, and exercise they do. So there I was, Angelica Donahue, at the mercy of an over-educated, underpaid woman with too much power and good intentions who sent me to the Sunnyside Assisted-Living Centers of New York, a chain of homes for the elderly and infirm that had started in Texas, where I was from, and had recently moved to New York State. The nurse at check-in had told me their motto was "We Make Things Right," but when I asked why, if the chain had originated in Texas, I'd never heard of them, she told me college graduates didn't know everything and shouldn't have to. I forgot to ask her how she knew I was a college graduate, but then again, I had a few other problems on my mind.

From the time I arrived at Sunnyside, I had one goal: getting out of there and getting home. I couldn't walk or crawl to the window to fling myself to the ground seven floors below, so I knew I would have to resort to some other form of escape. Just as I was about to strangle myself with the bed sheets, the door to my room creaked open and in toddled a little girl, naked as a jay bird (as my mother used to say) and babbling non-stop in baby-talk, a language I've yet to master.

"Hey, there's a baby in here," I screamed, but nobody answered. I could hear someone down the hall groaning and the nurses gossiping about the patients, but the more I screamed, the louder the nurses and the groaning got until I finally gave up.

"So who do you belong to?" I asked, trying to sound scary and dangerous, hoping she'd cry and her mommy would show up to help me get back to my apartment, broken ankle, shattered knee, and all.

"Waa?" she asked.

"Where are your clothes?" I said.

"Da goo ma mimi."

"Oh, you're a big help," I answered, rolling my eyes.

"A doo mimi dada," she said.

"Sure," I answered, making a noose out of the sheet and slipping it over my head.

"Doo doo on you," she said.

Had she really said shit on me? Now I had a baby insulting me. "Shut up, you little twerp," I said, forgetting about the noose and remembering my cell phone. I could get out by calling my neighbor, who I didn't know but whose husband, I knew, was an orthopedic surgeon.

The damn phone was in the pocket of my coat, which was draped across a chair on the other side of the room. The least the kid could do was make herself useful and get it for me.

"Nice girly, girl," I said to the toddler.

"Ah soo mima bebe," she said.

Just my luck. She spoke a foreign language.

"Oh, googy tuff, tuff," she said.

"Googy tuff, tuff yourself and shut the hell up," I said. "You're no help."

"Fuckyoutoo, biggie doo doo," she said.

"What did you say?"

"Ooh, two booboo," she answered, pointing to my legs.

"That's right," I said. "I've got several big honking boo-boos."

The little girl giggled and said, "Ooh, bad boo."

As she spoke she appeared to be getting taller. I was going to tell her I didn't see anything funny about my broken leg and messy knee, but then I realized that I was probably talking to a figment of my imagination, and if Nurse Knit-a-holic came, I'd never get out of there. That's when I told myself that she had to have been conjured by my imagination, so I might as well enjoy the entertainment. Maybe I'd hallucinate I wasn't in pain, too.

"Are you growing?" I whispered, just in case we had a visitor.

"I am," she said, looking all of seven. Gradually, a t-shirt and pants appeared. "I'll dress myself," she said. "Maybe that will make you feel better." Suddenly, she was wearing clothes. Her long black hair braided itself. Ribbons appeared at the ends of the braids and she looked several years older. She pulled something out of her shirt and tossed it aside. A pink skin resembling her younger self crumpled to the floor.

"Old skin," she said. "I'm like a snake that way."

"No, you really didn't just shed your skin," I said, forgetting to whisper.

"Yep, sure did."

"I'm hallucinating," I whispered again, hoping I was talking to nothing.

"No, you're not," she answered.

"You read minds, too?"

"You'd be surprised by what I can do," she said, as a pair of sneakers appeared on her feet.

"You're not a snake, are you?" If I was hallucinating, my guess was I could imagine a snake as a person, although I didn't know how a snake would get into a New York City nursing home. I was pretty sure pets weren't allowed.

"No, I'm not a reptile. I'm a real person, sort of."

"Good. Then if you're a real person, would you please get my cell phone out of my coat pocket so I can get some help to get out of this dump?"

"You don't need it," she said.

"Are you related to Nurse Mary?" I asked. The night was going from bad to worse.

"Things aren't getting worse," she said. "They're going to get better than you ever thought they could, if you do what I ask." She grew a couple of inches taller and looked about ten years old.

"Listen, Alice, I need some help, not conversation."

"My name is James, thank you very much," she said, narrowing her eyes.

"Apparently, you're not very well read." I said, shutting my eyes.

"Let's not get personal," she answered.

My ankle was throbbing and my knee ached so badly I wanted to cut off my leg because a blade put to skin and bone would have made me feel better. I was sure of it. *Just let the pain subside and put me to sleep*, I wanted to say, but I was in so much pain I couldn't speak.

"You got it," James said.

When I awoke, there was a teenager sitting across from me in the chair where my coat still lay slung across the back. Her hair was in a black curly tumble over her shoulders and her t-shirt was so short it showed her belly-button.

I pinched my arm to make sure I was awake, because that's what writers always have their characters do to see if they're awake, and because I couldn't feel my legs anymore. I lifted the covers to see if I still had legs, and I was relieved to see I did.

James laughed. "I thought I'd give you some relief. You know, no pain?"

New hallucination, but still a talking one. "Excuse me, figment of my imagination, but since I'm imagining you, could you reach in the left-hand pocket of that coat behind you and take out the cell phone. I'd like to get—"

"My name is James," she said. "Don't you remember anything? I thought you'd be cool, but you are *so* not cool."

"Oh, yeah, right. You're the hallucination that grows and speaks."

"If you want to call me that, go ahead, but the truth is, I'm here to make things right."

There's that motto again. "Then get me to Beth Israel Hospital in Manhattan, get a cast on this ankle, and get my knee fixed, but most important of all, get me home."

"You always wanted to be a famous writer, didn't you?" she asked, aging until she looked as if she were in her mid-twenties. Her clothes changed as she aged. After a few minutes, she was wearing a pair of slacks and what looked like a pale-blue cashmere sweater that changed colors every few seconds.

"Cashmere?" I asked.

"Yes, but I can't decide what color suits me," she answered. The sweater changed from blue to pale yellow. Her hair was stylishly bobbed and she was wearing large, gold hoop earrings that looked fashionably correct with the yellow.

"Stop there," I said. "Yellow does it for you."

The sweater turned a rich, buttery color and stayed that way.

"You were always stuck teaching writing, weren't you?" she said.

"I wouldn't call it stuck. I liked teaching. Still do." Had I ever thought I was stuck? I couldn't recall saying anything like that or even thinking it. Teaching was fun, but now that I thought about it, it was time-consuming, low-paying, and not well-appreciated, as far as I could tell.

"You never had time to write that novel you told everyone you were working on." She sighed as if resigned to something out of her control. "Always the bridesmaid, never the bride."

"Something like that," I said. The truth was painful, but at least my legs didn't hurt anymore. I could have made time to write, but I hadn't, and now I was too old. Maybe I wouldn't have been famous, or maybe the *idea* of writing a novel was more appealing than the work involved in cranking out 80,000 words. I couldn't say.

"Too late for me now," I said, trying to figure out how to wiggle out of the bed and get to my phone.

"It's never too late," she said, rising from the chair and walking over to me.

"So you say. You're not real, so what would you know?"

"I'm real enough. I'm as real as you are, though the Hindus would say this is all illusion, so neither of us is real. Go ahead, touch me. See for yourself."

I lifted her hand. She *felt* real. I squeezed her fingers. Maybe Nurse Crazy Lady had given me medication while I was asleep. If that was what was causing this, then I was grateful.

"How about that cell phone?" I asked. As long as I was hallucinating, I figured I might as well try to get home. *Am I ever going to get out of this place? How much can one person imagine and still not get anywhere?*

"I'll make a deal with you. I'll tell you a story and you write it," she said. "It will be one of your best novels."

"Where's the deal in that?"

"You get everything you want as soon as you start writing."

"Nice idea, but how am I supposed to write a novel here, even if I wanted to?" I asked.

"On your laptop," she said, pointing to my lap.

Sure enough, there was a laptop, lit up and ready for me to write.

"Wow. This is some hallucination," I said, "but you forgot the writing table."

"No problem." James waved her hand and I was back in my apartment sitting at a large cherry desk with a new computer and a twenty-inch flat-screen monitor. Maybe I should have asked for a penthouse apartment and a cherry-red Jaguar.

"I'm ready when you are," she said.

"But it won't be my story. I mean, I didn't come up with it. It wouldn't be original."

"Holy goose crap," James said. "I can't believe you're worried about whose story it is."

Why was I complaining? This might be the first time in history somebody got something for practically nothing. I was sure I must have earned such an opportunity, even if I couldn't remember what I'd done.

"It'll be your story when you're finished," she said. "You'll have to trust me."

"Trust you? Are you my guardian angel?"

"I'd like to think so," she said, sounding more mature by the second. "But some would say I'm an imp or worse—and there's a princess and her sidekick who will be tweaked that I told you what happened in Hog Temple. But you'll be famous, just like you wanted to be, because it's a true story and people will believe it."

"A princess and her sidekick? What does that mean?" I asked, stretching my mended legs. She didn't answer, because the phone rang. It was my agent. I didn't even know I *had* an agent. As I said "hello," I looked for James to help me out, but she was gone.

"When do you think you'll be finished?" my agent asked, sounding exactly like James.

"In a couple of days," I said, wondering where those words had come from and how I knew what she was talking about. "I'm working on the prologue." I glanced at my computer screen and there it was: "Prologue."

"Just in time to pick up your Jaguar," she said.

I own a Jaguar? Had I already written the book? I must have. Whatever I had or hadn't done, I somehow knew I understood James's story as if I had lived all the parts myself. *Had I really had an accident and broken my legs? What was happening?* I closed my eyes.

When I awoke, it was three years later. Don't ask me how I knew it was three years later; I just did. I was sitting in my penthouse living room in front of the fireplace where a toasty fire flickered and popped. As I admired one of my recently published novels, James, aged about to eight, with her hair in braids and wearing a t-shirt, jeans, and sneakers, appeared beside my chair. "Hold me and read me your book," she said.

I sat her on my lap, knowing that long before I was done, she'd grow into an old woman and become much too large to stay seated there, but until that moment, I'd do as she asked. I lifted the novel from the table next to us, and with James snuggled in my arms and leaning against my shoulder, I read …

~SATURDAY~

1
Henry

Lou-Ella was gone and there was nothing he could do about it. If only he had said something to her about how much her friendship had meant to him before she died. But wasn't that always the way it was? You waited until your loved ones were gone to remember to tell them how much they meant to you and then you prayed for forgiveness for not having done so every night for the rest of your life. Oh, the failings of humanity.

Henry's life was full of "should'ves" and "could'ves" just like everyone else's. He hadn't gotten to know Lou-Ella like a real pal until they found themselves at Sunnyside. She had made the things he ruminated over having not done seem as if they hadn't been worth worrying about. She had been funny and optimistic, despite the stupidity of her caretakers. Now, life was a big, fat zero. Henry was so sick with grief he had to force himself to talk about something else.

"I'll tell you what a fling is," Henry Calhoun said to his friend, eighty-year-old Lee Donahue. "A fling is what I had when I was eighteen and shared more than one midnight risky-frisky with my mother's best friend, Isabella. She was only twenty-eight with a husband the size of a small mountain and the disposition of a rattlesnake, but my, my, my, being with her was worth every minute. And I was in love with that woman. You know, I built her a cabinet for her china teacups—hand-carved it and rubbed it down with Tung oil. It was the prettiest thing I ever built for anybody, and I was some proud to have done it, even if she and I were the only ones knowing where the thing came from. Sweetest time in my life, I have to say. Damn near killed me when she decided her old man was more to her liking." Henry gave a little shake, as if the memory had given him a shiver. "I thought I'd go to my grave a happy man back then, but I can see I won't. Now, I'm about as happy as an orange peel dropped in a corner."

Lee shook his head and made an "hmm" sound, but didn't look at Henry.

"Are you listening to me?"

"I always listen to you, Henry," Lee said, keeping his eyes on his work. "Hell, Henry. An orange peel can't be happy. It's an inanimate object."

"Thanks for the information, Lee. Don't you think I know that?"

Lee pasted another picture of his cousin's great-granddaughter in his scrapbook and then made a sound as if he were shaking off a chill himself. "You think they're trying to preserve us by keeping the air-conditioning up so high?" he said, wiping some glue on his pants.

"Nope, that ain't it," Henry said, pointing to a woman in her early fifties organizing art supplies at a corner table. "Most likely she is going through the change."

"You think?" Lee lifted his head slightly, squinted, and then went back to fiddling with the glue.

"Just listen to her," Henry said, looking around the room to see what the other residents were doing. "The woman flies off the handle about every little thing. That and she's hell-bent on making us as crazy as she is."

Henry had complained many times about the woman in charge of coordinating the residents' entertainment being too damn fussy. He suspected he had driven Hodges, his favorite orderly, damn near crazy by pissing and moaning about the room they used for arts and crafts being too small and too cold, but he knew Hodges couldn't do anything for him. Maybe he went on about the room to hear himself talk or to remind himself he was still alive. *Jeez, I don't know why I go on so*, he had said to himself on several occasions, but he did it anyway.

Hodges, the only staff member to do anything that mattered for the residents, had no great influence with management, as far as Henry could tell. Now that he was thinking of management, he couldn't remember anyone, not Hodges, the Princess, or that sourpuss at the front desk ever mentioning meeting with the folks in charge of the place—whoever they were. "Nobody knows anything around this place," Henry enjoyed telling anyone who would listen, but the residents had tired of hearing him and the staff only waved him off—an act that irritated him no end, he often told Lee.

What tweaked Henry worse than being ignored was being treated as if he were just learning how to use Crayons. He wasn't interested in art for children or by children, even if the crafts lady, or Activities Coordinator, as she called herself, thought children meant folks in their seventies and older. He was a man, and men needed *men* things to do. How about a weight room? How about a bowling alley? He squirmed in his chair, trying to get comfortable, but he couldn't because the soft thick cushions curled up around him, making him feel as if he were slipping away. Every few seconds he would try to scoot closer to the table. He was going to have to say something to Hodges about the chairs being a pain in the ass to get in and out of, too.

"Y'all, listen up," screeched the Activities Coordinator. "I brought y'all some glitter-glue and some happy face stickers to put around your photos." She reached deep into the pockets of her red apron and brought out a handful of bright orange stickers with those smiley faces that Henry thought were stupid. "These will liven things up a bit and put a great big ole smile on your faces. Now, Mr. Calhoun," she said, "let's turn that frown upside down." She stuck two fingers in the corners of her mouth and lifted them until she had a smile. "If you're good, I'll give you some balloons to share with your great-grandchildren."

"If she isn't careful, I'll tell her what she can do with those balloons of hers," Henry said to Lee, snarling. "I'll tell you what I'd like to turn upside down. I may be eighty-five, but I ain't forgot I'm a man through and through." As soon as the words "upside down" were out, he was sorry. The visual he conjured by imagining himself in a compromising position with this woman whose name he'd never bothered to learn was enough to send him to church—and church was the only place he'd ever been bored. Nope, he didn't need any more boredom than he already experienced daily.

"Ain't a day goes by I don't forget something," Lee laughed.

"Look at that woman with her pasty white face and her long stringy hair—and that ugly gauze skirt. She thinks it's still nineteen-seventy-four. I take it back—what I said about turning her—you know."

"I don't look at her much," Lee said, examining the wooden tabletop.

"What do you say we bust out of this place, Lee? I been thinking about it all day. Let's have a little fun. Take a ride across country on the rails. Come on. What do you say?"

"Are you crazy? A week on the road without my mashed prunes and I'll be stopped up like a cheap toilet."

"No, you won't. That's just a lie young folks tell us old folks to make us afraid to leave home. They need to keep us close, so they can keep an eye on our money."

"What about my walker?

"Your walker? You ain't going to need a walker in a boxcar, Lee. Sheesh."

"Forget it." Lee said, rolling his eyes. "Oh, yeah, that's right. All I've got to do is give you a couple of minutes and you'll forget what you were talking about. We both will."

"Funny," Henry said, clicking his false teeth. "You're hilarious."

"I ain't going anywhere, Henry. I like it here. I'm happy."

"I heard the receptionist—what's her name?"

"Day manager."

"What?"

"Her name is Katherine and she manages the day shift," Lee said. "She ain't a receptionist."

"How in hell do you know that?"

"I'm not dead, Henry, in case you haven't noticed. I get around. That girl has worked here forever. It might be about time you learned folks' names."

"Don't lecture me, Lee Donahue," Henry said, examining his fingernails and then slapping his hands on the table. He sure wasn't in the mood for a lecture from Lee on getting to know the staff, especially with breaking out of Sunnyside on his mind. Holy smokes, he wouldn't give a calf's hide for anybody in the place besides Lee, the Princess, or Hodges.

"Leave me alone, Henry, or I might have to bust you in the mouth," Lee said, balling up a fist and shaking it in Henry's face.

"You just do that, Lee, and some nurse will shoot you so full of mood-altering juice you'll sleep for a month."

Lee dropped his fist and looked around.

For the first time in their fifty-year friendship, they were about to fight over a dang woman. Henry patted Lee's fist. "Put that away, old man. We ain't fighting over a woman this late in our lives."

"You need a knuckle sandwich in general, Henry. Always have."

"What kind of way is that to talk to a friend who's trying to help you in your last days? I just wanted to say that that Miss Katherine of yours told Hodges that for a man my age, I'm surprisingly lucid, and being the lucid man I am, I say we hit the road."

"Come on, Henry, we can barely make it to the shitter without Hodges's help. We don't have any business jumping on a train, much less thinking about it. I can't remember the last time I jumped on anything, now that you mention it."

A group of residents pointed at Henry and Lee and giggled. Henry winked, although he wasn't sure who he was winking at because his eyesight had deteriorated. "That's what happens when a person ages," a nurse no longer working there had said when he had asked why his sight was going wacky. He wasn't sure she was telling the truth, but whatever the reason, he was afraid he was going to have to get glasses with lenses as thick as double-paned windows. Eighty-five or not, he still had some vanity left, even if his vision was shot to shit.

"Now y'all hurry and finish up. Right after crafts, we will be showing *One-Hundred-and-One Dalmatians* in the TV room and I know y'all don't want to miss that," Miss Activities Coordinator said, giving Henry the evil eye—at least he thought that's what she was giving him. "Do you, Mr. Calhoun?"

"No ma'am," Henry said, turning to Lee. "That's just what I'm craving to watch. How about you, Lee?"

"You are such a comedian, Mr. Calhoun," she said, whipping around so her back was to him. "There's no need to scream."

Henry checked the volume on his hearing aid. It was down so low it was almost off, but just a second earlier it had been fine. "Damn," he said, fumbling with the volume until he could hear snorts and sputters coming from some residents working at a nearby table. The women covered their mouths, stifling their laughter, irritating him all the more and making him itchier than ever to get out of Sunnyside. *This home is my coffin*, he would have said if there had been anybody around who cared. The realization that he and Lee were as good as dead to the outside world made him want to kick the walls and scream for help, but what would be the point in that? If he behaved badly, he knew a disinterested and overworked nurse would sedate him, so he decided to keep his anger and disappointment to himself, as he had gotten in the habit of doing early on.

Henry turned to Lee breathing as heavily as a man might if he were about to fly out of his skin and said, "Come on, Lee. When I was a youngster, I rode a horse from right here in Hog Temple, Texas, into the heart of Mexico. Just like in that movie the Princess smuggled into us the other night—the one about those boys who rode into Mexico to break horses and got themselves in all kinds of deep ca-ca. You remember that one, don't you?"

"I remember that pretty little Mexican girl."

"Yeah?"

"Oh yeah," Lee said, "I sure enough do—"

"I guess you boys need something to do," the coordinator snarled, slamming a tube of red glitter-glue on the table in front of them. She pressed herself against the table between the men and yelled into Henry's ear. "Here's some glitter-glue for you, Mr. Calhoun. That ought to make you happy."

Henry snatched the tube off the table, ripped off the cap, and squeezed it so hard its contents shot onto the tabletop in one shimmering glob. He dipped two fingers in the glittery goop and, using them as if they were artists' pens, sketched a likeness of Rodin's *The Thinker* in the middle of the table. "Now that's artwork," he said to Lee, grinning.

"Am I going to have to get the orderly?" the coordinator asked, as Henry's version of Rodin's *The Thinker* glistened and pulsated in the bright light.

Henry looked closely at the drawing just in time to catch it wink, or so he thought. This place was driving him crazy and now he was seeing things. He had to get the hell out. "Do as you please," Henry said. "That's just what we need around this beef cooler. A little excitement before the meat wagon shows up."

"Mr. Hodges," she screamed, heading for the door, "take Mr. Calhoun to his room. He is misbehaving again." But just as her back was to him, Henry smacked her on the fanny with a loud whack, leaving glitter fingerprints on her skirt.

The exasperated woman turned back to Henry and wagged her finger in front of his leathery face. "I have complained more than once about your freshness. You are now officially banned from Saturday Night Craft Fling, and that's all there is to it. No movie for you, either."

Mr. Hodges, his keys rattling, trudged across the room toward them. Henry saw him coming, but chose to watch Lee dip his fingers into the same shiny red puddle and then give him pointers on how best to use the glue to make the designs in the book Miss What's-Her-Name had given him.

Lee smeared the glue over the bridge of his nose and across he cheeks. "Check me out, Henry," he said. "The heck with the book."

"Good work, my friend, but you missed the tip of your nose."

"Don't be a critic, Henry," Lee said, going back to his scrapbook. "You always were a critic. Couldn't a soul do anything right but you."

"You best pull that burr out of your butt, Lee," Henry said, but Lee didn't answer. Yep, it was time for both of them to ditch good old Sunnyside, because as far a Henry could tell, they were sinking fast.

Hodges had been at the Center since Henry and Lee's first days at Sunnyside. They had been dropped off by their fat, over-educated, money-grubbing relatives, as Henry liked to point out. Now that he was thinking about it, it made sense that he'd have a grandson, and Lee would have cousins many times removed whose reason to be was to count the money the two of them had made over the years. After all, Hog Temple had been named after its first settlers—the men who had made millions mining gold in California and the whores who had accompanied them to this part of Texas filled with rocks, trees, and—the real treasure—water.

His grandfather told him that the miners and the girls had come to Hog Temple, at the time unnamed, to build their own version of heaven and had hidden their gold, only pulling it out on New Year's Day to celebrate their good fortune. Outsiders had dubbed the place Hog Temple because over the years the original settlers soon grew fat in girth and wealth.

"Our forefathers worshiped their gold and rejoiced over their good luck and beautiful land," his grandfather had told him, "and outsiders were jealous. Even so, the name Hog Temple stuck. You come from common folk, son, but they were hardworking and as honest as they could be expected to be, so you should be proud." And proud he was, but of himself and Lee, not his useless grandson and Lee's cousins.

How Hodges had landed in Hog Temple, Henry hadn't figured out. Hodges was a skinny man without any fat or a first name, as far as Henry could tell. At least Henry had never heard anyone call him by a first name.

The way Henry remembered it, the day Samuel, his overstuffed grandson, had packed him up and moved him into Sunnyside, he had been ready, He had been itching to get away in those days, too, especially from the sweaty, stinky house where he had to listen to Sam's ongoing summation of whatever news show was splashing across the TV screen. Back then, he had complained, too, mostly about the smell of cat piss and the kitty fur that covered the furniture, the food, and him. God, now that he was thinking about it, the dozen or so cats Sam kept, and the endless dull nights glued to the news channels, didn't seem so terrible, because Sunnyside was no better, maybe even worse, and he knew Hodges knew that was how he felt. But now Lee had called him a critic and said that he always had been and that had stopped him cold. Was he nothing more than a cranky old complainer? Had he become the stereotype of an old man in a nursing home? No, no—his complaints were valid. Nobody could have lived happily in either place. Lee had to be wrong—dead wrong. *Oops, there's that word again.*

Henry looked Hodges over. The fellow was a clean man. Hodges once told Henry he was twenty-eight and had never been further than the Hog Temple City limits, but Henry couldn't remember knowing any of Hodges's family. If Hodges had been telling the truth back then, then that would explain why the tattoo on his right forearm read, "Home is where the heart is," because who wouldn't have loved Hog Temple with its hot summers, its cottonwoods, and its super-sized Wal-Mart?

On his left forearm Hodges had a tattoo of what looked like Jesus with the words "Jesus ain't Santa Claus" scrawled just below the beard. Lou-Ella Whitehead, Henry's friend from childhood and now former resident of Sunnyside, used to swear that the tattoo, called Mr. Tattoo by the staff as well the residents, winked at her now and again, but how that could happen and what "Jesus ain't Santa Claus" meant was as much a mystery to Henry as why he, Henry Cole Calhoun, had lived as long as he had. Too bad Hodges was a man who stuck to the rules, at least the major ones, anyway. Henry could have used him to help him escape.

"How do I look, Henry? Hodges?" The bridge of Lee's nose and cheeks were dotted with shimmering specks of red.

"Mighty fine, sir," Hodges answered. "Now, the two of you come along to your rooms. The arts coordinator lady is in some kind of state and y'all know she's on the edge of no longer being able to contain herself. She's on the other side of being a spring chicken and worrying there ain't no place for her."

"There's a place for her, Hodges, but it ain't here," Henry said.

"Don't be unkind, Mr. Calhoun. That's not like you," Hodges said.

"You don't know him like I do, Hodges," Lee answered.

"What is wrong with you, Lee?" Henry asked.

"Nothing. I'm right as rain, but in case you haven't noticed, time is running out for some of us — the name Lou-Ella ring a bell?"

Lou-Ella. It rang a bell, all right. Henry was missing her like crazy and she hadn't been gone even a day. Turning to Hodges, he said, "There's no need for the crafts lady to worry about what I think. You can tell Miss What's-Her-Name she don't need to worry about nobody thinking she's a spring chicken. Hell, everybody under sixty looks like a spring chicken to me."

Hodges laughed. "You don't want the poor woman to have a stroke on account of you two — do you?"

Henry and Lee shook their heads.

"Mr. Calhoun, grab that walker and give your buddy there a hand. Y'all don't need to worry me or anybody else by having Mr. Donahue fall down and crack a bone."

Henry grabbed Lee's walker, handed it to him, and whispered, "You want to die in Hog Temple, Texas, in the Sunnyside Assisted-Living Center? Is that how you want your life to end?"

"No, I do not, but I don't see what other options I got."

"I do. Let's make a break for it."

Mr. Hodges had his back to Henry and Lee. Without turning around to look at them, he walked toward the door. "Come along, gentlemen. Don't make me have to come get you."

"Let's head for Mexico," Henry whispered.

"What?" shouted Lee, cupping his ear. "This thing is crackling and popping. Can't hear you no more."

"Let's head for Mexico," Henry shouted back. "Holy smokes, Lee, you're acting like every dang old person I ever saw."

"There's no need to yell," Hodges said. "Turn up your hearing aids. You're not heading anywhere but to your rooms, so come along."

Lee turned up the volume as ordered, but Henry didn't.

"We'll break out of here one of these nights soon and get us a ride to the train yard," Henry whispered in Lee's ear.

"How are we going to do that?" Lee asked, walking slowly beside Henry, talking into Henry's ear. "They got this place wired up like Ft. Knox."

"That's what we are, ain't we?" Henry whispered back into Lee's hearing aid. "Gold in a sack of skin and bones. I hate to say it, but it's Hodges's job and the duty of the other folks who run this deposit box to make sure we die and stay dead and then make sure the insurance people are notified right off. Can't fault them for doing their jobs. That fat, blubbering fool of a grandson of mine can have the money. I just don't want to go out watching Disney movies, eating baby food, and listening to Miss Activities Coordinator, or whatever she is, rave about the benefits of Crayons over colored markers. I want to meet the Big Rancher in the Sky doing something that don't involve cutting and pasting."

"I'm with you," Lee said, leaning on his walker as they shuffled down the hall behind Hodges toward their rooms, taking their own sweet time.

"The Princess will help us. I know she will."

"What are you boys whispering about?" Hodges asked.

Henry grabbed Lee to keep him from tripping on the nubby brown carpet.

"I've had enough trouble out of you two to last me a lifetime," Hodges said. "Especially you, Henry Calhoun, so please, boys, please, don't be causing any more ruckuses around here. Please."

Henry could tell from the way Hodges's chin twitched that he wasn't really mad, but he wasn't in the mood to test him because he knew before long he was going to get Hodges in a twist for real.

"Don't you worry about a thing," Lee answered. "We are planning on being good as gold from now on. Cross our hearts and hope to die."

"Shut up," Henry said, smacking Lee on the arm. "We ain't hoping to die. What he means, Hodges, is that we'll be as good as girls in church. Yes, sir. You can count on us."

"Here's something that will perk y'all up," Hodges said. "The Princess will be here tomorrow. She said to tell you boys you're her first clients."

Henry and Lee look at each other and grinned.

"Mighty nice of her to spend her Sundays fixing hair instead of only coming on Wednesdays. She don't get paid for the extra day, you know," Hodges said, opening the door to Henry's room, or "suite," as Sunnyside advertised it.

"Come on, Lee, let's sit a spell," Henry said. "I got a couple new books I'd like to show you."

"I need my magnifying glass, Henry. You know I can't read nothing without it."

"I'll get it for you, Mr. Donahue." Hodges said. "You all have a seat and I'll be right back."

As soon as Hodges was out of sight, Henry turned to Lee. "What's the matter with you? I wasn't really planning on reading. Now get in here and sit."

"I'm sorry, Henry. I thought that's what you were up to. I forgot for a minute what we were talking about."

"I can see you're going to be a big help," Henry said, dropping into an armchair by the bed, thinking about how accustomed to his mess of a room he had gotten over the years.

Henry's room was crammed full of gum wrappers, newspapers, magazines, comic books, stacks of old *Wall Street Journals*, and maps of Texas and Mexico. Every few months, the staff locked Henry in the cactus garden while they cleaned his room. He didn't mind sitting with the cactus, but he hated folks rummaging through his belongings. Who were they to say what was worth keeping? As soon as the attendants and cleaning crew were gone, he'd begin collecting all over again because it made him feel a part of the world outside the center.

Quilts given to Henry by the families of deceased residents were piled on Henry's bed, and a collection of photos of Henry wrangling horses when he was seventeen stood in hand-painted clay frame on a bedside table next to a blue plastic telephone with red oversized numbers on white plastic squares. A desk sat in front of a picture window overlooking the street-front parking lot. Henry had a single bed, a battered pine dresser with a mirror, a TV with a used VCR, and a bookshelf bending in the middle from the weight of the Louis L'Amour westerns he had collected over the years. A Donald Duck calendar hung on a hook by the bathroom door next to a picture of Henry's daughter Angelina wrangling horses in the same corral where Henry had broken his first thoroughbred. Angelina was seventeen when that picture was taken, but was long since deceased, killed in a riding accident at eighteen, racing her twenty-one-year-old husband through the desert. Her horse had stumbled into a ravine breaking his neck and hers, and leaving behind Angelina's baby boy, not two months old.

Even Henry's cat had died of a broken neck. Sometimes life was full of ironies, he thought. His daughter had died a month to the day after his wife, MaryLuz. All that remained of Angelina was her now chubby thirty-eight-year-old son Samuel, a boy Henry had raised alone after the child's father found himself a new girl and left Texas, once and for all. Samuel was no prize, but Henry had loved him as best a man like he could, even if his thoughts about the boy suggested otherwise. At least that's what he told himself.

As an adult, his grandson Sam was an embittered middle-aged, self-employed accountant, living alone with his computer and seven cats to keep him company. As far as Henry could tell, the boy didn't even get dressed anymore. The last time Henry had visited him, his grandson had spent the day sitting in front of his computer dressed in only his jockey shorts, talking on the phone with his clients, and looking at naked girls on the Internet. If only I could have spent more time with the boy, Henry thought, but running the ranch took so much of my time—but I guess there's no point in beating myself up over what I sure as hell can't change.

"Sit down, buddy," Henry said to Lee. Lee did as he was told. "Now listen up. We can't miss the Princess. We have to remember our appointments. Hodges might get busy and forget, so we have to do something to make sure we don't. Talking to the Princess is critical to getting off this kiddy farm."

"Yeah, so what are we going to do?"

"We're going to write messages to ourselves on our bellies."

"What in the world for?"

"You got to pee about a hundred times a day, don't you?"

"Yes, but I don't see—" Lee said, looking, to Henry, more than bewildered.

"Me, too," Henry answered. "And that's why we're writing on our bellies." Henry was always coming up with some plan or another that Lee couldn't understand, and Henry knew it. "Remember that movie the Princess brought us about that fella who couldn't remember who he was, or what he had to do, or where he had been and so he tattooed himself all over to be able to remember?"

"No," Lee answered. "Too far back."

"Good God Almighty," Henry said. "That was just three days ago. I'm eighty-five and I remember."

"Well, I don't," Lee said, raising his voice.

"Never mind the movie, then. I liberated a marker from the activity room for a time just like this. Lift that shirt up and let me write the information on your belly."

"Let me do it. If you do it, it'll be upside down," Lee said. "Besides, you might get tangled in my hair." Lee lifted his shirt, baring a potbelly covered in white curly hair.

Henry pulled the black marker from his pants pocket and handed it to Lee.

"This ain't going to stain my good shirt, is it?"

"Hell, no. And hurry up. Hodges will be back any second."

"What am I supposed to write?"

"Christ Almighty," Lee said. "Write 'Hair Princess, 3 P.M., Beauty Room, Sunday.'"

"What if I forget tomorrow is Sunday?" Lee asked, writing on his belly.

"I'll remind you," Henry said. "Now hurry up and give me that thing."

"Henry, can I ask you something?"

"Yeah, but make it fast."

"You ever think about Maryluz?"

"Not much. I think more about Angelina, when I'm thinking. Why?"

"Just wondering," Lee answered. He finished scribbling the words between folds of skin and tufts of hair and handed the marker to Henry. "Did you have everything you wanted? I mean, if you died tomorrow, could you say you were satisfied with the things you had?"

"You know I didn't have everything I wanted," Henry said. "What about you?"

"I had all but one thing," Lee said. "Guess I can't complain."

"Why are we having this conversation, Lee? You ain't planning on kicking the bucket tonight, are you?" Henry asked.

Lee got this way sometimes and Henry found it unsettling. Death was only a breath away and everybody at the center knew it; there was no way not to know it. Sometimes Henry thought they should rename the center "Sunnyside Death House: Here today, gone tomorrow," but he kept this thought to himself—always. *Death house is right. Was I having a spell this morning when was I out by the pool? I swear Lou-Ella was nineteen again and wearing that old hat she got on her birthday about a hundred Julys ago. Maybe it was that crazy little thing she was wearing. Was that a bathing suit? Thong. That's what that piece of string was. And I know I saw her wrestling with a lasso trying to get it to cooperate, but what was she planning to do? I don't remember. Did I ever know? I'm sure I saw her waving that pistol her daddy gave her when she was fourteen. I didn't even know she still had that thing, much less had it here at Sunnyside. And where did that baby-*

faced fella come from? I've never seen him around before. And where did he go? Did I think him up, too? I can't ask Hodges. According to Lou-Ella, you can't trust anybody around this place. Now who am I going to talk to besides Lee, whose brain just plain shorts out twelve times a day? I've got to get Lee and me out of this bone yard. I'm so in need of a normal damn minute I'm starting to lose my mind. I swear I am.

There was a knock at the door.

"Just a minute, please," Henry called out, writing quickly on his stomach: HP, 3 p.m., B.R.

"Come on in," Lee shouted as Henry threw the marker under the bed.

Hodges entered carrying the biggest magnifying glass Henry had ever seen.

"Good God, Lee," Henry said. "How blind are you? That thing is the size of a dinner plate."

"I use it to read fine print on contracts," Lee said. "Like the print that says how they decide when to send us to a nursing home."

Henry grimaced, his leathery skin folding in tiny layers around his eyes.

"It took me a while to find it, but here you are, Mr. Donahue," Hodges said. "Give me a buzz when you're ready to go to your room. I'll be at the front desk cleaning a spill."

"Yes, sir," the two men said, patting their bellies. "Yes, sir."

"Sure is a pity about Mrs. Whitehead, ain't it, boys?" Hodges asked, staring out the picture window.

"It's more than a pity," Henry said, shaking his head.

"I'm going to miss Lou-Ella. I reckon she's been here as long as me and Henry," Lee said. "Why, I remember—"

"Don't start with that remembering business," Henry said, looking around as if he expected someone else to appear. "You don't remember nothing."

"You got any idea where that rope disappeared to, Mr. Calhoun?" Hodges asked, turning around and looking at Henry and then at Lee. "Because Miss Katherine is having a hissy-fit over that thing."

"Nope," Henry answered, snapping back. "It went its own way during the fuss. Maybe one of those EMTs picked it up."

"No, they didn't. I asked them," Hodges said, turning to go.

"What's the big deal about the rope?" Lee asked.

"The uppity-ups are worried one of y'all will take a hankering to—" Hodges used a finger to draw a noose around his neck and pretended to hang himself. He made a choking sound. "You know what I mean?"

"Gotcha," Lee said, looking at Henry.

"What are you looking at me for? I don't have it," Henry said, trying to appear as innocent as he knew he really was. "You might ask Miss Arts Coordinator. She don't seem a bit too stable to me."

"Already did." Hodges turned to leave. "See you boys later," he said, closing the door behind him.

"Henry, you were the last one to see Lou-Ella alive," Lee said, after Hodges was out of hearing range.

"Yep, and what a sight that was."

"I miss Lou already," Lee said, rubbing an eye.

"Me, too, buddy."

"Yeah?"

"Sure do." Henry grinned, but not because Lou-Ella was no longer with them. "I wish you'd seen her in that itty-bitty thong. It was something else. And those red cowboy boots. Oh, yeah. That's why we've got to get out of this place."

"Because of Lou-Ella in a thong and cowboy boots?"

"No, because she went out yipping and yelling and trying to lasso me with that rope everybody wants. You notice Lou-Ella didn't drop dead hanging over her glitter-glue, did she?" Henry asked, shaking his head. "And we ain't either, my friend. One way or another, we ain't either."

2
Katherine

As far as Katherine Wilson could tell, her day as the receptionist and temporary weekend manager at the Sunnyside Assisted-Living Center could have started on a better note. Things would have been fine, she kept telling herself, if her day hadn't begun with finding eighty-three-year-old Mrs. Lou-Ella Whitehead lying dead next to the pool dressed in a pair of red cowboy boots, a thong bikini, and a gun tucked in a holster that hung from a belt around her sagging waistline.

"Her flabby old stomach is probably just as loose as that belt," Katherine had said to the EMT. "And that bruise, right there at the base of her throat—it's probably a hickey, or worse." The EMT hadn't responded, but had gone about his work as if finding dead women in their eighties with hickeys on their necks and wearing thongs was a daily event. *Well*, she wanted to say, but didn't, *this nonsense might be something you're used to, but it most certainly does not happen in my world—at least not until today—and nothing like it had better happen around here again.*

By the time Katherine got to Lou-Ella's body, somebody had put a pillow under her head and a matching red, white, and blue-sequined cowboy hat over her face. Katherine assumed Lou-Ella must have been wearing the hat along with the rest of her outfit, but these days nothing was for certain, so she couldn't say.

If you asked her, Katherine would be quick to tell you she wouldn't be caught dead *or* alive dressed like any old Western yahoo after ten too many cocktails, even though she was a shapely sixty-six with a belly as flat as a chalkboard and a behind as firm and tight as any forty-year-old. At least she, Katherine Louise Wilson, could get away with wearing such a naughty getup, unlike that old fool who had to be wrapped in black plastic, loaded into an ambulance, and driven straight to the morgue.

And what was she doing with one of those ugly blue-black bruises a girl got back in the 1950s when a boy sucked on her skin too hard to show her how much he wanted her? What was *that* about? Everybody knew those hideous symbols of a man's conquest had gone out with bobby socks and drive-in movies. This was the twenty-first century, for heaven's sake. What was wrong with people? If this was what dementia did to folks, then they could just take her out back and shoot her, because she was going out of the world in style and with some dignity.

The way the other residents told it, Mrs. Whitehead had died trying to lasso Mr. Henry Calhoun, a cagey coot only too happy to accommodate her request for one last roll in the hay—providing he could remember what it was he was supposed to do. Mrs. Whitehead had dropped dead in mid-swing, the old folks had whispered to Katherine from behind withering, yellow-skinned hands cupped around their mouths.

"The nerve of that horny old bastard," she had said before thinking, setting the whole crowd scurrying away as fast as their walkers, canes, and anti-slip chenille slippers would allow. She had gasped at the realization that she had been so candid, but her shame was short-lived. "If folks think I was put on this earth to tend to frisky old men and women," she had yelled after them, "they are dead wrong. I don't know what I was put here for, but that ain't it. Go on, run away. The whole lot of you."

It doesn't matter what I say around this bone palace, she reassured herself later. By the time those old pains in my ass turned around, their minds were probably on who was going to get double-dessert at lunch, or some such hooey old folks trouble themselves over.

In any case, this unsavory business, in Katherine's opinion, was the fault of Miss Lilly Beale, better known as the Hair Princess, the girl whose job every Wednesday was to cut, wash, dye, and style the residents' hair. If you asked her, Lilly ought to think about doing something about her own ratty hair. What girl in her right mind would dye her hair Crayola red, blow dry it until it was the texture of straw, and then style it with what anyone with half a brain would swear had been a Weed Whacker?

Katherine was glad she wasn't Lilly Beale, because if she were, she'd have a heck of a lot more to worry about than an unpleasant curse word or two tossed in the air. After all, wasn't the motto on the sign hanging over Sunnyside's main entrance *We Make Things Right*? Hadn't she heard Lilly once tell Lou-Ella Whitehead to "let the girl in you loose"? What was right about that? Worst of all, Mrs. Whitehead had taken that silly girl's advice and had gone one-hundred percent loosey-goosey. Instead of things being made right, like the sign promised, they had gone as wrong as wrong could get. "Tsk, tsk," Katherine clicked. *When you get right down to it, I'm not Lilly Beale and I'm not a princess, hair or otherwise, so I might as well forgive myself for cursing in front of those old folks, because letting a curse word or two slip is not committing a crime—and it's not something I normally do around here, not like some people.*

Every time Katherine thought of Lilly, she got steamed. She knew the girl hadn't directly killed Lou-Ella, but she'd bet a year's pay the Princess was responsible for putting those two old folks up to such wickedness, which was a way of killing her indirectly. Even if the authorities couldn't find fault with the Princess or charge her with murder, she knew damn well God would. Nobody had to say a word. She knew whose fault it was, as sure as she knew it was a sunny day—and in Hog Temple, it was always a sunny day. Always.

Katherine also knew she'd need the help of someone without any connection to the center if she was going to prove the Hair Princess was the "burr under the saddle of wrongdoing," because there wasn't another Sunnyside employee or a single resident who would rat that girl out. Not now, not ever.

She rifled through the pile of paperwork left by the former manager who'd disappeared without even giving one day's notice, much less two weeks. Some of the residents swore the woman aged throughout the day—came in a youngster and then turned into an old lady, got real sick and left—so maybe that was why she quit. Whoever heard of something so ridiculous?

Katherine once asked Hodges and Lilly if they had met the woman, but they said they never had. Naturally, she didn't believe them. Of course, everybody also knew the residents of Sunnyside imagined all sorts of things, so whatever the sick, decrepit, and nearly dead said didn't matter, couldn't matter. Maybe the woman was plumb sick to death of the place and had to die to get out of here. Katherine laughed. *I am too damn funny.*

Whatever the reason the manager had taken off, Katherine wished they'd find a new one soon. She didn't want the job, had never wanted it, even when her boss had suggested it a few days before Miss Unreliable showed up, took the work, and then disappeared. "You're so organized," her boss had said. "You're just the one to control the gates." He'd said this as if she were a levee of some sort. The idea that she could be compared to something that rigid, even if it did open and shut, made her uncomfortable. If there was one thing Katherine hated, it was having to record deliveries and incoming and outgoing visitors. Being the gatekeeper was for someone else, someone more attuned to worrying about the world at large.

Katherine picked up the visitor logs and flipped through them. The last month of logs had to be filed before she could leave for the day. She sighed twice: first out of annoyance and then second because she knew she might as well resign herself to her new status. Life had been so much easier when she had been the administrative assistant for the Director of Resident Records—in at nine, out at four-thirty, and four weeks vacation a year. Until now, life had been good.

Katherine opened the page for Mr. Henry Calhoun. He hadn't had a visitor in over six months. She flipped over to Mrs. Lou-Ella Whitehead who, on the other hand, was a different story. She'd had all kinds of male admirers from the man who did laundry on Saturdays to the pizza delivery boy from around the corner, to the professor down the hall who brought her the chocolate his daughter sent him, even though he had to have help to find his way back to his own room, and God only knew how many more. From the looks of the men lined up regularly at Lou-Ella's door, you'd have thought she was some kind of love goddess, but of course, that was silly. Who could possibly find an eighty-three-year-old sexy?

Just the thought of what Henry and Lou-Ella might have had on their minds turned her stomach. And what had they been planning to do with a loaded gun? Imagine that: a real gun strapped to the hip of a woman older than dirt, and loaded, no less. And the rope—even a fool could guess what she had planned to do with that. But where had that thing gone? Lord, all she needed was for some poor thing to get tangled up in that wayward piece of cowboy history, fall into the pool, and drown.

Hell fire and damnation. She suddenly realized that the mark on Lou-Ella Whitehead's throat could have been—*Holy Mary*—a rope burn. Great God in Heaven, she thought, shuddering. *Mrs. Whitehead could have been strangled* – murdered – *while I was in charge.* Katherine whipped out a piece of paper from under the counter. Terrified, she scratched out her orders to Hodges as fast as she could.

Hodges,
Find that missing piece of overgrown hemp before the center loses another resident and we find ourselves looking for new jobs. You get your butt in gear because we don't know what might have taken place here –

Katherine had almost written "yarn" instead hemp, but if she had, Hodges or somebody else she worked with might have accused her of being a knit-o-holic, which she was. Working at a place like Sunnyside required that a person be obsessive about something when not on the job, and knitting was about as harmless a thing she could indulge in as she could think of. If asked, she wouldn't have minded saying so, but today she had bigger things troubling her. Just as Katherine was about to suggest in her note that Hodges speak to the sheriff about the missing rope, she heard a *tap, tap, tap* coming from outside. A deliveryman pushing a cartload of bottled water stood at the front door of the center, tapped on it, and waved to Katherine through the smoky glass. She stuffed the incomplete note into Hodges's message box, fluffed up her hair, licked her lips, gave him the sweetest, most inviting smile she could muster, and buzzed him in. There's no point in worrying about where the rope is now or what people think of my relaxing hobby, she told herself as she pointed to where the water was kept—but she knew there was a point, and knowing that the whereabouts of the rope was a mystery yet to be solved gnawed at her as she watched the deliveryman struggle with his cart.

This was the fellow's first week on the job and only his second visit, so Katherine couldn't expect him to remember where everything was; even so, it was annoying to have to remind him, because she was a busy woman with a lot on her mind. Besides, he had arrived late in the day just before she was getting off work. His only saving grace was that his babyish face was so soft and delicate she found it hard to yell at him. Baby faced or not, one of these days, she promised herself, if the boy didn't pull himself together and act like a professional, she would sit him down and give him a good talking-to.

After the morning's events, Katherine was looking forward to leaving on time. It was four in the afternoon and Saturday to boot; it was time for her to head home, and still nobody had found the rope that had been missing from the time Lou-Ella hit the pavement. At least that's what Henry Calhoun told the coroner. If Katherine had to bet on it, she'd say nobody would ever find that thing, but even so, the missing twine called to her, wouldn't leave her alone. She decided she'd better pick up the phone and give Hodges an order to locate the rope as soon as possible. It was one thing to have a resident die, but to possibly lose another one through just plain carelessness—well, that was unacceptable. Besides, when the owners found out about the thong, Lou-Ella, and God only knows what else, they'd get their knickers in a twist and the whole Sunnyside staff would get their asses fired, including the silly Princess, who probably needed her job as much as anybody.

Whether she was crazy about her current position was irrelevant. Katherine needed to work, and she was damn well going to keep her position one way or the other.

Katherine picked up the intercom pager and shouted into the mouthpiece, "Mr. Hodges, call the front desk. Call the front desk immediately."

Some cranky, addle-minded rodeo-wannabe had probably stolen the rope to keep it for what Katherine's mother used to call "a memory builder," without understanding that it might well be evidence in a crime. Not that he (and it had to have been a man, because rope snatching was a man thing to do) would keep it long, because memory was a quickly passing thing among the residents of Sunnyside. She knew the drill. The thief would wake up one morning, find that overgrown piece of string, throw it in the trash, and then not five minutes later be found sobbing into his pillow about the rope that had meant so much. Before you could say, "Pour me a shot of Jack Daniels," you'd find the culprit caught up in a crying jag dredged up from a youth he no longer had, although he couldn't tell you what the thing had stood for, or where he got it. Katherine shook her head. She had seen the same scenario repeated too many times—the doctor would have to be called in and the poor slob, whoever it was, would have to be given medication to calm his nerves. At least this was the scenario she hoped would be played out this time, but lately life in Sunnyside had been unpredictable, and today her insides were knotted, a sign that something bad was just around the bend. *What a damn waste of worry time. All this upset because that skinny girl with the lip ring and the pierced cheek puts crazy ideas in old folks' heads while fixing their hair.*

A few minutes later, Hodges appeared at the front desk. "Hodges," Katherine said. She didn't have time for niceties. "I want you to locate that missing rope—now."

"Miss Katherine," Hodges said "you know I always do what you ask, but I am up to my nose hairs in folks needing help getting showered, so while I am as hopped up on finding that rope as anybody, I am shorthanded right now. You got to believe me when I say I can't drop what I'm—"

"Stop. Stop it, Mr. Hodges," Katherine snapped. "We're going to get our rear-ends yanked out of this place if somebody gets hurt with that thing, so find it before I get back here Monday morning. And as soon as you have the thing locked up someplace safe, call me at home and let me know. Get yourself and that Mr. Tattoo of yours to work. And quit twitching so much. It always makes that damned Jesus tattoo of yours look as if it's winking and blowing kisses. See what I mean? There it goes again."

"I ain't twitching, Miss Katherine," Hodges said. "And the tattoo ain't a picture of Jesus, even if folks think it is."

"Listen, I don't have time to argue with you. We don't know how Mrs. Whitehead passed any more than we know why you twitch."

"I *don't*."

"Hodges, that rope might belong to the scene of a crime."

"There ain't no point in troubling yourself about that rope, Miss Katherine, 'cause it ain't no weapon," Hodges reassured her. "The rope wasn't used for anything other than to lasso Henry Calhoun. That was all it was used for and there ain't no question about it."

"Is that so, Mr. Hodges?" Katherine asked, making sure her tone was such that Hodges would know she didn't believe a word. "And how on God's one green acre would you know that?"

"I ain't lied to you yet, now have I?" Hodges grunted. "Excuse me, but I got to go, Miss Katherine. I got a fella here fixing to race buck naked down the hall."

Katherine stared as Hodges rounded the corner of the nearby hallway. How in hell did he know he had a fella "fixing to race buck naked" anywhere? That was the problem with everyone she had worked with at Sunnyside—they all thought they knew more than she, or said they did, when they most certainly did not. *And that Hodges—what a weirdo.* He was likable enough, but there was something off about him, not in a bad way, but off nevertheless. The residents had often accused his tattoo of coming to life, of blowing kisses and winking at them when Hodges wasn't looking, which was why she had started calling it Mr. Tattoo. She was the first one to give the thing a name—a move she took pride in. *I am so clever.* If asked, even she would have sworn she saw it wink, but because she was sure that such a thing wasn't possible, she decided what she had seen was his skin fold over at the eye when he flexed his muscle, or twitched, as she put it. There was no point in dwelling on that silly ink splotch on his arm, she reminded herself. Whatever Hodges was doing, she hoped he would find time to locate that rope so she could dispose of it safely, even if that meant turning it over to the police.

Katherine glared one last time at the receiver resting in its cradle, brushed her hands together as if she were knocking dirt off her palms, and looked up just in time to see the night manager pulling into the parking lot. "Done," she said, relieved to finally be able to leave.

As she packed up her purse and snuck an unopened box of tissues belonging to Sunnyside into her knitting bag, Katherine kept an eye on the night manager, who was outside, fiddling with a sprinkler gone haywire. She glanced at the yarn unraveling in her bag and admired the blue-green ripples of fuzzy wool bunched in loops and swirls against the box of tissues. The yarn reminded her of the pattern of wet spots the crazy sprinkler had left on the sidewalk and of the Gulf of Mexico and the summers she spent with her mother and older sister splashing in the cool water under the sizzling Texan sun. There was nothing like Padre Island in July.

The sound of spraying water and the ball of yarn made her tingle with the memory of seawater beading up on her arms, legs, and face, her body thick with suntan lotion slapped on by a mother worried about her girls' fair skin being aged by a warm but relentless sun.

"Drink lots of water and wash that sea salt off your skin—and rinse off that sweat, too," her mother used to say. "Salt water will kill you once you're out in the world and no longer in here." Her mother had patted her abdomen. "Once you're outside, though, you'll have to rely on fresh water, the essence of life."

Katherine had thought at the time it strange that the one thing that gave you life and nurtured you could later kill you. It didn't seem fair or right, and now that she was an older woman herself, she still found it wrong, so wrong.

"Nature's perfect product," her mother had always called the water from their spring. "What that means for those of us in the world—well, I will leave that for you two to grow up and figure out," she told Katherine, while adjusting her beach chair. Had her mother been keeping a secret? What was it that her sister and she were supposed to uncover? Katherine had been too afraid to ask because her mother had never tolerated lots of questions. Later, when she asked Mora, who was ten years older, what their mother had meant, she only shrugged her shoulders, rolled her eyes, and picked at the polish on her toenails.

"What could be better for the body and soul than pure, clean water?" Katherine remembered her mother asking one afternoon on the beach. Her mother had pointed to the opened Thermos she held in her hand and offered it to Katherine. She couldn't think of an appropriate response, so she nodded, grabbed the Thermos filled with spring water her mother had brought from home, and took a big gulp. Now, companies bottled water and charged a fortune for it, and Sunnyside was having water delivered just so visitors could sip on something that made them feel—what? Good that Sunnyside was spending their money on fancy water for them to drink while their relatives dried up like peaches left on a windowsill too long?

Katherine stared at the night manager, who had gotten the sprinkler back in working order while she was daydreaming, and watched as the water sprayed in a circular direction, giving life to everything in its path. Now that she thought about it, every sweet memory she had from childhood was tied to water. For a second, she was overcome with sadness. Maybe one of these days she'd start drinking eight glasses of water a day like her mother had long ago recommended.

Meanwhile, there was no time to relive the past or decide whether she needed more water in her diet. It was time for somebody to put a stop to the twaddle spreading amongst the residents like a viral infection. She knew nobody within a fifty-mile radius would dare say a word against that no-good, high-heel wearing, hair-clipping piece of trouble called the Hair Princess, so she was going to have to be the one. Here she was in the prime of her life, and now this. Just the thought of having to take charge of such an unpleasant chore made her mad. Damn mad.

Old folk were old folk, and they were supposed to settle into their golden years and stay old until their skin dripped off their bones and their brains wilted under the strain of dissolving cells. They were entitled to age gracefully, damn it, and not die trying to recapture the lost pleasures of youth. That's why women went through menopause and middle-aged men sat around watching exercise shows with skinny girls in tights sticking their behinds in the air as they stretched and jumped.

Did those silly boys with their failing eyesight and their tender innards think those girls barely out of diapers who were famous for shoving their breasts, bottoms, and bared midriffs at the viewers and offering the promise of a glimpse of skin were really going to deliver what those muddle-brained men hoped for? No, they were not, but every last one of the male residents had cable in their rooms—the center had cable TV all over the place. Ridiculous, she thought, not to mention disgusting.

The way Katherine saw things, old men had one job, and that was to tend to their bellies—bellies that would eventually grow so big their grandchildren would swear they were about to deliver triplets. Men in places like Sunnyside were supposed to be grateful for the generosity of the women they once loved, not go for one last hidee-ho out by the swimming pool in broad daylight. And women—eighty-something women were supposed to be free from men playing grab-ass and oohing over the size of their rah-rahs.

Old age was the time for women to settle into flat shoes, utility bras, and comfortable panties that didn't creep up the crack of your you-know-what. Old folks were supposed to be enjoying the reward of years of hard work by lounging in front of the TV, eating Jell-O, and pasting pictures of their great-grandchildren in rainbow-colored scrap books like the ones the activities lady brought to the Sunnyside Saturday Night Craft Fling twice a month. That girl, the

Hair Princess or whatever she called herself, had no right to interfere, no right to mess with nature and the way of the world. No, she certainly did not. Why, Lou-Ella Whitehead once told her that the Princess could whip up a salad that made everyone see you as a pouty-lipped sixteen-year-old virgin. If that wasn't the craziest thing she'd ever heard, she didn't know what was.

If I was running this place, she told herself, folks would sure as heck be attending to a different set of rules and those dimwits who let Lilly Beale take over the hair salon — well, their heads would be spinning from the speed with which I'd put an end to that little reign.

When Katherine got home, she was going to put the events of the day behind her. Tonight she just might have to have three glasses of wine instead of her normal two.

3
Lilly

The last time Lilly worked on the residents' hair, Wednesday night, nothing unusual had happened, as far as Lilly could recall. She had washed their hair using her favorite shampoo, Betty's Orange Soufflé, a locally made shampoo that promised to "bring life to hair, old or new," and she had towel-dried their tender heads, using towels Hodges had washed using three times as much fabric softener as necessary to ensure that no one's scalp would be rubbed raw. One of the many things she admired about Hodges was his empathy for the residents at Sunnyside and the care with which he attended to their needs. As they had cleaned up the shop, Hodges had grown steadily agitated until he blurted, "Lilly, we haven't heard from you-know-who in a long, long time."

"What's a long time, Hodges?" Lilly had asked.

"Thirty years or so—you know, in this time," he said, waving an arm around the room to indicate earthly time. "I'm thinking it's been too quiet for too long. That ain't right. Not that I'd like to have to clean up their messes, but it don't feel natural."

"I wouldn't worry myself over a good thing," Lilly said. "Maybe we're finally free of the Jameses and their nonsense."

"Thirty years ain't more than a blink, Li, but they've never kept their noses out of our business for as much as a blink. That's what worries me."

"You aren't missing them, are you, Hodges?" Lilly laughed.

Hodges shook his head, but didn't laugh, so Lilly stopped laughing and patted his back.

Maybe what was bugging Hodges was the same thing that had been eating at her for days, but she hoped it didn't mean that the Jameses were on their way. Their silence was a good omen, an indication that the Jameses had moved on. She hoped her agitation, and Hodges's, too, was nothing more than a shift in the universe, the natural evolution of beings in the throes of rapid change, but before she could say this to Hodges, a soft rapping interrupted their conversation.

She turned in the direction of the knocking, twisting her lip ring slightly, hard pressed to return to her role as hairstylist. But the tapping was persistent, so even though it was after hours, Lilly responded to the knocking. Two of her regular customers, Mrs. Neely Gill and Mrs. Lou-Ella Whitehead, peered back at her through the door, tapping their knotty fists against the glass, obviously in distress.

Hodges opened the door.

"I know the Princess is closed already," Mrs. Gill gasped, clinging to Hodges, "but my hair is flat in the back. Flat, flat, flat and I can't stand it. Miss Lilly took care of Lou-Ella here. She said she did, and Miss Lilly did it after hours."

Hodges glanced back at Lilly, who waved them in.

Mrs. Lou-Ella Whitehead, a tiny woman barely over five feet tall with a head full of bushy white hair, patted Mrs. Gill on the arm. "Now, now, you don't need to worry."

"We can't have Mrs. Gill with a flat head, can we?" Lilly asked, taking her by the hand, leading her over to her hairdressing station, and sitting her down in the soft red vinyl chair. "Tell me what I can do for you."

"We have dates," Mrs. Whitehead said. "With two hotties—I heard someone on TV say that that's what all the young girls are calling good-looking fellas—and I can't go out looking like this."

"Is that right?" Hodges asked.

"Sure is," Mrs. Whitehead said.

"And who might you ladies be passing the evening with?" Hodges asked.

"We've got plans with Henry Calhoun and Lee Donahue." Lou-Ella said, laughing and slapping Mrs. Gill on the back.

"I hope you two aren't planning on wearing those boys out," Lilly said. "Mrs. Whitehead, I believe the back of your 'do has gone wild." She pressed a hand against the back of Lou-Ella's head, pretending to adjust her hair. In actuality, she was calling out her suffering. Lilly absorbed the pain Lou-Ella carried—her "albatross," Lilly knew Lou-Ella would have called it, if she were able to talk about her loss to anyone besides her friend Henry. The memory of the death of her child fifty years earlier was burrowed under her skin like a tick. Because her grief, sorrow, and guilt were lodged so deep, Lilly shook slightly as she drew them out. Her teeth ground together, and she ached so violently it was as if her own bones were dissolving.

The child's death could have been prevented had Mrs. Whitehead not been occupied by a bottle of bootlegged whiskey and a boyfriend not worth his weight in dog biscuits, as Lilly had so often heard her say. By Lilly's estimation, Lou-Ella had suffered enough. Because these exorcisms took time, some of the guilt would eventually creep back, but it would not return with nearly as much strength as before. Little by little, Lilly would eliminate every last bit of Lou-Ella's agony, making them both happy, all under the pretense of doing her hair.

Lou-Ella shuddered and then sighed.

"Have anything you want to tell me, Mrs. Whitehead?" Lilly asked. This was her test question. The answer would reveal whether or not Lou-Ella had relinquished the guilt she cradled like the child she had once borne.

"I did, but I can't think of it just now," she answered. "It'll come to me, I'm sure of it, and when it does, Miss Princess, you'll be the first to know."

Almost eliminated, Lilly thought. One more session ought to do.

"No, Princess. I don't have anything to tell you, unless you want to know what movie Henry and I are going to watch, or whether or not we're going walking in the moonlight." She laughed again. "You want to know, Mr. Hodges?" she asked.

"No, ma'am," Hodges answered. "As far as I can tell, a woman with secrets is a woman most of the fellas around this place want to get to know better, so it's best you keep your lips sealed."

"Lou-Ella is part of the 'in crowd'," Mrs. Gill said.

"What do you mean, Neely?" Lou-Ella asked. "The way things have been going around here, pretty soon I'm going to be the whole damn crowd."

Mrs. Gill looked for a second as if she were going to cry, but Lilly stroked her neck. With each passing of her hand, she lifted Mrs. Gill's fear and replaced it with a calm not felt often enough in the universe, at least in Lilly's opinion.

Mrs. Whitehead chuckled. "Didn't mean anything by it, Neely."

"Lou-Ella has a secret," Mrs. Gill said, smirking, but before she could make another sound, Lou-Ella threw her hand across her friend's mouth.

"You'd better hush up right now," Lou-Ella snapped.

At the sharpness of Lou-Ella's tone, Lilly tried to read what she was thinking, but all she got was a craving for strawberry shortcake, followed by an unpleasant memory of the time Lou-Ella was twelve and received a painful switching from her grandmother for breaking a china plate during a temper fit.

"Secrets make you more desirable, they say," Hodges whispered, putting his head between the two ladies. "Keep it under your hat."

"You are too young to know what you're talking about," Mrs. Gill said.

"Mr. Hodges is how old, Miss Lilly? All of twenty-five?" Lou-Ella asked.

"A little older," Lilly said, leaning Mrs. Gill back in her chair and washing what was left of her hair. If she only knew how much older, Lilly thought. "Twenty-eight, he tells me."

"He is barely out of diapers," Mrs. Gill gasped.

"Come on, Mrs. Gill, you know that ain't the case," Hodges said, patting her hand. The practically bald woman blushed and patted his hand in return.

Mrs. Gill had no hair on the back of her head. Not a strand. Her scalp was pink and sprinkled with freckles. A couple of white curls hung over each ear and a few sprigs of hair stuck straight out of the top of her head. "There's nothing wrong with my hair, is there?" Mrs. Gill asked in what seemed to Lilly to be a moment of remarkable lucidity. "I'm bald, ain't I?"

"I'm afraid so, Mrs. Gill, but I was thinking of you just the other day and I bought something just for you."

Hodges grabbed a soft cotton towel from a stack nearby and gently dried Mrs. Gill's head while Lilly went to what she called her "goodie closet" and retrieved a snow-white wig with delicate shoulder-length curls. "What do you think of this?" She held it under the light.

"It's gorgeous," Mrs. Gill answered, sitting up. She took the wig from Lilly and fingered the curls. "Looks just like my hair when I was a girl."

"I thought it might," Lilly said "Let me plump it up a bit and you'll be good to go."

"What's this going to cost me, Princess? I only have three dollars." Mrs. Gill pulled a change purse out of the side pocket of her dress, opened it wide, and showed the contents to Lilly. Three gold one-dollar coins stared back.

"Well, you're in luck, Mrs. Gill, because that's exactly the price of your new 'do."

Mrs. Gill giggled. "Can't say as I believe you, Princess, but I'll take your word for it."

"Guess you'll have to," Lilly said, combing and curling. Mrs. Gill's conscience was clear, but it had taken more sessions than Lilly had anticipated getting it that way. She was almost ready for the next step, but not quite.

Ten minutes later, Mrs. Gill was out the door on the arm of Lou-Ella Whitehead, wearing her new hair and a new smile.

"You sure ain't no financial genius," Hodges said, once they were alone again.

"I'm not trying to be," Lilly said. "That's not my job, or yours, either."

"Yeah, yeah," Hodges answered. "But you live here long enough, you start worrying about 401Ks, health insurance, whether your teeth will last a lifetime, and what you're going to leave to your kids."

"We're ethereal beings, Hodges. We're Protectors, not people," Lilly said, enjoying the sound of the word "ethereal." But as she passed a mirror and caught a glimpse of herself, even she had to admit it was hard to remember. "And we can't have children, remember?"

"The worry business is catching, Lilly. You know it is."

Lilly ran a hand through her red spiked hair.

"You'd better be careful, Li. Speaking for myself, I feel more like them everyday."

"No, Ha, you don't," Lilly said. "You can't."

"Think what you will," Hodges answered, "but I'm telling you I do. Mind your thoughts—you'll see it sooner or later."

"You're imagining things, Hodges," Lilly said.

"That's how we got here, ain't it?" he answered.

"Be that as it may, we aren't them," Lilly said, her stomach coiling around itself in what Hodges always referred to as a "worry knot." They weren't supposed to worry. Hodges and she were beyond worry. They were in the world, but not *of* the world, so where was the origin of this worry?

"You save them old folks, and what do you get for it? You turn into one." Hodges shook his head.

"No. I haven't, and you haven't either," she said. Lilly was no savior, either, not really. She considered herself a simple soul doing the only thing she knew how to do and that, in her mind, kept her humble. She twisted the new diamond piercing her cheek and gave her lip ring a little wiggle. She was young like Hodges, only she and Hodges were older than any of the residents, employees, or even the owners. "How old are we really?" she had asked Hodges the week before. He couldn't remember—not even his tattoo could remember, and if anything could have recalled their true ages, it would have been Tattoo.

Even if she had known how old they were, it wouldn't have mattered. What was age when you could be any age you wanted? Hodges and she "were," and always would "be," as far as she knew, and life would go on as usual until time came to a screeching halt, or until the universe, and all its many universes, rotated in a new direction—if such a thing were possible.

What amazed Lilly was that for the first time during the eons she had been in the world, she felt sad about the things Hodges and she could not do. She didn't want to grow old and die, and she didn't want children because heaven knew humanity as a whole was work enough, and she certainly didn't want the troubles of having lovers because the whole relationship business humans had to go through frightened the wits out of her. But something special roiled about in the human process of loving, living, and dying, and she knew it. For the first time in her long life among people, she wanted to understand exactly what their experience was from their point of view. For the first time, she thought she might be feeling envy or regret, and she wondered how that was possible.

Maybe this really is what regret feels like. Maybe Hodges is onto something. Maybe the human habit of worrying is catching. Maybe the whole range of human emotion is like a virus—once it latches on to you, there's no cure. Maybe the things that wore down Lou-Ella, Henry, Lee, and the others are beginning to wear us down, too. Maybe we've been here so long we're imagining that we're human. Maybe, maybe, maybe. Lilly shook her head. At least their lives were back on track; at least the Jameses, or whatever they were calling themselves now, were out of the picture, or seemed to be for the moment, and she had managed to right a number of mistakes Hodges and she had made. At this point, they were in good standing with their overseers and she planned to keep it that way.

But that had been Wednesday. Here it was Saturday afternoon, and Lou-Ella had slipped to the other side with her guilt partially intact. Lilly had not saved her from an emotionally painful passing, and knowing that Lou-Ella had dropped her body carrying the sting of a life lived wrong, at least in Lou-Ella's mind, sent Lilly into fits. This incessant nagging that she should have done something, that she could have done more and hadn't, shocked her more than anything else about the incident.

Lilly didn't care about thongs or sex or the fact that Lou-Ella had died—all creatures on Earth had to die—nor did she care about the ways people found to connect with or to comfort each other in order to relieve themselves of the pains associated with living. The problem was that she hadn't helped Lou-Ella, not to the fullest, and she couldn't stop wondering, couldn't stop reviewing Wednesday night's events. Why had this happened, and where had she gone wrong? After all, no one in her charge, in all the time she had been on Earth, had slipped away without Hodges's or her help.

Lilly had to admit something had been heading toward her for a long time. As the collective unconscious raced toward consciousness, she knew the universe was changing. She had felt it coming, felt it in her bones, felt the unknown swirling, twirling, and winding its way toward them—and this thing, whatever it was, had disturbed her sleep and hovered over her, much like the memories of youths misspent hovered over so many residents of Sunnyside. And now whatever it was had made its presence known. Lou-Ella had died before her time under Lilly's watch, and while the coroner had seen nothing unusual in her passing, Lilly and Hodges knew everyone at the center had felt the rumblings of something ominous simmering beneath them.

Earth was where Hodges and she had first been imagined. Earth was the place where souls spun from the untamed thoughts of a God still imagining a self connected across time and multiple universes, knotted themselves into silver webs containing the whims of a supreme being not yet fully realized. When they awoke, they had been confused and fresh, like human babies are when they first arrive, but with a power growing within them that would one day surpass the power of all the other creatures; thus, they had been born in their own way with no understanding or sense of their own supremacy. At least that was how it had been in the early days, and thus they were humble.

When the gathering of ethereal beings began among humanity, Lilly and Hodges found themselves face down in the gritty dirt, in a place and in bodies previously unknown to them.

Until the second they felt the first pang of hunger and thirst, they had been nothing more than a wisp in the eye of God—if they had existed at all.

In the early days, they had been charged primarily with the care of the humans, creatures they neither understood nor wished to understand because it was all they could do to understand themselves—at least that was how Lilly remembered it—so how, they wondered to each other back then, could they be held accountable for anyone other than themselves? Thus the two had ruminated over the best way to carry out their duties—until they happened upon *Them*. But it was the yet unimagined who would eventually cause the trouble yet to come, the unimagined who simmered in the human unconscious, who once imagined could spring loose the essence of all creation, and who would test Lilly and Hodges's strength, and the testing would never stop—as Hodges would remind Lilly at the least little sign of trouble.

These entities Hodges had named *Them* had been born, Lilly suspected, from the darkest, most troublesome region of humanity's unconscious and were, therefore, vile in her estimation. They had to be cast out of the world. "Our job, as I see it," she told Hodges, "is to protect humanity, even from itself, if need be."

Hodges and she, new to life and encumbered by the bodies in which they found themselves, combined their power as they understood those powers, which was barely any power at all in those days, compared to what they would come to know. Yet, with those meager combined powers, they had remanded *Them* to the outer regions of the worlds, to that place of neither time nor light.

During the great battle that had precipitated their exile, *Them* conjured up three spirits whose only *raison d'être* was to free *Them* from beyond the boundaries of time and propel them back into the earthly world, and thus back into the hearts and minds of humanity, to create chaos. Once released, however, these niggling spirits reveled in their freedom and came to realize their free will. The three lost their fear of *Them* and did as they pleased. Doing as they pleased, they soon decided, meant abandoning their duties and leaving *Them* in the place where they had been cast by Lilly and Hodges, who were then called Li and Ha.

It was during the time human beings were learning to walk upright that these three reckless, undisciplined renegades with nothing but time on their hands took to tormenting Lilly and Hodges for no reason that Lilly could surmise, other than to amuse themselves.

Centuries had passed and now here Li and Ha were as Hodges, an orderly, and as Lilly Beale, hair dresser, at Sunnyside Assisted-Living Center in Hog Temple, Texas, on the edge of Big Bend National Park and the Mexican border, still protecting humanity from itself, an unending chore made complicated by those pesky troublemakers. Their job had never gotten easier, as Hodges had hoped it might. To the contrary, their work had grown more difficult with the passing of time. Lilly had once predicted this would be how things went—and it was these difficulties she ruminated over as she sat on her porch staring at the cottonwoods.

What Lilly hadn't said to Hodges back then was that as a result of humanity's undisciplined and immature consciousness, the next few million years would be filled with newer and bigger terrors, none of which they could adequately prepare for. But those beings yet to come would arrive with powers possibly greater than any Hodges or she might wield. How she knew this she couldn't say, but it was her conviction that she was right in her vision of the future that strengthened her resolve to stay alert and tend to her job to the best of her ability.

This time around, Hodges and she were not only in charge of protecting and making things right for the residents of Sunnyside, they were also bound to an eternal game of high jinks initiated by the Three Jameses, those three pesky spirits whose only joy, she had concluded, was to make as many people as they could as miserable as possible.

As far as Lilly could tell, Hodges and she hadn't done a great job of mastering their powers, but they had gotten by with a minimum amount of embarrassment. They were down to only a few occasional mistakes. That was better than…there was no need to delve into their many early errors now. The others like them, who could rewrite memory or rearrange history or even cause groups of people or things to reconfigure themselves, having mastered their particular gifts, took great pleasure in pointing out the snaps and pops of a command gone wrong, especially when it came to the two who made the most mistakes: dear old Hodges and Lilly, herself. But this was not the time, she thought, to dwell on the musings of others. Hodges and she had larger, more pressing problems at hand. At least the Jameses, as far as she could tell, weren't part of these recent troubles—not yet, anyway. But there was Katherine, the temporary day manager who wasn't taking her job as seriously as she ought or as seriously as she would have to one day. What to do, what to do, Lilly ruminated.

Lilly and Hodges had had their share of run-ins with spirits feisty in their confusion and spirits seeking entertainment at the expense of humanity. They had dealt with them swiftly, creatively, and with force, but whatever was about to be unleashed was unlike anything, Lilly suspected, that had gone before. She was unusually apprehensive. Even Katherine was more agitated than usual. So what had happened? Lou-Ella had died under her watch and out of her control. Eventually Lilly was going to have to help Katherine, who hated Lilly and who referred to Hodges as "Hodges and Mr. Tattoo" in less than flattering tones. Yes, she was going to have to have Katherine uncover the secret she had hidden from herself, and that was probably going to shock the poor woman silly.

Lilly sat on her porch thinking over what had happened the Wednesday before while watching two rabbits hop among the rocks dotting her front yard. She found her psyche tuning itself with acute precision into their rabbit frequency. The rabbits, tiny brown bunnies with oversized ears, stopped and turned toward her, their hearts beating so fast and hard it was as if she were listening to a chorus of white water pounding the banks of a North Texas river. *What's wrong?* they asked telepathically.

Lilly knew that if Hodges had been there, he would have assured them all was well in the world. He would have coaxed the tiny bundles of bone and fur into the open and fed them carrots or some other vegetable to their liking. He had a way with animals. They were drawn to his goodness, she thought, just as the old people in Sunnyside were. But she wasn't Hodges, and she didn't have time to tend to anything other than her own troubles—tonight she wanted to know why this new thing swelled in her gut—the feeling that all was lost in this one death. Perhaps there was a clue somewhere in her memory that would reveal the *why* of Lou-Ella Whitehead's untimely end.

What did I miss? What was the clue? How did this take place without my knowing it was coming? she asked herself over and over as she sat watching the bunnies. *Is this what guilt feels like?* She was gripped by fear, the kind of fear that steals your breath, that says to be careful, and shouts, "Look right here, right in front of you." *See what's right in front of me? What does that mean? What if the Jameses had changed their minds and rescued* Them*? What if they had gotten loose? After all, Hodges and I cast* Them *out in the early days when their powers were much less than they probably are now.* Had those hideous contemptible monsters finally broken free and somehow found their way back?

Don't ask us, one of the bunnies said. *Just give us some food.*

There is one way to find out—if Lou-Ella has "the mark," the real mark, it will be the sign they've returned. She glanced at her watch.

Food, the little creatures shouted, thumping their feet on the hard dark dirt. *"We're hungry."*

"Yeah, yeah," Lilly said, grateful for the distraction. "I heard you." Where was Hodges when she needed him?

4
Katherine

Katherine's apartment was sweltering when it should have been almost as cold as a meat locker. She threw her purse on a nearby chair and rushed to the thermostat to check the temperature. Ninety degrees. *What the hell is going on?* She examined the digital automatic timer to see what time she had set the air conditioning to go on, but the timer had never been set. *What?* She could have sworn she'd set it before she went to work. *Damn.* She had been looking forward to a nice cool apartment, pouring herself a tall glass of wine, and relaxing in front of the television with her knitting. She had a new knitting book written by a couple of twenty-something New Yorkers, whose following consisted of college girls across the nation. Katherine was itching to read the sweater patterns they claimed you could knit in two days.

Girls were knitting in class and, according to the book, on the subway, in their doctors' offices, and on their way to school and back again. Administrative assistants, college professors, dental assistants, and even girls in their teens had given up smoking, chasing boys, chewing bubblegum, going to Weight Watchers, and watching MTV to knit sweaters, hats, purses, afghans, and dresses. As far as Katherine could tell, the union of needles and yarn was going to result in fewer teen pregnancies, fewer cases of lung cancer, and a nationwide lessening of female angst. Folks are finally getting somewhere decent, she thought.

"Knitting is the rage, the new art," the authors of another popular knitting guidebook, *Your Knitting Vacation,* told a Dallas reporter, "and the rage is growing at such a rapid pace only God and the tax man can predict where our store will be in six months. We've had to expand three times in the last year."

Katherine was proud of herself. She had always said knitting was more than an experienced woman's hobby. *Isn't that just like me?* Katherine stood a bit straighter. *I am light years ahead of my time.*

She looked around her living room. Coral-colored afghans, turquoise-blue slippers, electric-yellow shawls, and pillows of alarming shades of greens, blues, and cantaloupe—the colors of the waters of the Gulf of Mexico and its inhabitants—were piled on chairs, in the corners, and in oversized wicker baskets designed originally to hold dirty laundry. Even the curtains over the dining room window had been knit with fine hot-pink cotton. She admired her handiwork, wiping the sweat off her brow. *I am such an artist. Somebody ought to give me a reward.*

"Hello," a deep voice said from behind her. "I'm here to reward you for a hard day's work."

Katherine gasped, turned, and stepped away from the direction of the unfamiliar voice. A tall gray-haired man with the blackest-bluest eyes she had ever seen stood with his head and one leg sticking through the opened doorway. "Excuse me," she said. She could have sworn her door had been designed to automatically lock behind her once it shut after entry. She hadn't even heard the thing open.

"I'm sorry about the heat," the man said, stepping inside her apartment. He was dressed in snug fitting jeans, a red-plaid short-sleeved shirt, and cowboy boots. He carried what appeared to be an oversized tool kit, black with orange handles. He set the toolkit on the parquet floor, stepped confidently on the nearby carpet, and stuck out his hand. "James James James," he said, smiling. "Folks call me the Three Jameses, but that's not quite fair because I have a younger brother named James—he's the youngest of us—and a sister named James James James, also." He chuckled. "Together we make the Three Jameses," he said with considerable pride.

"I had a sister, but she passed away when I was kid," Katherine said *Mora Frances was her name. It must be nice to have brothers and sisters you get to see.* "She was a lot older. And my parents gave her a name of her own." *Your daddy must have been as crazy as that fella on TV who sells indoor grills and who named each one of his children after him. How silly is that? Besides, by your telling, you are really the Nine Jameses, and that's even nuttier.*

"Some folks accuse my daddy of thinking he was some kind hotshot, or some kind of wannabe, all because he named us after himself," the Three Jameses said, "but my father was around years before that fella, and he was bigger than any movie star or grill salesman will ever be."

Katherine was about to ask how the heck he knew she'd been thinking about that grill salesman when she realized that he probably got that all the time, so, instead, she said, "I guess folks make that connection a lot."

"Sure do. I've come to expect it," he said.

Mr. James was weathered, his skin softened like fine leather. He could have been her age, or ten years older—or even ten years younger, for all Katherine could tell. She had the sense that Mr. James had been around a long time but, at the same time, he had the air of youth—a timeless quality, as her mother used to say about folks whose age she couldn't determine. Katherine decided his age didn't matter.

"Just who do you think you are, strutting into my apartment?" Katherine sputtered, stepping backwards and grabbing a knitting needle out of a nearby basket. She held the blue aluminum rod with its pointed end up for him to see, waving it less than a foot away from his face.

"I'm the new super," James said. "Trying to fix everybody's thermostats. Something seems to have gone haywire in every dang apartment. All one-hundred of 'em." He stepped toward Katherine, offering his hand, smiling in what Katherine thought was a friendly demeanor, but could be devilish for all she knew.

"You step on back," Katherine said, whipping the air with the ten-inch needle. "Let me see some identification."

"Or what?" James said, backing out of her reach. "You'll knit me to death?"

"You take one more step in my direction and I'll stab you in the eye quicker than you can say 'don't.'" She jabbed at his chest with the needle, forcing him to jump out of the way.

"You've got some mean wrist action. I bet you're a master knitter."

"How would you know anything about knitting?" Katherine said, lunging forward.

James sidestepped the jab and answered, "I'm a master knitter myself. Took it up to calm my nerves when I quit smoking."

"Sure you did," Katherine said, backing away, but softening. If he really was a knitter like herself, he couldn't be all bad. "Now, let me see that I.D. Our super is a short, skinny kid with a tattoo of the Alamo on his arm, and you are not him."

James James James reached in his pocket and slowly withdrew a badge.

"Throw it on the floor where I can see it," Katherine ordered.

James did as he was told. "Were you a cop once?" he asked.

"No, but my daddy was the sheriff right here in Hog Temple," Katherine said, looking down at the badge with a photo of the man in front of her and the words "James James James, Super, Homestead Apartments" emblazoned on the front. Looking up at him, she asked, "Where's the regular super?"

"Passed away last night," James said, appearing to Katherine a bit sobered by being threatened.

"Passed away? He was only twenty-three."

"Yes, but these things happen from time to time. Got his head caught in a dishwasher in Number Two trying to dislodge a Barbie doll from under the main dish rack when the thing got going somehow and then 'snap.'" Mr. James snapped his fingers. "Neck broke like a stale cracker." He shook his head as if his sorrow over the incident was genuine, but he was still smiling, so Katherine had her doubts. She lowered the needle.

"Poor boy," she said. *That is a made-up story if I ever heard one. Nobody on earth would believe such a ridiculous tale, but maybe that's what makes it true. Seems this is a bad day for everybody. Folks are dropping like flies. Hope I'm not next.*

"Fortunately," James said, "those kinds of accidents are one in a trillion, so I think it's safe to say you can plan on living a long life."

"I guess," Katherine said, wondering if this man had some special gift that let him in on her thoughts. There were people, according to her mother, who could do such things, so she decided she'd better keep her thoughts in check, especially anything that bordered on frisky.

"Whew, today has been some kind of day," she said, "but I don't need to bore you with the details. Come on in and take care of my air because I am sweating up a storm." She shook James's hand. She felt, in that moment, as if she were the most loved woman on earth, as if the world had been created for her and her alone, and together James and she would discover what was yet to be uncovered. She let go of his hand and tried to relax, but she was still full of emotion, so all she could get out was, "Sorry about the needle. A girl has to be careful these days."

"I know what you mean," James said, a silly smile spreading across his face.

Katherine couldn't tell if James's smile was supposed to give her the creeps or if it was supposed to make her comfortable, because some people had body language that flat-out lied. She remembered meeting a man back in her thirties who was cursed with a face that implied danger when, in fact, he was as gentle as a mother handling her new baby. When Katherine wasn't smiling, she looked angry. Visitors to Sunnyside had, on occasion, accused her of being in a snit and had gotten on the defensive when she had been preoccupied with nothing more than a new knitting pattern she hadn't mastered. "Amateur mind readers" was what she liked to call them.

"No need to worry about me," James said. "I'm as harmless as a butterfly pinned to a board."

Did I say what I was thinking? "Are you really a master knitter?" she asked.

"You bet I am. Just ask me about my cables and my fisherman's knit sweaters. I won first prize in the last Dingle, Ireland, knit-off. That ought to tell you how good I am."

He can out-knit the Irish? He must be good.

James James James fiddled with the thermostat, then went back to his toolbox and took out some tools. "I need to get into the laundry room," he said, patting her shoulder. "To the fuse box and to where I can find the wiring."

Again, Katherine was flooded with joy, with the thought that life was a Merry-Go-Round with a gold ring dangling within reach of every rider on every horse. She felt like dancing, like making love, like wrestling on the floor with James, the new superintendent, and like giving him the very best of her and everything she had. She would knit him a sweater, even if they did live near the Tex-Mex border and Big Bend National Park where the coolest it got in winter was in the sixties. He could just turn up his air conditioner and wear the thing in the house while he watched television; after all, that's what she did. Oh, who was she kidding? The reality was that the man could knit better than the Irish, or so he said, but heck, she'd try knitting him a sweater anyway.

The more Katherine thought about it, the more excited she got. She'd knit her own brand of sweater, one she made up by herself. It wouldn't be the likes of any sweater he'd seen before. First, she'd have a couple of glasses of wine and then, just as soon as Mr. James James James was done fussing with her thermostat, she'd whip out the royal blue yarn she had been saving for a special project and put her knitting needles to work. She hoped he wouldn't take long to get the temperature set and the air in her apartment the way she liked it: as cold as an Alaskan ice floe in January.

"The fuse box? The wiring?" James asked again.

Katherine pointed to a door in a nearby hallway. For the first time all day she was speechless.

James nodded his head. "They got the fuse boxes in a different room in every apartment," he said, marching toward the laundry room door.

Dazed, Katherine watched as James James James disappeared in the crawl space behind the washer and dryer. Maybe Mr. James would like to have a drink with me after he's done, she thought. *Wouldn't that be a treat?* She ducked into the laundry room.

"Would you like a glass of wine when you're finished in there, sir?" she asked James, now squatting over a collection of wires pulled out from the wall. "I'd like to make up for the near-eye poking I gave you." She was surprised by her boldness. This type of behavior was out of character for her—not once, in her entire life, had she asked a man in she didn't know. She'd thrown plenty out.

"Wine with an upstanding gal like you? You bet I would," Mr. James said, rising. He looked every bit like the sixty-year-old movie star Katherine had always imagined having as her boyfriend, but had never been lucky enough to land. James James James took her hand and pulled her close to him, and whispered, "I'd like nothing better. Thank you for asking."

Katherine's heart pounded, her face warmed, and her body tingled. "You don't have more apartments to go to?" she stammered.

"This is the last one," he said. "When I'm done here, I'm all yours."

Katherine gazed at her reflection in his eyes. She blinked. The woman staring back was none other than Katherine at sixteen. Was this how he saw her? Was this how she wanted to be seen? She swayed. Her breath rushed out of her lungs, her knees buckled, and her body nestled against his. A few minutes earlier she had been threatening to kill James James James with her knitting needle and now she was nursing a fixation as big as the entire state. *What in heaven's name has come over me?*

James wrapped his arms around Katherine, clutching her against his hard, broad chest. "Whoa, there little lady," he said, picking her up and carrying her to the couch where he laid her down, resting her head against a collection of pink and green cable-knit pillows. "Let me fix you some of that wine you were talking about, and while you sip, I'll get this place cooled off. Can't have the heat getting to such a lovely young woman."

"Kitchen, box of wine on top shelf of refrigerator," Katherine whispered, her heart racing like a teenager who'd been caught sneaking out. "You won't miss it." *I am a sixty-six-year-old woman. Why am I behaving so girlish?* It was embarrassing.

James returned with a goblet filled to the brim with the best rosé Katherine could find in a box. "Here you are, Miss—"

"Katherine," she said. "But you can call me Kat. That's what my friends and family call me." Katherine hadn't been called Kat in over twenty years.

"Okay, Kat," James answered, examining the goblet he held in his hand. "Nice set of wine glasses you have here. I own a set just like 'em."

The wine goblet had come packed inside Katherine's favorite laundry detergent. She had collected the whole set because they were prettier, she thought, than the real crystal her neighbor next door had picked up at an estate sale.

James extended his hand and by extension the wine she was ready for. She took particular notice of his arms; they were muscular in the way she had always imagined her dream cowboy's arms would be. The men of Katherine's past, the cowboys who had ridden through her life thus far, had never come close to looking the part, never measured up. Finally here was a man, scoured and tough, who at least looked the part. Strong jaw, brown skin, sharp cheekbones, hard chest, no beer gut, blue-black eyes, sinewy arms, and a look on his face that said all was right in the world. *Honey, where have you been all my life? I put in my order ages, I mean, ages ago.* Katherine shut her eyes briefly, dizzy from the heat and her good luck.

"You just lie back on these pillows and rest while I fix things up, Kat," James James James said. "And when I get back, you and me are going to get to know each other." His cheeks flooded with color and his eyes darkened. "Seems we got two things in common already: we live in the same apartment complex and we have the same taste in fine crystal." He looked around her living room. "I reckon you're going to be plumb surprised how much we have in common."

A chill crept up the back of Katherine's neck—the kind of chill you get that says bad news is on the way, the same creepy ripple she felt just before she broke off her six-year relationship with a banker eventually busted for depositing money into his bank account, taken from every woman over seventy this side of Mexico. *Please let me be wrong this one time.* Pleading had never become her, but if she were saved this one time from bad judgment, she'd never beg God for another thing—a least that's what she told herself.

As the goose bumps began a systematic pop along her arms and shoulders, James bent over her, stroked her cheek with his fingers, and pushed her hair off her forehead. "You need anything, anything at all, you just holler."

Katherine hardly heard a word James said because as soon his skin met hers, the only thing she could think of was how she wanted to pull him to her, to place her wet mouth on his, and to beg him to touch her in places she hadn't been touched in years. She closed her eyes. *Oh, yes. Something special has finally come my way. My prize for putting up with the likes of fake bankers, men searching for a womb, and men wanting someone to mama them, my reward has finally arrived in the form of Mr. James James James. God is good. This time there is no mistaking it — what I have here is no ordinary man, no ordinary man, at all.*

5
Henry

Henry lay on his back staring at the ceiling. This was what his life had come to— staring at a speckled ceiling with notes written on his belly in Magic Marker. Of course, no one was making him lie there. He was clever enough and ornery enough to come up with an interesting way to bide his time at Sunnyside. He could trot down to the craft room once the movie was over and everyone was back in their rooms and then—out of sheer meanness—draw caricatures of the activities lady on the tables. Better yet, he could steal a pad of paper, sit on the visitor's porch, and draw a graveyard under the shadow of hills that rambled along the horizon and dot it with headstones for Miss Activities Coordinator and anybody else he didn't like. But he didn't have the energy for meanness, or anything else, for that matter. He hardly had the energy to breathe—all because he was sick of being at Sunnyside.

In his youth, Henry had had quite the reputation as an up-and-coming cowboy artist. "A freak of the range," one underground art journal called him, as if cowboys weren't supposed to know how to do anything but round up cattle. He had even had his own show at a gallery in Dallas, sponsored by an art collector out of Houston. The gentleman had purchased the bulk of his work, a series of horses and cowboys working under a blazing sun and a series of abstracts drawn while visiting his uncle's ranch in northern Mexico.

Henry had lived up to his name and had become what had been expected of him. After all, his mother had given him the middle name of Cole, naming him after the great painter Thomas Cole, whose paintings she had admired. Henry wondered where his paintings and sketches were now. He had put pad after pad of sketches and boxes of paintings in storage after Maryluz, his wife, had died, but that was a long time ago, back some fifty years ago or more. He couldn't remember the exact time, but he was sure it was back when his daughter Angelina was still alive. Or was she? His memories had blended into one solid mass, and remembering the good parts of his past required a magic trick or more when he was tired—and tonight he was tired of every damn thing.

Worn out or not, he had to ask himself what had stopped him from picking up a drawing pencil the last few years. Not that dumbass lady hired to invent things for the residents to do, that was for sure. She'd probably go bonkers if she knew she had a real artist in the house. She hadn't recognized the copy of Rodin's *The Thinker Statue* he'd drawn on the table, so she probably wouldn't realize he could do anything of value, even if he had drawn it on his forehead. She was a puddle-brain, in Henry's humble opinion, but a man couldn't fault a person for being dumber than dirt, so he decided there was no point in agitating her further.

Even if he didn't have his sketches or paintings, at least he could draw if he really wanted to, and he had his memory, as muddled as it sometimes got. Old Lee didn't have that. Couldn't remember where he was half the time, much less that every last one of his friends was dead, except for Henry. It was a good thing, too, Henry thought, that Lee couldn't remember what his family had really done. Call it what you will, but they had abandoned him. Shameless. Folks were downright despicable these days when it came to old people, the sick, and the disabled. Henry had done the right thing: he had taken care of his parents in his house until they died, just as he should have.

Henry counted the specks of chipped paint on the ceiling. Life without Lou-Ella was going to be terrible. Though the woman had damn near talked his head off on more than one occasion, she always had something smart or entertaining to say, always had insightful observations about other folk's behavior, and could explain unkindness by reminding him people were, at times, simply full of shit. Just like Lee, Lou-Ella had known Henry a good many years and had seen every side of him there was to see. Lou-

Ella had been comfortable to be with, which wasn't something he could say about most people.

There were times when Henry could have sworn that Sunnyside was Hog Temple's version of an old timer's high school reunion. Most of the folks had either grown up in Hog Temple, had been raised nearby, or had been dropped off by folks who'd always wished they'd grown up there. At least these last folks, the ones who dreaded going back to where they came from, usually had visitors and money for things like a bus ride to Wal-Mart with an accompanying attendant. One day, facing reality, Henry finally was forced to admit that Sunnyside was nothing more than a fancy garbage heap, piled high with the aged and infirm.

Henry was all too aware of his state of affairs. Sometimes he wished he were more like Lee, concerned primarily with his bowel movements. If he had to live his life over again, he would make some major changes. He would have snatched the real love of his life from her husband and run off to Mexico to paint, to raise babies, and raise racehorses, and been a better husband and a kinder father and a more attentive grandfather. Yep, he'd live the life he'd meant to live but hadn't, if given a second chance. Not that Maryluz hadn't been a good wife, and not that Angelina hadn't been a daughter a father could love. No, it wasn't because they weren't good enough; it was because being able to look back, he could see that a man's greatest risk was in following his heart, and so was his greatest joy.

Isabella Martine had been the love of his live, only ten years older than he, and on top of it, his mother's best friend. His mother had been sixteen when she had given birth to him, so her girlfriends were never more than ten to sixteen years older than he was, and they were as exciting as all get-out, as he remembered it. He knew it was wrong, those feelings he had had for Isabella, but they were what they were, and there was nothing he could have done about it back then.

He could still smell the lavender soap Isabella used every morning, could still feel her plump red lips on his—if Isabella showed her face right that second, Henry would tell her he still loved her, and would love her until the day he died. He would tell her his one regret was not snatching her up and hightailing it for the Mexican mountains; he would tell her he had been young and stupid. If he could be with her one more time, young again, and with what he knew now, things would be different.

Yes, Henry thought sadly, not running away with Isabella was his greatest regret. If he had fought for Isabella, he might not be in Sunnyside with its groaning, lonely, dying old people. He'd be lying next to Isabella or living in the home of one of his grandchildren, the grandchildren he might have had, the same grandchildren who would now be running his ranch, and who would see to it that he was comfortable in his old age. So many fantasies, so many dreams to dream, and so much free time in which to dream them. He closed his eyes and dozed for a second, only to be awakened by a howl that launched him from his bed to the floor. Henry awoke to find he was standing but wasn't sure why, until he remembered where he was.

In the room across the hall, Miguel Rodriguez was wailing and, every now and again, coughing violently. Rodriguez gurgled, sniffled, and howled every night, all night. Poor old Miguel, a man who had never done anything in life but tend to horses, Henry's horses.

Henry sat down on his bed. He had overheard a doctor say to Hodges that Miguel would be gone soon. Henry shivered with the thought of losing Miguel, too. He reminded Henry of an old cat he had once. He had named the cute little ball of fur Pappy but later changed it to Howler. The damn creature had been the best mouser in the stables and a loving pet, but when he got to be about sixteen or seventeen he wandered the barn in the middle of the night howling his head off. Henry loved that cat—he never had been a dog man. Dogs got on his nerves with their barking, shitting, getting in the trash, and chasing chickens.

"It's an old age thing," the vet told him when Henry had asked about Howler's caterwauling. "Won't stop till he dies. Folks do the same thing. Go to an old folks' home in the middle of the night and you'll hear for yourself. You ought to put him down." But Henry never could. He didn't believe in taking an animal's life just because it had grown old, but as much as he missed that ratty old cat once he was gone, he was still glad when Howler died. One afternoon Howler managed to get under the feet of a horse heading back to its stall and got stepped on. He died of a broken neck in a matter of seconds. Finally, Howler had been put the hell out of his misery.

While he would never wish the same thing on Rodriguez, the vet was right. Here Henry was in the old folk's home and, sure enough, his buddy, his friend from the time he was four years old, Miguel Rodriguez, pissed and moaned like a colicky baby night after night, begged for his mama and papa, and cried from dusk until dawn because he was afraid of the dark. Miguel's most pitiful act was to plead for someone to tell him where he was, but no matter how many times Hodges told him he was living in Sunnyside surrounded by old friends, he still asked. Long after Hodges put a nightlight in Rodriguez's room, he still cried and moaned so loud Hodges swore he could hear Rodriguez as far away as the north wing. Henry shook his head; Miguel and he were housed at the southernmost point of the south wing.

Nobody really cares how much noise Miguel makes, Henry told himself. Most of the help left for the day around 5:30 in the evening. Besides, half the center's residents cried out at night. The halls were filled with a chorus of nighttime caterwauling, screams for missing parents, and brothers and sisters, not to mention moans, groans, and heavy sobbing. For the amount of racket that went on during Sunnyside's darkest hours, you'd think the residents were anticipating the devil's fire being stoked just for them. Why else would they weep and howl so? These were the questions Henry ruminated over late at night, every night.

Miguel Rodriguez had been the best horseman in Texas during his time; he'd won more prizes at the rodeo than even Henry could remember, he had raised and sold prizewinning cattle, horses, and pigs— and now here he was, alone and babbling like a baby, probably wetting himself on top of everything else.

In his old age, Miguel was enough to make Henry cry. If he could live his life over again, he would treat Miguel better; he would give Miguel the recognition that he deserved. Now that there was no opportunity to make things right by his best buddy, and though he had nothing to do with Miguel being treated like a baby, he felt responsible. That was what being dumped in a place like Sunnyside did to a man; it made him an infant again, humiliated him, made him angry, and, worst of all, made him *want* to die. Maybe some of the residents needed to be here, but not Henry. His only crime was running out of money and having a grandson whose only interest in him was how much money he could make selling off Henry's property. Why should he care, anyway?

Dead or alive, the ungrateful fat boy was going to get his property one way or the other and spend the dough that came along with it. He knew the boy swore that most of the money went to Henry's care, but he didn't believe that for a second. That tub of butterfat was probably buying up stock in computer companies or porno sites. Sam told Henry he couldn't have him painting up the walls of the house—it wasn't normal.

So what if he had painted scenes from Greek history on his living room walls? They were *his* walls; he, Henry Cole Calhoun, had built and paid for them. And so what if he had set fire to his house on more than one occasion? Anybody could have forgotten a pot of beans cooking on the stove and done the same thing. Lots of people had made the same mistake—men much younger than he, and they hadn't ended up in an assisted-living center. But Sam hadn't been as worried about the fires as he had been about the paintings on the walls. "I can't have you painting on the walls or furniture," Sam had said. "It's not normal." That hadn't made a lick of sense to Henry when the boy had said it, and it still didn't.

Henry gripped his pillow and covered his face. In his heart of hearts, he knew it wasn't the painting or the fires that landed him at Sunnyside. Nobody wanted him anymore. Lou-Ella was gone, Lee was damn near feeble-minded and unable to walk without his walker, and Miguel was racing toward the grave. The realization sent Henry Cole Calhoun into a sobbing fit. At least *he* cried softly into his pillow so no one could hear him. If he'd had somebody to talk to, he'd have confessed what was weighing on his mind, but he didn't, so he thought and mumbled and carried on as if he were his own best friend.

Hank Cole, as Henry was called in his youth, was not giving up the ghost any time soon, and while that might be a large part of his problem, he knew on some level he wasn't croaking in the near future. He glanced at his oversized clock. It was midnight. Tomorrow this time he would be on his way to Mexico with Lee — hearing aids, walker, and all — to some nondescript border town packed with *señoritas* as old as they were. They'd find a place where men and boys butchered the pigs and goats and where women their own age were still capable of whipping up hearty meals of beef enchiladas, corn tortillas, crispy beef tacos, piles of red beans and fluffy rice, and pans of sweet flan for their families and visitors in a matter of a few short hours. Maybe they'd even lay out a pan of goat meat — his favorite — or even have it ready and waiting for him.

The town of Henry's dreams would be a place where Lee and he could die lassoing a horse or drinking cactus juice, where they could guzzle tequila and smoke until their lungs felt like ashtrays. They were going someplace where they could eat salsa for breakfast if they wanted and draw pictures in the damn dirt if they felt like it. Maybe they'd land in a rugged Mexican mountain village where they could listen to men play their favorite music on acoustic guitars until the sun came up.

Henry wanted the company of a woman, but not a young thing put in his path to satisfy his urges. Although that had an appeal he couldn't deny, if the truth be known, he wanted the company of a woman still working, one still feisty enough to round up her grown sons and daughters and command a brood of rambunctious grandchildren to the table for a family meal, a woman with stories to tell. Hell, he wanted a woman with whom he could reminisce about the way the hills turned purple and the way the fireball of a sun used to look when it was dropping off the edge of the earth at the close of the day during the time when folks still spent daylight outside, instead of inside watching news shows or a televised war. But who was he kidding? Lee couldn't lasso a horse if his life depended on it—the man used a walker, for God's sake—and, for that matter, neither could he. *Jesus. Am I asking for too much? Am I?*

Tomorrow he would throw open the door to this airless tomb. Tomorrow he would put his crying days in the past—where they belonged—with the help of the girl the day manager, Katherine, hated, but who the rest of the staff and residents loved: the Hair Princess. Of course, the Princess had no idea she would be helping Henry and Lee escape, because she was too decent a person to do anything she thought might be dangerous or bad for them. No, Miss Lilly Beale, Hair Princess, would have to be tricked into helping them skedaddle, but he had no choice—he'd sooner fling himself into a canyon rather than stay another day at Sunnyside. As far as Henry was concerned, three o'clock Sunday afternoon couldn't arrive soon enough.

Henry held his breath, trying to catch Miguel's familiar gurgle and cry, but he didn't hear a thing. *Nada.* Miguel had quieted. Maybe Miguel had—no, he didn't want to think that. He didn't want to know he had lost one more friend. He strained to catch a whimper, but silence prevailed. Miguel was asleep for a change. He had been known to drop off occasionally, sometimes in the middle of a groan. Maybe tonight Henry could afford to feel sorrow for Lee and Lou-Ella, for Maryluz and Angelina, for Miguel, Isabella, and even himself, too. Yes, tonight he would bury his head in his pillow and sob for all of them. And sob he did.

~SUNDAY~

6
Katherine

Katherine rolled over in bed, bumping into James James James. *That's right; I'm at James's place, and I'm colder than an ice cube.* Not only was she was freezing, but he was, too. When her arm met his back, he was so icy cold she feared he was dead, but her fears were put to rest when he opened his eyes and said, "Good morning, Miss Kitty."

She laughed and buried her head in his arms. "It's Kat," she said.

"Miss Kitty to me," he said, sounding to Katherine like a man one-third his age, full of testosterone and the manliness of a young bull rider.

"Lordy, we have some sun in here this morning," James said, shielding his eyes with his arm.

James had, apparently, forgotten to close the curtains the night before. "Sorry about the light, but it's one of the things I love about this apartment," he said from under his arm. "It's why I picked this one when they told me I could have any one I wanted."

"Can't blame you for that," Katherine said, admiring the knit coverlet hanging over the arm of a nearby chair. Who would have thought James James James was a knitter like herself? She ran her toes over the corner of the baby-blue afghan with a series of intricate cables knit throughout—an afghan James himself had knit. He could do the most complicated cable work she had ever seen. *The man is downright impressive.* Not only was he the super and could repair appliances, electrical systems, and more, but he was, of all things, a master knitter. Who would have thought this babe magnet, this taller, older version of younger men she had seen only in magazine ads, was so talented? Anybody could tell from looking at James he was a man's man, but a master knitter? How she loved life's surprises.

James James James had done a great job of adjusting his own thermostat. When Katherine first walked into the room, the cold hit her so hard her breath was almost taken away. Her legs and arms felt as if millions of tiny icicles were piercing them—she was too cold, but she wasn't about to tell James. She giggled until her giggle turned into a goofy snort. *Why am I being so silly? And my snort. Oh Lord, why do have to do that?* She was a sixty-six-year-old woman behaving like a schoolgirl whose crush had gotten the better of her. What could she say to explain away her youthful exuberance? Could she tell James James James she hadn't felt so head over heels about anybody since that boy in eighth grade asked her daddy if he could take her to the state fair?

What was that boy's name? Could she remember after so many years? Yes, yes. Garrett. Yes, that was it. She closed her eyes. She could see and hear Garrett as plain as day—his soft brown hair, his muddy green eyes, his top teeth overlapping slightly, as if they were a pair of hands folded in a lap. Garret was telling her that he and his family would be moving, leaving her forever, leaving her without a boyfriend. She felt like crying every time she thought of that last day with her first heartthrob.

None of the other boys at school had shown any interest in Katherine, probably because her father was the sheriff and they didn't want him hunting down his daughter while they were busy doing whatever it was teenage boys did. Katherine ended up alone and lonely for the next two summers, even though, at fifteen, she had girlfriends to hang with, Hog Temple United Methodist Church Bible School to attend, and, at one point, three babysitting jobs, which gave her enough money to make her feel as if she were a girl from a family of means. She loved her father but hated his job. *Why couldn't he have been a ranch hand, a plumber, an electrician, or even a truck salesman or banker, like the other fathers?*

The summer of Garrett, as she referred to it, had been the state fair, hot dogs, cotton candy, scary rides, handholding, and endless days at the movies where they sometimes kissed when the screen had darkened and they were sure no one was looking. Once, she ate so much at the fair that she threw up while they were on top of the Ferris wheel, sending them both into fits of laughter and getting them banned from the stomach-churning rides for the remaining fair days.

The summer of Garrett had been the last carefree summer Katherine could remember having; every summer since then had been downright murder on her love life. If somebody was going to break up with her, it happened in summer; if she was going to unload some no-good, triple-timing, nose hair-trimming son-of-a-gun, she did it in the summer. It wasn't that marriage had been her life's ambition; then again, it wasn't as if she'd had any ambition at all. Katherine had always felt as if she were waiting for something, as if the answer to who she was and what she was to become would materialize out of thin air. But here she was, approaching seventy, and there was no longer anything to wait for, because her life would probably be coming to an end in a few years. And what she had become, an administrative assistant, and finally the day manager at Sunnyside, was all she was ever going to be. Well, at least I didn't become a serial killer or a bad mother, she thought.

"Miss Kitty," James said, interrupting her memories and giving her a squeeze. "Today is a new beginning."

Hell. The past is the past. Let it go. James James James is right: this summer doesn't have to be the same old summer and I don't have to worry about becoming anything anymore. The past is over. "Yes, it is," she answered. *I believe I've lassoed myself a new wrangler. Something is changing. I can feel it. Finally,* finally, *a man who can appreciate hand-spun Merino wool, a man who subscribes to knitting magazines, and can knit.*

James sat up, rolled toward Katherine, and gave her a kiss on the top of her head. "Now, tell me, honey bunch, what do you do when you're not knitting?"

"Oh, that? My job is about as interesting as watching water boil," Katherine said. "I'm the temporary day manager at Sunnyside Assisted-Living Center." She stretched and then pulled the covers up around her shoulders. "It pays the bills, and keeps my yarn fund filled. That's about it."

"My brother delivers bottled water there," James said. "Maybe you know him."

"Well, what do you know," Katherine said, wiggling out from under James, "New, right?"

"Just started," James said. "He told me there was a lot of excitement at the place yesterday. Something about a resident in a thong dying—"

"Yep. It's all because of the Hair Princess, but that's a long story," she said. *Damn it. The Princess is interfering with my love life now. Everybody somehow always gets around to that stupid girl.*

"I think James is a bit taken with her," James said, laughing. "He says she's prettier than a box of money on Christmas morning."

"She may be, but she'd better cough up that damn rope she's got hidden someplace," Katherine said. "Before somebody gets tangled in the thing and hangs himself, or breaks a leg tripping over it. *Why is that silly hunk of twine bugging me so much?*

"Rope?" James asked.

She was instantly gripped by the need to spill everything she knew to James. He's just that kind of man, she told herself. "Yeah. There was a rope involved. It was the primary plaything in a romp that had no business being thought about, much less taking place. And to tell you the truth, I wouldn't be surprised if the coroner decided the woman had been strangled with that very same hunk of hemp, because there was a tiny brown bruise about the size of a quarter—same as if somebody had given her a hickey for good measure, or had choked her to death by knotting that thing around her throat and giving it a good tug." Katherine imitated pulling the imaginary rope tight. "When I think about what goes on around that place—well, I could go on for hours." She shook her head. "You wouldn't believe the things I've seen and heard working there."

"Is that so?" James James James asked, rolling out of bed and putting on his pants.

Katherine stared at his hairless chest, his hard buttocks, his firm shoulders, and his muscular pectorals. She noticed a few cellulite dimples on James's ass but overall, he had it going on. Not bad for an old man. *Hardly looks a day over fifty. Not bad at all.* "The stories I could tell. I bet some of them would make your hair curl," she said, distracted by his sinewy arms. *It's damn refreshing to be distracted for a change.*

James James James crossed the room, picked up a blue chenille robe off a rocking chair, and laid it on the bed beside her. "Put this on, Kat," he said, taking Katherine by the hand to help her out of bed, "and let Number One of the Three Jameses buy you some fried eggs and grits."

Katherine sat up.

"Come on now, baby," he said, helping her to her feet.

Katherine stood, dropping the covers on the floor. Chill bumps popped up all over her body and her nipples did their best to stand at attention. They stretched, reaching north for all they were worth, but they were on a permanent route south and there was nothing anybody could do about it, short of plastic surgery.

Katherine grabbed the robe and pulled it on as quickly as she could. She didn't mind being naked in front of a boyfriend, but it was broad daylight, and James James James would be taking a hard look at her for the first time. She wasn't as perky as she had been in her youth, and a girl's flaws, as small as they might be, were always too, too visible under the glow of the Texas sun.

"Let me treat you to breakfast over at IHOP," he said. "And while we're refueling," he added, winking at her, "you can tell me all about what goes on at that place you work—Sunnyside, is it?"

Katherine nodded.

"I'm dying to hear some of those stories aimed at curling my hair—what I got left of it." James James James shook his head, but not one hair moved.

Katherine laughed. *Who'd think a couple of sixty-something year-olds could be as frisky as teenagers?*

James pulled her into his arms and gave her a long, wet kiss.

A man like James could get a woman to tell him just about anything he wanted — and that is a fact. So why doesn't he have a girlfriend or a wife?

"What's a pretty girl like you doing without a honey to see she's got all she needs?" He flashed his movie-star smile and swayed slightly, as if he were about to break into a slow dance. He stared into her eyes with his arms still around her and she felt the same way she supposed Cleopatra felt in Caesar's arms.

"Well, let me tell you," Katherine said, taking in a deep breath, forgetting about breakfast and about being naked in the sunlight, "There was this banker once …"

7
Lilly

"Lou-Ella had the mark," Hodges whispered to Lilly as she set up her supplies, preparing her work area for her first customers, Henry Calhoun and Lee Donahue.

"I know. You've told me about a dozen times, remember?"

Hodges nodded his head. "But—" he whispered.

"Honey, you don't need to whisper. Nobody is here but us."

"You don't know that," Hodges muttered, looking around the room.

"You worry too much," Lilly said, as worried as Hodges. "Don't you think I should repaint my sign?" she asked, pointing to a cracked, peeling painting of a girl wearing a crown, holding a comb in one hand, scissors in the other, and standing under the words, *Lilly Beale, Hair Princess*. Right now she wanted to distract her lifelong friend and partner. She could see the conversation that was coming and resigned herself to the fact it was unavoidable. She had wanted to ask Hodges if he was certain about the mark, but she didn't want to upset him. She would have to disguise her doubt.

"I told you, you should have used some kind of primer on the thing before you painted it the first time," Hodges said. "Wish we'd used some kind of primer on the whole thing. But we didn't, and now what we got here is a truckload of paint-peeling trouble. *They* have been here." He whispered the name so softly she had to read his lips.

"I don't know what took *Them* so long," Lilly said, trying to sound normal while removing the sign from its hooks. "You knew it was going to happen sooner or later—that is, if the mark is real and not a fake one. To tell you the truth, I never was sure about that last one—" Lilly waved her hands in the air and drummed her fingers "—never sure that last invocation we did would hold."

"Well, I sure as heck thought it would," Hodges said. "The way they shrank back, I thought they were gone for good."

"Nothing is ever gone for good, Hodges. I've come to see that's so," Lilly said, running her shoe over a scuffmark. "This floor needs mopping," she said. *No, they aren't gone for good. I suspected that the moment they were banished.*

"Forget the floor. We've got more pressing things to tend to. You know He'll send us back if we mess this up," Hodges said, taking a hanky from his pocket and wiping his forehead. "The mark is real, all right; you can take my word for it."

"Is that so?"

"Yes."

"You're sure?"

"Of course I'm sure." Hodges ran his hand over his face as if he were wiping something away. "You know they like marking what they think is theirs, and it's always that same little bruise-type thing."

"You might be right. Then again, you could be wrong," Lilly said. "It's something to think about. If it's *Them*, they can't help but leave the mark. If I remember correctly, it comes from crossing over and touching human flesh. I think it's one of those biological interactions that could be explained by a scientist, if it had to be explained."

"Damnnation, Li, I don't give a hornswaggled cowpoke's pocket money why the mark shows up. You don't understand where I'm going with this. Let me be clear, so listen up." Hodges wiped his forehead again. "You and I are getting a reputation."

"And what's that?"

"For being royal screw-ups, and if we keep this up we're going to get called back and made to do things like watch plants grow or be in charge of rocks. I got to say, I ain't too damn happy about the prospect of spending the next hundred years watching rocks evolve, although that would be a damn sight better than wandering the streets of Calcutta or Delhi begging—if you know what I'm getting at."

"Then I guess we'd better find out what they're after," Lilly said, "before somebody else does."

Blisters of sweat rose on Hodges's forehead, bursting and sending droplets of perspiration careening over his eyebrows and down his nose. He buried his face in his handkerchief, then pulled it away, balled it up, and tossed it in the trash. He replaced his hanky with a ragged washcloth taken from a nearby shelf. If there was one thing Lilly wished she could do, it was to be able to relieve Hodges of what had become a propensity for worry, the same worry they weren't supposed to experience.

"Don't worry, be happy," Meher Baba had said, and then some Rastafarian guy named Bobby McFerrin cut a CD singing the same phrase, but Hodges and Lilly seemed out of sync with Baba and Bobby, unable to get back to that original state of being in which they had first arrived. *What has happened to us?* She felt her thoughts slip in Hodges's direction.

"You tell me," Hodges said.

"With Lou-Ella having a mark, I'd have to say either Henry gave her a hickey in a moment of hormonal overload, or we've had a visit by the Three Jameses," Lilly said, climbing off the chair and laying the wooden sign on a nearby table. "I really don't think the mark you saw is the real one, Hodges. You know how the Jameses are. If they put it there, they did it to worry us. If that's the case, they're having fun again at our expense. As far as I can tell, we don't have anything the Jameses could possibly want, and neither did Lou-Ella. Most likely, the mark isn't the mark at all but a plain old hickey. Simple as that."

"But the Three Jameses have been itching for I-don't-know-what for as long as I can remember. And even if they really are only after some fun at our expense, I don't think I can take any more from those—whatever they really are. Honest to God in Heaven, Lilly, I can't."

Lilly couldn't figure out when James, James, and James were the most dangerous—when they were feeling devilish, when they screwed up, or when they were simply trying to be themselves. She hoped that Henry had been feeling particularly youthful and had given Lou-Ella the mark, but it was quite possible the Jameses had been up to no good. They hadn't heard a peep from the tiresome trio in decades, so it was likely that they had decided to surface from whatever dung heap they had been lying low in. In any case, Hodges's jangled nerves made sense to her, but she couldn't risk Hodges getting too wound up or he'd be useless.

"Those fools? If they're up to no good, we are not suffering at their hands. Not now, not ever again."

"But those boys, girls, or however they appear these days are—"

"Trust me, Hodges, you're getting yourself all worked up over something we can fix in a flash if we have to."

"But Lou-Ella passed before we were finished. That's what's worrying me, Li, and it should be worrying you."

What she didn't say, and wished she could have, was that the more Hodges talked about it, the more she was inclined to agree with him that something bigger was at work, but this time their dilemma had the earmarks of a much larger force, not simply a frisky old man or that little gang of Jameses with their three same names, their nasty tricks, and fancy smoke screens. She knew their mode of operation. If the three Jameses were the culprits, she was positive they'd have shown themselves by now, because the one thing they loved more than anything was being able to show how devious, powerful, and full of mischief they could be, and get credit for it right off the bat. But Hodges would have blown a gasket if she had told him what she was really thinking—as arrogant as the Jameses were, they would have scattered with a simple well-placed threat from Lou-Ella Whitehead, so the reason for the gun had to have been—Lilly couldn't bear to face it. *I hope this is some silly trick the Jameses have cooked up to scare Hodges, because if it isn't, we've got major trouble.*

"The Jameses must have scared Mrs. Whitehead something terrible. She had a *gun*, Lilly, *a loaded gun*. You know the woman was dead-set against weapons. Why, Mrs. Whitehead thought a fork was too dangerous to have on the dinner table." Hodges wiped his forehead vigorously with his already soaked handkerchief. "So what does the gun mean?"

Lilly went to the refrigerator, took out a carton of prune juice, and held it out in front of her so that Hodges could read the label. "Want some?" she asked.

"No, thank you. And please don't change the subject."

"Maybe the gun was simply for effect."

"I doubt it. Didn't you hear me when I said she was against weapons? I say it was the Jameses, and then some."

"I heard you."

"Why don't you want to face facts, Lilly? Why do you keep trying to get me sidetracked?" Hodges was shaking.

"Calm down," Lilly said. "Maybe the Jameses frightened her. They're capable of that, as you know."

"You don't think they went back to …." Hodges was sweating even more profusely than he had been earlier.

"Don't even think that, Hodges," Lilly said, looking at the carton of prune juice, trying to distract herself as well. "I love this stuff. The only thing I like better are the prunes themselves, fresh from the market."

"Of course you do, because nobody *makes* you drink it. Ask any of the folks around here and they'll tell you they don't want it, don't need it, and wish they weren't forced to drink it. Now, let's get back to the subject at hand." Hodges pursed his lips. "Come on, Li."

Lilly returned the unopened carton of juice to the refrigerator, shoving it to the back, next to a giant chocolate Hershey Kiss she was saving as a gift for Henry and Lee. *If the Jameses haven't released Them, who or what did? And what if what we're dealing with isn't Them, but something or someone brand new?*

"I don't know why in the world you drink that when you don't need to," Hodges said, shaking his head.

"I didn't. Didn't you see me put it back? I'll have some later. It makes me feel more in touch with the folks in this place," she said. "You should try it."

"I have. Can't get used to the stuff," he said, running his hand over the tabletop. "You know what Henry always says about prune juice—it's just a plan cooked up by young folks to keep their elders from getting too far from the toilets and thereby not be able to get to the bank to withdraw every last penny of their money."

Lilly laughed. "Only Henry would see constipation as part of a conspiracy." In her heart, she had to admit that maybe Henry was right. Young people had old people all wrong—in many cases—even when these seniors had enough physical problems to land them in Sunnyside.

Hodges straightened a stack of towels that had tipped over. "Listen, Lilly, I'm worried."

"Hodges," she said. "When we get frazzled, things get complicated. If the Jameses have something wicked up their sleeves, then they're waiting for us to work ourselves into a knot and that's how we get screwed every time. You know it, and they know it."

A no-nonsense voice boomed over the intercom. "Mr. Hodges to the activity room, please. Mr. Hodges, please come to the activity room."

"Yeah, yeah," Hodges said, shaking his head and muttering to himself on the way out the door. "But Li, the thing of concern is that Lou-Ella had a gun *and* the mark—it feels like *Them* are back, if you ask me."

"Try not to worry, Hodges," Lilly said. "Please. If *Them* are back, they're probably after the Jameses for failing to help them escape."

"Unless them boys or girls or whatever they are this week brought *Them* back," Hodges said. "You know they might have."

"I doubt it," Lilly said, but thought, I hope not.

"I just want one minute when there's nothing happening we need to tend to, just so I can make heads or tails out of this mess. One minute—that's all I'm asking for," Hodges said, rolling his eyes toward heaven and then waving his hands. "Just one."

Lilly watched from the door as Hodges trudged down the hall, fluttering his fingers, still muttering to himself. She hated seeing

Hodges upset. He was too softhearted for this business, but you get the job you're given and there's nothing you can do about it. At least there never used to be a way to ditch your assignment and get a new one. Maybe the universe really had taken on a whole new spin, and maybe they would be reassigned again. This time she wanted to step up, not be sent to some remote, disease-ridden corner to learn yet another lesson about what it meant to be human. But what were the chances of that happening? The way things were headed, Lilly was afraid that trying to conduct daily business was about to get as pleasant as walking naked through a blackberry patch. But if she and Hodges shined a bit brighter this time, if they could resolve the current situation without massive destruction or the death of innocent people, maybe, just maybe, they would be recognized with an opportunity to better their circumstances.

The last thing she wanted was for them to be blamed for yet another James-inflicted disaster. She and Hodges had had to put up with being blamed for Atlantis slipping into the sea when it had been the Jameses who had caused the disaster. Then there was the time Hodges and she had been ordered to guard the children of a small village in northern England. The Jameses came to town, pretended to be Pied Pipers, lured the children away in the night, and returned them in the morning to the villagers as loaves of bread and fruit pies, which their parents subsequently ate. For that, she and Hodges were sent to the darkest regions of a universe no one had heard of, not even the Jameses, and for a full two decades they were made to clean what would now be considered the equivalent of toxic waste. It rotted their edges, made them glow a sallow gray, and left the taste of rotting anchovies in their mouths. Lilly had had enough, though she knew she could take whatever was dished out, just as she was sure Hodges would wither under another James induced punishment. Yes, Hodges and she were going to have to resolve this situation on a positive note.

Hodges approached two women arguing in the hallway and then stopped beside them. Lilly considered what she might do for the two ladies once they got past Hodges and to the hair salon. One of the women suffered from dementia and the other was a friend who, out of love, tolerated her sick friend's angry tirades. Lilly stuck her head out the door just in time to hear Hodges burst forth with a recitation of lines from Shakespeare's *The Tempest*. The woman with dementia clutched Hodges's arm and recited right along with him. Before Lilly could say a word, voices poured into the hall from adjacent rooms, each offering their own quotations from great writers, joining Hodges and his partner, who recited with such enthusiasm it was as if she had never been anything other than full of joy. No matter that they weren't in the theatre. No wonder the residents love Hodges so much, she thought as she shut the door to the salon and dropped into a nearby chair.

Whatever was going on in Sunnyside, Hodges was wrong about one thing: it was going to take a lot longer than one minute to sort this mess out— she was sure of that. Now, if she could only get rid of this nagging feeling that she could have done something more for Lou-Ella.

8
Henry

Henry grabbed Lee by the arm with one hand and his walker with the other. "It's our time, Lee."

"I wanted to take a nap," Lee grumbled, shuffling down the hall toward the Beauty Room. "And tell me something, Henry. If you knew you were coming to get me, then why did I have to write all that shit on my stomach?"

"You never know when a man's mind will go kaplooey," Henry said.

Three women, a collage of red, blue, and yellow ruffled skirts and blouses with a collective age of 270, leaned on canes and walkers, blocking the entrance to the space that the residents had named the Beauty Room.

"I am in charge of telling him where the supplies are, Jane," a tiny woman snarled in the face of a much taller woman with freshly coiffed lavender hair. The tiny woman was twisted into a half-stoop and her teeth clicked as she spoke. She leaned over her walker to make her point.

"You got to tell him last time, Phaedra," the tall woman answered, tapping her two canes against the tiny one's walker. "And get those dentures fixed. Your clicking is driving me crazy."

"You have it all wrong—both of you," the third woman said, gripping her walker so tight Henry was sure he saw the aluminum bend around her fingers. "It's my turn. And for that matter, I'm going to be greeting the mailman on Monday. I heard he is as cute as one of them fancy country singers in Jockey underpants and as handsome as Adonis. That's what one of the nurses told me yesterday while she was helping me with my bath."

"I know his name," Phaedra said, her teeth, with every word, touching in a rapid series of short clicks.

"You do not," the third one said.

"I do, too," she answered, throwing back her head.

Henry thought she must have something up her sleeve, because to him she looked about as smug as a rat sneaking off with the cheese.

"No, you don't," the tall one growled.

"I sure as hell do," the tiny woman yelled, waving a hand in the air. Spit peppered the third woman's shirt.

"Damn you, Phaedra," she yelled, her voice cracking. "That's the fourth time this week you have spit on my clean clothes."

Henry turned his hearing aid down, and then tried to guide Lee around the ladies, but women were blocking the door completely and so engaged in their squabble that they took no notice of Henry, Lee, or Lee's walker.

"You never liked boys anyway, Phaedra," the tall woman wailed. "Everybody knows that about you. Always did know it, too. You've been a girl's girl since day one."

"Well, I ..." Phaedra sputtered.

"Everybody knows about you and that waitress from the Romp and Stomp Club," the third woman shouted.

"That was when I was eighteen years old. Besides, you don't know anything about us and she can't tell you because she is D-E-A-D," Phaedra shouted back.

For no reason that Henry could ascertain, the tall woman started crying. The third one cried right along with her and Phaedra sneered at them both.

"Ain't nothing sacred in this place," Phaedra said, looking at Henry and Lee. "A woman can't even go to her grave in peace. She's got to have some old biddy nagging her till the day she dies."

The other two women cried harder.

"Good afternoon, ladies," Henry said.

The ladies yanked tissues from their pockets and blew their noses simultaneously.

"Don't know if y'all know this, but the postman is making a special delivery right this very minute," he said matter-of-factly, lying.

Three heads whipped in Henry's direction. "And that cute little nurse, the one who wears those short skirts and those pointy shoes, Miss Phaedra, is down in the lobby helping him right this minute. The lobby, you might say, is holding something for everybody. No lie."

The two women wiped their eyes.

"Thank you, Mr. Calhoun. Afternoon, Mr. Donahue," Phaedra said and then, as quickly as she could, which in Henry's mind was an eyelash short of a snail's pace, she began a slow steady trek in the direction of the lobby, followed by a flurry of ruffles, canes, and walkers.

Finally, the entranceway was clear. The Hair Princess stood on the other side of the door, urging them to come inside.

"We're almost free, Lee," Henry said, pushing the door open and then turning his hearing aid back up.

"Howdy, gentlemen," Lilly said. "Come on in."

"Nice to see you, Princess," Lee said, dropping into a nearby chair.

The room smelled like a mix of prune juice, hairspray, soap, and powdered and perfumed women.

"I thought we were your first customers," Lee said, sounding disappointed.

"Hair emergency," Lilly said, looking at her watch. "Let's just say it's been a busy afternoon." She laughed. "But you gentlemen are right on time. It's 3 P.M. on the nose." She looked up at Henry, now leaning on Lee's walker. "What's on your mind today, Henry?"

If you only knew, he thought. "I was thinking maybe you could give us a ride up to the hills," he said, trying to appear innocent. "Lee here has been homesick for his old home. He's been complaining something terrible and he—"

"That ain't true, Henry. Not a word of it. I can't remember what my house looked like and as far as it being in the hills—I know I never lived in them hills. Wouldn't have considered it."

"Damn it, Lee," Henry growled. "I am trying to help you here."

Lilly put one hand on his arm and twisted her new eyebrow crystal with the other. "I suppose I could run you over to Wal-Mart for some frozen ice drink. I'm not supposed to take you off the premises without Hodges, but I don't think it would hurt to get you two out of here on my own for a couple of hours. I'll ask the nurse on duty if he'd mind." Lilly winked twice.

Everybody knew the Sunday nurse was addicted to Mexican soap operas and didn't like being taken away from the nurse's station where he watched DVDs on the computer of the latest episodes of his favorite shows. His cousin in Mexico City was a computer nut, according to him, and burned every show to DVD for a low monthly fee.

Imagine that—a fifty-year-old man obsessed with soap operas. What has the world come to? The only shows Henry watched were the exercise shows—the ones out of Hawaii where the girls jumped, stretched, and danced for an hour at a time in white sneakers, white socks, and bikinis. As far as Henry was concerned, those were the only shows on television worth watching.

"You think that youngster is going to say yes?" Henry asked, confident he would.

"You know he will, Henry," Lilly said, laughing. "Let's get going. I'll let him know where we're off to on the way out." She grabbed her purse. "Here, help me get Lee to his feet."

Henry knew Lee had grown stiff in the few minutes he had been seated. Henry could rely on Lee to get stuck in damn near every chair he sat in. For the first time, it occurred to him that maybe he shouldn't be including Lee in this escapade, but he didn't want to make his getaway alone, so Lee would have to do. Henry helped Lee get his hands on the aluminum bar. While Lee pulled, Henry shoved him from behind until he was standing.

"Meet me in the lobby," Lilly said. "I'll bring the pickup around."

"Yes, ma'am," Henry said.

Lee nodded. "Where are we going, Henry?" Lee asked.

"Jesus, Lee. Don't you listen?" *Great day in the morning. Lee is as dumb as a box of socks these days.*

"I listen. Yes, I do, you dried up old prune," Lee said, his face turning a sour reddish gray. "Don't you use the Lord's name in vain, Henry Calhoun."

"Come on, Lee. This ain't no time to argue. Miss Lilly is taking us to Wal-Mart for frozen ice."

"She is?" Lee was excited now.

"Yep, and we got to get our sorry asses to the lobby. So *vamanos*," Henry yelled, happy as a chigger stuck in an armpit. They were almost free, so free he was ready to quote Dr. Martin Luther King, Jr.

In less than an hour, Henry and Lee would be on their way to Mexico. And the Princess? He hoped she'd forgive him for what he was about to do.

9
Katherine

The restaurant was busier than usual, as far as Katherine could tell. It also seemed to her that there were lots of new faces among the staff. There was something familiar about the waitress, though, but Katherine couldn't remember having met her before. Maybe she's the daughter or granddaughter of one of the Sunnyside residents, she thought.

"How are those grits?" James James James asked, leaning toward her.

Katherine noticed a tiny black speck on his cheek, just below his left eye. "Best grits I ever had," she said.

"You just let me know if you need anything," he said. "Anything at all."

"You've got something under your eye," Katherine said. "Let me get if for you."

James James James pushed his chin forward and tilted his head back. It was just enough to allow the light to give Katherine a good look at whatever was stuck to his skin.

"That's good, honey. It'll take just a second," she said. With one of her long pink nails, Katherine scooped up the speck of what turned out to be glitter, but upon closer examination she noticed his skin had a shimmer to it, as if were made of billions of moving cells. She stopped for a second.

"What's the matter, babycakes?" James asked.

"Nothing." Probably the light is off in this place, she thought, and wiped the piece of glitter on a napkin. "There," she said, "all fixed."

"Are you sure?" James asked, leaning toward her again.

When Katherine looked into his eyes, she noticed the reflection of people moving. She felt as if she were watching a movie, so she pulled away and looked around to see if the reflection in his eyes was the wait staff shuffling plates around their table, but they had disappeared. Probably they're in the kitchen, she thought, but when she turned back, the pupils of James's eyes had gone white. Reflected in his now watery white pupils, she saw herself as a young girl at the state fair — with Garrett.

Katherine dropped her fork. James was gone and Garrett sat in his place.

"Thought you'd never see me again, didn't you?" Garrett said, laughing at what Katherine could only guess was a look of horror on her face. She closed her eyes. *I'm dreaming. I must be home in bed. I've dreamt everything. The problem with the air conditioner, meeting somebody named James James James. What is wrong with my mind that I would cook up a man who could knit? Maybe I'm having a stroke, or maybe someone put peyote buttons in my water at work and now I'm having the trip of a lifetime.*

"Kat," James said. "Open your eyes."

Katherine opened one eye and then the other. James James James was once again sitting across from her. She surveyed the room searching for Garrett, but he was gone, as were the other diners.

"So it *is* you," James said, his voice weary. "I thought it might be."

"I don't know what you're talking about," Katherine said, furious at being deceived by this man's parlor games. "Did you put something in my drink last night? Did you?" She shoved herself back from the table. "Damn it, that's what I get for jumping in the sack with a man I hardly know." Katherine grabbed her purse and stood. "I will get a cab home, thank you very much."

"There won't be a cab out there," James said. "You're no longer where you think you are."

Katherine was so angry she shook. "No shit, Inspector Clouseau—"

"I know you're upset, but—"

"Admit it, James—or whoever you really are. You spiked my drink with something despicable, didn't you?"

"No, Katherine, I didn't," James said, taking her hand and patting it, his words soothing but troubled. "I swear to you, I didn't."

"Lord help me, I have been a dumbass, the biggest dumbass of all," Katherine wailed, "but not anymore." She turned to run, but she was too dizzy.

"What's happening is out of your control now but not because of anything I did. You've got to believe me. If we work together, though, I think we can pull ourselves out of this. I swear I'm not going to hurt you, Miss Kitty. On my honor."

Katherine dropped into her chair, holding her purse on her lap. Everything was brighter than usual. Swirls of blue, gray, and purple radiated from the edges. Even James had a halo of blue around his head. "What's happening to me?"

"You've done this all by yourself," he said. "Take another look. Could I have brought back these people?"

The room, empty just moments ago, was now teeming with friends and acquaintances from Katherine's youth.

Garrett waved from a corner, where he stood chatting with the teenager once in charge of operating the Ferris wheel. There were some friends from high school sitting in a booth by a window, waving to a group of girls pulling up in a car in the parking lot. An old family friend sat nearby sipping coffee and chatting with one of her former Sunday school teachers. A woman she recognized from the Texas State Fair those many years ago stopped to offer her some cotton candy, but Katherine shook her head.

"You used to love this stuff. It was your favorite," the woman whined.

A little girl wearing a pink tank top, silver tutu, pink tights, and matching ballet slippers tapped the woman on the arm.

"Here you go, honey," the woman said, handing the swirl of pink to the child. "Katherine doesn't like cotton candy anymore."

The girl stuck her tongue out at Katherine, took the cotton candy and scooted away. "You sure grew up cranky *and* picky," she yelled over her shoulder on her way out.

"Oh, my God," Katherine whispered. "That little girl—she's me when I was six." She turned to James, bewildered. I'm having a stroke, she thought, or I've had the stroke and I'm dead. Or James is a liar and he's drugged me and now he—but James isn't that kind of man.

"You have to believe me when I say I had nothing to do with this," James said, tapping her on the forehead. "Everyone you see came straight out of here."

"Here?" Katherine asked, touching her forehead, too.

"Right there," James said, giving her forehead one last tap.

It was at that moment that Katherine saw herself as a teenager get up, wave to her, leave a crowd of girls waiting for a table, and walk over to where Garrett had turned away from the ride operator, and slip her hand in his.

"I cooked all this up?" Katherine asked.

"You sure did, Miss Kitty," James answered.

"But how? How is that possible? And how do you know?" Before Katherine could get an answer, she was overcome by a flush of heat that flooded her from head to toe. "You're not Christmas Past, are you?

"Christmas Past?"

"Am I having a Scrooge moment?"

"Is that what you think this is?" James asked.

"What else could it be?"

"You're talking about a book and a movie, Kat, not—"

"Oh, Lord, forgive me all the terrible things I've done, please," Katherine said, swooning.

"This isn't about—" James was saying, but as far as Katherine could tell, he never finished his sentence. His words ended abruptly, disappearing into the whoosh and slosh of blood pumping through her veins. Her arms and legs weakened, the room took on the glow of sunset and then faded into a dirty orange, and Katherine fainted—or so she thought.

10
Lilly

The twenty-four hour Wal-Mart was strangely quiet for a Sunday afternoon. Lilly tried to fight off the feeling of dread that clung to her, but it held tight. She had had this premonition of impending disaster only a few times before: once, just prior to having to fend off the Three Jameses in a battle of control over a cache of fireworks she was charged with keeping out of their hands, and once when she was pursed by *Them*. Her best bet, she decided, was to stop worrying. What was going to happen was going to happen, because until it did, there was nothing she could do. Instead, she concentrated on getting Henry and Lee back to the snack bar where the flavored ice was crushed, spit into a tall blue cup, and sold.

Lilly, Henry, and Lee negotiated the aisles, jammed with stacks of boxes of canned vegetables, juice, picnic supplies, and kitchen paraphernalia, with Lilly steadying Lee by cupping his elbow in her hand and guiding him and his walker with the other.

Henry shuffled along beside them as if the bottoms of his shoes were covered in tar, as if he were preoccupied with something, and this worried her, too. Maybe he had the same sense of dread—or maybe it was something simpler. Maybe he was mourning Lou-Ella.

"Henry," Lilly said, trying to be gentle, "I'm sorry about Lou-Ella. She was a sweet person. I'm sure you'll miss her."

"You're not going to ask about that rope, are you?" Henry asked, glancing from side to side as if he were searching for someone.

"No. Why would I ask about a rope?"

"Because Hodges said Miss Katherine was fixated on the thing and was worried somebody was going to hurt themselves with it," Henry answered, sounding agitated. "Now, how about a cherry ice? A large. What do you say, Princess?"

"I saw the rope," Lee said.

"What?" Henry asked.

Lilly thought the two men were getting silly, but she guessed they were entitled.

"It spoke to me last night. It said, 'Be at Wal-Mart no later than forty-thirty and you and Henry will get your wish.'"

"What?" Lilly asked. *Maybe the Jameses really are up to something.*

"He's crazy," Henry said to Lilly. "His medication must be bad."

"Did the rope say anything else to you, Lee?" Lilly asked.

"Nope, but it wiggled and was full of faces."

"You are not going to tell me you believe this old bag of raggedy-ass bones, are you?" Henry yelled.

Lilly stepped back from Henry and Lee. The feeling of dread grew. Something large and ominous was closing in. She looked around her but nothing looked unusual. "Come on, gentlemen," she said. "Let's not argue. Look, we can sit over there and talk about this." Lilly pointed to some tables and chairs in front of the snack bar. An employee stood behind the counter, preparing French fries for the deep fryer.

"I, I … I ain't a sack of whatever you called me," Lee shouted back. "I told you the rope came to me and spoke and I meant what I said. And it had faces in it. I saw them. The rope told me it was going to put the thought in your head to come to Wal-Mart today for a crushed ice snack and then it showed up in my room and said, "Lee, you make sure you and Henry do exactly what I say. I want the two of you to run away. You're going to run right out of Wal-Mart."

"Is that right?" Henry shouted back. "You are one sorry son of a dog biscuit. I should have taken Miguel Rodriguez with me instead of you. You can barely walk. Are you crazy? How in the hell was that rope planning on having you run when you need a walker to get from your bed to the shitter? Tell me that, would you?"

A small crowed gathered around them.

"You can't say what I can or can't do, H.C.," Lee shouted.

The air got icy cold. Lilly tried to shake off the chill, but she couldn't.

Henry's face was as white as a bridal gown and his lips were drawn so tightly across his face all that was left was a thread of red. "Run? You can't even walk, much less take your sorry self one step away from your precious prunes, so how are you going to do anything a piece of string says?"

"It's more than a rope," Lee screamed, sounding to Lilly more and more lucid by the second. His skin was tightening and the canyons of crow's feet were gradually disappearing. She was convinced Lee had found the one thing she had never seen but had heard plenty about. But the bigger question yet to be answered was what Lee had done with the rope.

"Lee, where did you put this rope?" Lilly asked.

"Oh, sweet Jesus, Lee," Henry screamed, pounding his own ashen forehead with his fist. "You done messed up all my plans. Come on, buddy, say you ain't seen nothing. Say you were dreaming, and let's get our iced drinks."

"I was not dreaming," Lee said, throwing his walker aside.

Lilly stepped back. The wrinkles in Lee's skin had disappeared and been replaced with the skin of a man in his forties.

Lee burst into tears, covered his eyes, and wailed into his palms.

The crowd stepped aside. A manager ran from the back. "What's happening?" he shouted.

"What *is* happening?" Lee asked Lilly, dropping his hands.

Lilly shook her head. Hodges and she were in big trouble now. They were going to be babysitting rocks for ten eternities instead of one. At the rate they were going, they were probably going to *be* rocks. She snapped her fingers, hoping one snap would put everything back to normal.

"Call the fire department," the employee in the snack bar by the deep fat fryer howled, running from behind the counter. Flames shot out of the kitchen all the way to the ceiling.

"Call the fire department," the manager screamed, wringing his hands on his apron.

Did I do that? Damn it, I must have. Nothing I do works, she thought, shaking her head.

"Is this a movie stunt?" a man from the crowd shouted, but before he got his answer, the fire alarm went off, dispersing the crowd and sending employees, customers, the manager, and visitors racing toward the nearest exits.

Henry rubbed the side of his head, fiddled for a second with his hearing aid, and then ripped it from his ear.

He must have normal hearing.

"We've got to get out of here," Henry said, stuffing his hearing aid in his pocket.

But Lilly couldn't answer, because she was frozen solid where she stood. She had become a porcelain-like statue, the kind she had seen in the same gallery where Henry's work had been shown many years ago.

"Princess," Henry said.

"She's hard as stone," Lee said, touching her cheek.

"Lee?" Henry touched Lee's arm. "You look — you look —"

"I know, Henry. I can feel it. You ought to see yourself."

"Me?"

"Yeah, you." Lee grabbed a metal spatula and held it up to Henry's face. "What do you see, Henry?"

"Holy cow," Henry said, a grin sweeping his jaw line.

Lilly watched, wanting to warn them, but her tongue was firmly planted to the bottom of her mouth.

"Ain't it wonderful?" Henry said, waving the shiny spatula, and then tossing it aside. "Let's get the hell out of here."

Don't go, she thought, as hard as she could.

"But what about the Princess?" Lee asked, running toward the front doors, which were now wide open.

"She'll be okay," Henry answered. "Don't worry about her."

"Guess I don't need this thing," Lee said, taking his hearing aid out and tossing it in a nearby trashcan.

Lilly wanted to call after them, to insist that they stay, but try as she might, she couldn't get her tongue to budge. *Shit. This has to be the Jameses again. How am I going to get out of this one?*

There was so much Lilly wanted to know, but she couldn't do anything but ruminate over the questions she couldn't answer while she waited to be released from her porcelain state. To pass the time, she concentrated on a cart loaded with hair dye standing nearby. She particularly loved the models' hair, a variety of reds and golden blondes. She admired the way they titled their heads and smiled with confidence, as if they would be young forever. Those glowing faces shouted to the world that they would never want for the touch of another person. Lilly knew from the look in their eyes and the coy dip of their chins that they believed what they projected to the world and, therefore, dared passing shoppers to ignore them. These girls could never imagine growing old, couldn't fathom that one day the touch of a hairstylist's hands against their scalp would feel like the touch of a recalcitrant lover making amends.

Lilly knew better than most that in old age the majority of this bevy of beauties would rush to their weekly hair appointments where their would be washed, their heads massaged, and then towel-dried, while their hearts pounded like teenagers on a first date. These models, in their later and final years, would flock, just as their contemporaries would, to the local salon—not for the dye, the perm, or the cut, or to have their nails done, but because they craved something much more basic—they would come simply to be touched by another human being.

If asked, Lilly would have said that hair salons, throughout time, had shared the same purpose: they were places of spiritual refuge for the shy, the old, the dumbfounded, the disfigured, and the lonely. Hair salons had always been the one the place where people could partake in the communion of touch and, for a brief period of time, be healed of whatever ailed them—the hair salon had been, and would always be, the temple of love.

"And hairstylists will always be the ministers of love," Lilly had once told Hodges. "We place our hands on the people no one touches or wants to touch and, by doing so, ease their suffering, even if only for the time they are in our care—any hairstylist on the planet can tell you that."

Once Henry and Lee were out of sight, the store filled with firefighters intent, it appeared to Lilly, on covering every square inch of exposed floor, ceiling, or shelves and everything in between with foam and water. Somebody get me out of here, she thought as thick white foam coated her from head to toe.

A female firefighter wiped the foam from her face.

Great, Lilly thought, once she realized she knew this particular public servant.

"What do you know," the firefighter said. "For once I'm saving you instead of kicking you into a new era."

Why is that?

"Because we're on the same side for a change," she said, removing her hat. Black curls shot in every direction, as if a collection of shiny black springs had been sprung loose. It was an act the other firefighters didn't notice.

I bet.

"I wish you were a gambler because if you were, that's a bet I'd make. I'd like to have you doing my work so I could be sunning on some luxurious beach right now instead of standing here watching you get harder and harder. But you're in luck," she said, clapping her hands.

Girl James's hair had always reminded Lilly of the inside of a mattress, but she didn't dare say so. She shivered, shook, and became herself again, only now she was soaking wet. "James, you little creep," Lilly said. "What the hell did you freeze me for?"

"I didn't," the sister of James James James said. "Golly, gee whiz. How silly of me to think you might be grateful for being rescued."

"Don't screw with me. I've had enough of you and your brothers."

"Hey, I'm your savior, so be nice." Girl James wagged her finger in Lilly's face.

"Girl James, Saint. I can't picture it," Lilly said. *But you did free me, and for that I'm grateful.*

"You're welcome," Girl James answered, distracted by the firefighters making one last sweep through and around the Wal-Mart snack bar.

Seemingly satisfied that everything had been taken care of and the fire they had rushed to put out was in no danger of reigniting, the firefighters began their exodus back to the front of the store, rolling up hoses as they went.

Lilly had no idea where Henry and Lee had disappeared to, but just in case unknown forces had snatched her two old friends, she would raise a wall of protection around them. She rolled her eyes, held her hands in the air, and recited a petition of protection so old she couldn't remember when she'd first learned it or even who'd taught it to her. The thing that was supposed to happen would now take place, but without Lilly's presence. Henry and Lee would be safe until they made the decision that only they could make.

"The Petition for Safety, huh?" Girl James said.

"Protection," Lilly corrected.

"Whatever. Let me do one, too. Those two are going to need it." Girl James chanted something in a language even Lilly had never heard, jabbed at the air with her forefinger, slapped her hands together twice, and then said, "Double whammy. They're safe, as far as I can tell."

"Thanks," Lilly said, sounding as if she were softening, but she wasn't. "Why did you do that?"

"I have to."

She has to? Ordinarily, Lilly would be curious about why James had to help, but all she wanted was to figure out what was going on. Girl James, she was certain, was only around for one thing: trouble.

"Ever think of changing your name?" Lilly asked, trying to divert Girl James's attention from whatever she was really up to.

Girl James grabbed some paper towels off a shelf, tore them open, and gave a handful to Lilly. "Why would I change my name?" she asked. "What's wrong with James James James?"

Lilly wiped her face, hair and hands. "Isn't it a little hard for people to differentiate you from your brothers? You're all named James James James, aren't you?"

"I know who I am, and you've got eyes, don't you?" Girl James said, as if Lilly had asked a stupid question. "Just because we have the same name doesn't mean we are the same. Besides, I'm a girl."

So you present yourself—but I'm not sure what you are and I've never been sure what you are, Lilly thought. "We both know that's not what I'm talking about," she said, looking around, expecting to have another James James James appear and to be turned into a kitchen utensil. She could usually deflect their efforts when she had at least a second's notice, but she so rarely did.

"We are the least of your worries," Girl James said.

"I've heard that before."

"Not from me you haven't," Girl James said, rolling her eyes. "Maybe you heard it from Number One James, or Baby James, but not me. I'm the lady of the bunch."

"You're the same family, the same scamps responsible for tricking Hodges and me into accidentally setting off Mt. Vesuvius. Don't think for one minute I don't remember all those people in Pompeii going up in smoke ... or the next two hundred years Hodges and I spent in darkness." Every time she thought of those wasted years spent wandering the dark side with wailing souls searching for the one thing they had loved the most while on Earth, she was sad and angry. Hodges and she had felt the pain of longing and existing only as longing with no vessel, no body to absorb their grief. *And exactly what were we grieving? What was it that generated that terrible ache?*

Their time among the discarded had been excruciating. After all, Hodges and she had been imagined by the light and out of the glow of all goodness, and to be cast out—no, Hodges and she could not take being cast out again, could not go through another time of longing; the pain would be too great. *Had it been goodness we so desperately missed? Or was it having no purpose that compelled us and made our separation so intolerable? Why can't I remember?*

"The why of things isn't important—that's all done, but I am sorry about what happened to Hodges and you," Girl James said. "It was a little joke, an accident. How were we supposed to know what would happen?"

"And what about the time the three of you tricked us into serving beef to those old people in that village in India?"

"Those people were going to starve to death," Girl James said. "And Hodges and you were slow as molasses in getting around to taking care of them."

"But we were told to work within their belief system and you all knew it."

"Who told you to let a bunch of old folks starve to death?"

"No one. We had a plan, and things would have been fine if you hadn't interfered."

"Who were you taking orders from?" Girl James was beginning to vibrate in a way that made Lilly nervous. With the Jameses, you never knew what was really going to happen until it happened, but in this case, Lilly was betting that this was a signal that the little imp was worried.

"You know I can't tell you that."

"Because you don't know. You two have been here so long, you don't know who you're taking orders from. For all you know, the Protectors could be worse than us. That's who's really in charge, isn't it?"

"No."

"Then it's Citibank."

"Citibank? Are you crazy? What are you talking about?" Dealing with the Jameses had always been difficult, even when they were coherent, but Lilly was not in the mood for games. Not today.

"The big corporations. They run everything down here."

"Don't underestimate me, James," Lilly said, her face darkening and the muscles in her neck tightening. "Even I have limits when it comes to patience, so stop with this nonsense. We need to get to work on the task at hand." She spun her lip ring and glared at James.

"For all you know, there could be some other group, like us, disguised as Citibank executives and ..."

"You're ridiculous. You sound like Henry and all the other conspiracy theorists," Lilly said, gritting her teeth. "Henry worries about how drinking prune juice is a plot by relatives to steal his money, and now you." *How did we get sidetracked?*

"Letting those cows get fat and sassy while people were starving didn't make sense to me," Girl James said. "Anyway, we had the best intentions. Chalk it up to another accident. I still say somebody had to do something."

But, Lilly remembered, the Jameses had had a good laugh when they saw the reaction of the village elders when they discovered they had eaten the very things they worshiped. Hodges and she had been horrified, but the Jameses had had no sympathy for the human anguish that followed in the aftermath of their so-called "good deed."

"Shut up," Lilly snarled. "I shouldn't have trusted you back then and I shouldn't trust you now."

Hodges and Lilly had been disciplined for this "grave error in judgment" by being made to wander the streets of Calcutta as beggars until they had forgotten who they were, and why they existed in the first place. Who had put them in the dark, dank city where the air was thick with human suffering? Funny, but that was one thing she couldn't remember. Had they been remanded to Calcutta to learn to understand their charges, or had it been to intensify the sorrow of being separate and alone? Lilly couldn't remember that, either. She did remember that Hodges and she had developed sores all over their bodies, that they had appealed to the more fortunate for scraps of food and scrounged the city for fresh water, and that Hodges, penniless and in rags, had taken to wearing old coats he found on the streets. After several years of wandering Calcutta's alleyways and marketplaces, they had finally been awakened and returned to their true selves by a smack on the forehead from a passing Hindu Master. On that day, Hodges was delirious from the heat—he was wearing twelve coats at once—and Lilly was suffering from head lice, a staph infection that covered over half her body, and an open wound on her foot. Yes, Hodges and she understood human suffering, and in the end it had made them more alert, more compassionate.

Because of their own suffering, Lilly now felt forced to embrace the Jameses, who had been born out of darkness and who had originally found themselves in the world understanding nothing except corruption. Had it not been for what the Jameses had seen in the spirits of the humans and the realization that arriving in this world brought with it free will, they might have done as *Them* had wanted and been forever condemned to darkness.

Girl James and her brothers had chosen to stay in this imagined world and as close to Hodges and Lilly as possible because, Lilly guessed, of the tiny peek at goodness and mercy they had had, the possibility of redemption from their foul and rudimentary origins, and their ability to choose. Although the Jameses would never admit to being attracted to the idea of free will or kindness, Lilly was sure these were the reasons they hovered so close. Girl James was right when she said they couldn't have known what would happen as a result of their antics, and Lilly understood their ignorance was a forgivable offense. Had it not been for the Jameses' "accidents," as they so blithely referred to them, perhaps Lilly and Hodges would not be as caring for the residents of Sunnyside as they were. So she decided she would forgive the Jameses, but she didn't have to like or fully trust them. *Why is every decision so complicated?* She adjusted her blouse. "Now, what did you do with Henry and Lee?" she asked.

"Nothing. I swear."

"You are such a liar."

"I'm not lying, Lilly," Girl James said.

"I've never known you to tell the truth."

"Well, for once I'm being straight, honest, truthful—all those things I find distasteful." Girl James laughed, her curls threatening to leap off her head and onto the nearby shelves.

Undisciplined and immature consciousness, Lilly thought. If it wasn't Girl James who drove them off, then *that's* why they took off without me. Henry and Lee think they know something, and they do, but they only have part of the picture. I wish this whole business was a result of humanity's slow crawl up the evolutionary trail, but it's not.

Knowledge, as powerful as it is, could be dangerous when acquired by the uninformed or unprepared, but in Lilly's mind this did not make an increase in knowledge a bad thing—only a thing to be handled with respect and care. Henry and Lee were overwhelmed by the excitement of being freed by forces stronger than themselves, but they were not thinking, and this made their situation precarious. For a moment she longed for the early days, when she was Li, Hodges was Ha, and all things earthly were new—but when she gave it a bit more thought, those days were filled with scary creatures and humans who ate raw meat and whose only form of communicating consisted of grunts and growls. No, she didn't really want to return to those times. *But why do I have to be the one in charge? Why was I asked to care for these people? Why couldn't I have been given an easier job? Is this regret and dissatisfaction with my life I'm feeling? But these feelings are what I remove from the residents at Sunnyside. Are they somehow attaching themselves to me?*

"I don't know what happened to Henry or Lee, but I know why I'm here."

"And why is that?" Lilly asked.

"You won't believe me if I tell you."

"Try me." *Hurry up. Get to the point. I'm running out of patience.*

"Okay, okay."

Lilly crossed her arms and scowled at Girl James so that she would know she meant business. "I'm waiting."

"James James James sent me."

"Why? To do what?"

"Okay," Girl James said, grinning as if she had just been named Queen for a Day, "but when you hear why I'm here, it is really going to raise a blister."

11
Henry

Outside, Henry and Lee inhaled the hot humid air. Waves of heat rippled upward from the pavement, giving Henry the sensation of standing in a sauna. He tugged at his wet, sticky shirt, clinging to his chest.

"Refreshing, ain't it?" Lee asked Henry.

"Hell no, it ain't refreshing," Henry said. "It's stale and muggy, but it's the air of the free, so it's all right by me."

Lee nodded, looking somewhat dazed to Henry. "You all right, Lee?" he asked.

"Never better, never better," Lee said, looking himself over. "I can honestly say I never felt better in my whole life. Just surprised is all."

"Good." Henry examined his hands, now hard, tanned and youthful. "I'm feeling mighty frisky myself," Henry said, running his tongue over his teeth. "No dentures, Lee. Look, no dentures." He pulled back his lips so Lee could see.

"Well, I'll be damned. Would you look at that?" he said, peering into Henry's mouth, and then stepping back. "Did you notice we're wearing new clothes, too?" He pointed to his boots and then his pants.

"They ain't exactly brand new, Lee. Ain't that shirt you're wearing the same shirt you got for your twenty-first birthday? If I remember correctly, you wore that piece of cotton every day for damn near a year."

Lee glanced down at his chest. "No wonder I'm feeling so good. I'm wearing my favorite shirt." He looked up at Henry, appearing to be the happiest Henry could remember seeing him in years. "This day is getting better and better," Lee said.

"I'd have to agree with you there," Henry answered. "No more white rags Sunnyside calls shirts — and I am some grateful for that, even if this one here does have long sleeves." Henry was now wearing a western shirt with roses embroidered on the front yokes and red piping accents on the yokes and front arrow pockets. Pearl-covered snaps ran down the front of his shirt in place of buttons and similar pearl snaps held his sleeves together at the wrists. He took his hearing aid out of his pocket and tossed it onto the ground. "I sure don't need this anymore, either."

"It's a wonderful thing," Lee said, "whatever the hell is happening."

Henry turned around a couple of times to see if they were still in front of Wal-Mart and sure enough, they were. Nothing on the outside of the store seemed to have changed; it was still blue, with its standard Wal-Mart sign, in white and red trim on the building in various spots. "Everything looks normal," Henry said. "But it can't be. Think we're dead?"

"I don't believe so," Lee answered. "We could be having the same dream, though. I've heard of that happening. If that's what we're doing, all I can say is, it's a damn good dream. I don't reckon I want anybody to wake me up, at least not yet."

"Hey, Lee, check that out." Henry pointed to the far end of the parking lot, where a beaten and bruised green pickup truck without a driver sat, its engine running. Henry looked for the people who had been in the store earlier but the lot was empty and, from the looks of things, so was the Wal-Mart.

"It's kind of creepy out here," Lee said. "You don't reckon the devil is going to show up and roast us over a fire, do you?"

"You know, Lee," Henry said. "I thought you were feebleminded in your old age, but now I'm seeing that maybe you were a touch slow from the git-go."

"Shut the hell up, Henry. You don't know where we are or what's happening to us any more than I do. I've been taking crap from you my whole life, and I ain't about to start all over again, if that's what's happening here. You understand me?" Lee stubbed the ground with the toe of his boot, taking a nick out of the fine leather. The hurt on his face was too much for Henry.

"Relax, Lee. I don't mean anything by it, and I don't think we're starting over. Maybe we're starting somewhere in the middle or maybe not. Maybe we're part of a medical experiment at Sunnyside. Can't say. All I know is I am forty years younger and that works for me."

But Henry could see Lee wasn't listening. He was gazing off in the distance.

"Hey, Henry," he said pointing at the ratty, banged-up pickup, "ain't that your old tin bucket, the one you used to sneak off with Isabella in? Look at that—it's got a ding on the door just under the handle—same as that old pickup you drove into the ground. "

Henry looked at the truck, examining it thoughtfully. "Damned if you ain't onto something, Lee. Let's take a look," he said.

"Henry, how do you suppose we got like this?" Lee asked, admiring his middle-aged hands as they headed over to where the pickup sat purring over the sweltering asphalt.

"You tell me," Henry said. "You're the one with the talking rope." He laughed. "Maybe we really are dead." *But I don't believe we are.*

"Wait, Henry," Lee said. "Don't go over there. If we're dead, this might be the devil's work."

"Well, if it is the devil's work, then I'd say we are already up shit creek without a paddle." Heat rippled in waves all around the truck and them and, for a split second, Henry wondered if maybe they really had died and gone to hell. Wherever they were, though, he decided, there was nothing he could think of that they could do about it at this point, so as far as he was concerned they might as well enjoy themselves. "The way I see it, Lee, good or bad, we're here, wherever 'here' is, and there ain't nothing left to do but enjoy what we can, so we might as well go ahead and kick up our heels."

Lee examined the stiff leather boots he was wearing and then jumped, clicking his heels together ripping the air with a boisterous, "Yippee."

Henry strutted over to the pickup, snapping his fingers for the sheer joy and ease of doing so. As he approached the familiar truck, he did a little jig.

Henry peeped through the glass on the driver's side and then stepped aside so Lee could take a peek. "What do you think, Lee?" he asked.

Lee pressed his hands against the glass, looked over the door, and then pressed his face against the window for one last look. "It's yours. Ain't no question about it," he said, dropping his hands and turning back to Henry.

Hanging from the interior mirror was a beaded necklace with tiny red hearts dangling from its center. It was exactly like the one Isabella had always worn, until she took it off one day and hung in on the interior mirror of his truck—a mirror exactly like the one in front of him. *This has to be my truck.*

"Climb in," a sugary female voice said. "You drive."

Henry sniffed the air, now filled with the odor of lilacs and freshly soaped skin. "I'd know that smell anywhere," he said to Lee.

"Afraid to look behind you?" the voice asked.

Henry and Lee whipped around, until they were facing the owner of the familiar voice. Henry gasped and Lee clutched Henry's arm.

"What the hell?" Lee sputtered.

Henry tried to speak, but all he could manage was "Uh, uh, uh."

12
Katherine

Katherine blinked just long enough to catch the spin of what looked to her like a tornado tearing a path across the desert toward her. *Funny, I should be running for shelter, but I don't want to.* The tornado cut through a rock garden, the same one she remembered from childhood as being her sister's, and came to a swirling, pulsating halt not two feet in front of her. Amazed by her newfound fearlessness and determined to stand her ground, she shut her eyes, fully expecting to be swept up with the rocks, dust, and anything else the roiling twister had snatched up along the way. *I'm not going anywhere and you can't make me.* But once in the center of the raging coil, she heard voices appealing to her for freedom, so she opened her eyes to find a parade of ghosts passing, each summarizing the state of the life they had lived when alive. They spoke as they passed by, reviewing lives lived wrong, and reciting their mistakes and regrets over and over to Katherine as if they were searching for a new mantra. Katherine fell to her knees. *Who's talking? Am I crazy? What's happening here?*

"Kat," a familiar voice said. "Kat, it's Mora."

Katherine opened her eyes and gasped. "Mora?" The twirling conglomeration of voices and mournful faces was gone and in its place stood her sister. Mora's soft brown hair swept over her shoulders in a delicate flip, just as Katherine remembered it, and she wore her signature faded jeans and the same pale yellow blouse with her name embroidered on the pocket she had worn the day she died. In Mora's shadow, Katherine hung her head, feeling insignificant, small, and childlike.

Mora took Katherine's hand and lifted her to her feet. She held a mirror in front of her face. "Look, baby," she said. "You can begin again if you want to."

Kat leaned forward, staring into the eyes of a young girl of around twelve years old. "Mora," Kat cried, shoving the mirror aside and then in a child's voice cried, "I didn't mean it that time I said I hated you. I didn't mean any of those terrible things I said. I love you, Mora, I love you; I do.

"I know you do, Kat. You always loved me," her sister answered, "just like I have always loved you."

"Oh," Katherine whispered, closing her eyes, and throwing her arms around her sister. "I miss you so much. I'm sorry. Sorry." Katherine held her sister as tight as she could, sensing she might leave. "Don't go, Mora. Don't leave me again," she cried.

"Kat? Kat," a voice boomed.

Katherine opened her eyes. She was slumped in a heap at James's feet, clutching his legs, the mirror on the ground beside her. She looked first at James and then at the mirror. A child stared back.

"Oh, my God, James, is that me?" she asked, pointing to the mirror.

"Yes, ma'am," he said.

"I'm a child again?"

"I'm afraid so."

Katherine released his legs and scooted backwards, staring at her legs and feet, now petite. "Damn it," she said, speaking in a grownup's voice, "how in the devil's name did this happen?"

"First guilt," he said, helping her to her feet.

Every time James James James touched her, she was flooded with love; it made her question how she could have suspected him of wrongdoing in the first place.

"First guilt?" she asked

"That's correct," he answered, and let out a sigh that sounded to her as if he were burdened with the woes of the world.

"I think it's time to fill me in," Katherine said, clenching her fists as the feistiness she had felt at twelve came back. "Tell me what's going on," she demanded.

"I'm not really sure," he said. "But don't worry. I have an idea...I think I'm on the right track, but..."

"Don't worry? Are you insane? I was sixty-six just a second ago and now I'm—"

"Some people would be happy to be young again," he said, looking, Katherine thought, somewhat annoyed.

"How about twenty-five? I'd even take sixteen, but this?" She was overwhelmed by the urge to buy some licorice sticks, her favorite thing when she was just the age she now appeared to be. "James, I'm starting to think like a kid. Tell me this isn't happening." Katherine threw her hands up to her face.

"I'll get this under control, I promise," he said, taking her hand.

The warmth of her hand in his, and the feel of her small pink hand lying against his thick, callused palm, was comforting. His touch seemed to absorb her fear. Katherine wanted to believe him, had to believe him.

"You have to believe me when I say I'll take care of this. What's happening is a long story and much too complicated for a gentle lady such as yourself."

"Try me," Katherine said, tearing her hand away. "If I'm not dead or drugged, then I'm supposed to live until at least sixty-six. Right?"

James nodded.

"Then you'd have to agree we've got nothing but time at this point. The way I see it, I've got about forty-eight years ahead of me." *Damn it. Why do men always think they know everything?*

"Not really," he said.

"No?"

"No, ma'am. I don't know everything, but I know you've got somewhere around a few hours, your time, to figure things out. A few hours, max. Maybe."

But I'm only twelve. What does he mean? Oh, my God, I must be drugged. I have to be. Where's Mora? I want my mama and daddy. Daddy is a sheriff and he will put him in jail for doing this. What am I thinking? I'm so confused. That trickster drugged me. Yes, he did. "You," she said, but she was so disoriented she forgot her words.

"Honey, I did not feed you hallucinogens," James James James, said. "This is as real as anything else you've experienced — that much I can tell you. And while I don't understand exactly what's going on, I can make an educated guess about our time frame — and it's not long."

Katherine backed away. She had been a fool for so many men that she had begun to feel as if she had entered adulthood with "All assholes and dimwits check in here" tattooed on her forehead.

"Let's sit on Mora's bench," Katherine said, pointing to a rickety, blue wooden bench her sister had left too long in the sun so that the paint had begun to bubble and peel. *I have to be calm.* She was sounding and acting twelve again, which frightened her. The last thing she needed under these circumstances was for her sixty-six-year-old self to disappear entirely.

"You don't need to worry," James said, dropping onto the creaky wood. "I don't think you'll lose the memory of who you are, although you're going to bounce between twelve and sixty-six."

Not quite relieved by his answer, Katherine sat beside James and then turned, leaning against the arm of the bench, facing him. "You think, but you don't know?" she asked.

"This is a first time for me, too," he said.

She drew her knees up until her feet, now dressed in a pair of black leather cowboy boots, rested on the bench. "These are my favorite boots," she said, hugging her knees. "My parents gave them to me for my twelfth birthday."

James patted the toes of her boots. "I know," he said.

"This has something to do with that idiot Hair Princess, doesn't it?"

"Why would you say that?"

"She hangs out with that weirdo, Hodges, with the tattoo that blows kisses. I never said anything about it before, but I'm saying it now because everything has gone cuckoo around me. The two of them are into witchcraft, aren't they?"

"Not hardly," James said.

And then sounding more like a child than herself, she said, "Magic. They do magic, right?" And she thought about how witches and magicians could conjure up anything, even dead people. Didn't I just meet with my sister? she thought. The ache in her heart was unbearable.

"Something like that, but I wouldn't call it magic. A normal human being might not fully understand what they do, so I guess it's better just to call it magic. Better to think of them as angels—a special breed of strange angels. Just like you."

"Like me?"

"You don't know, do you?"

"Know what? That my sister is dead? I want my sister back," she said, pouting.

"You'll see your sister again, so try not to worry."

"Who are you, really? And why do you call yourself James James James?" she asked with the authority of a woman in her sixties. As she spoke, she felt herself swell with an anger and hatred so intense she thought she felt the roots of her hair begin to sizzle.

James waved his hand over her face as if he were removing something. The anger and hatred dissipated briefly, surged through her again, and then disappeared. For a moment, Katherine's heart raced and her fingers twitched. James touched her hands and they relaxed. "We took our name from King James, the English king who had the Bible translated to suit him," he answered. "He hated the Catholic Church because church authorities were always trying to do away with him."

"I thought you said your father named you."

"No, I said that's what people say. I said that people accuse our father of trying to be like a television personality. I didn't say we even had a father. But if you could identify such a person, I'd have to say he was bigger than anybody you'd ever see on TV."

Is he joking? "So you don't have parents?" she asked. It was clear to her that if she hadn't been drugged, she had to be dreaming because she didn't believe in otherworldly stuff, and in order to believe she was doing anything other than dreaming, she'd have to believe in devils, angels, fairies, Santa Claus, or at least magic, but she didn't, so she might as well enjoy her dream.

"We had parents—we just never knew them because they weren't like your parents," James said. He smiled and then patted her arm the way a parent pats a child's arm to offer comfort. "Let's just say we were raised by tutors. The best you could find in the universe."

She loved it when he touched her—she felt protected, and as if she would never lack for anything. If she believed in the supernatural, she'd have to say that James James James made her feel this way on purpose, because he was working toward some end she couldn't identify—not yet, anyway—but she didn't, so all she could say was that she hadn't felt so cared for in her whole life. *Why knock a good thing when it lands in your lap?* "You must have gotten a good education," Katherine said, not knowing what else to say.

"The best. You can't imagine the depth to which we were educated." He shook his head, still smiling.

Katherine thought his smile seemed to grow right along with the satisfaction of remembering his youth, so at first she couldn't take her eyes away from him. But under his gaze, she felt small and vulnerable. It was that feeling that brought her back around to her present circumstances because it had been the same way she felt when she first saw Mora. *Who's going to take care of me?* she thought, coming to her senses and realizing she still had a lot of growing up to do—again. "Damn it," she said, looking herself over.

"You're safe with me," James said. "You'll always be safe with me."

Katherine examined James's face with a child's eye. His nose seemed unusually large, his eyes had grown muddy, and wiry tuffs of snow-white hair poked out of his ears. *Yuck*, she thought. The crow's feet cradling his eyes crept from the corners, crawling into his hairline. *Disgusting.* She ran her fingers over her forehead and the area around her eyes. *Smooth as silk.* Katherine examined James's hands comparing them to hers—his were wide, the skin crinkled. His fingers were thick and their tips callused. Her hands were delicate, pink, and soft. "You're old," she blurted.

"So are you," he said.

"Not anymore," she answered.

13
Lilly

"I told you what I had to say would raise a blister," Girl James said. "Now, calm down. Like it or not, it's true."

"You're telling me that James James James sent you to save me?"

"That's correct."

"You really expect me to believe that, after all we've been through together? After—"

Girl James held up her hand. "There's no need to repeat what we both already know."

"Sure, he sent you. Or *They* did. And which James are you talking about anyway? You're all named James James James. I never know when you're telling the truth or what the hell any of you are talking about half the time, or which one of you the other one is referring to. If you ask me, you're all the same entity, just different aspects of the same thing."

"Do you really think so? I mean, I've heard of people having multiple personalities, but you'd think we'd be above that kind of simple biology or psychology, wouldn't you?"

Girl James sounded a lot like her older brother James James James to Lilly. *You three really are the same entity, aren't you?*

"Interesting theory, isn't it?" Girl James asked, wearing an expression resembling the elder James so exactly that Lilly had to look away.

"You could say that," Lilly answered.

"But how would you prove that we're the same?" Girl James said, sounding like herself again. "Any ideas?"

"I don't have time to chat," Lilly said, looking up, and then shoving Girl James to one side. "One thing I can always count on, whether you all are one and the same, is that you are always up to no good." She was surprised to see that James didn't flinch. Girl James never let anyone touch her.

"Lilly, you have to believe me. I'm here to help," Girl James said, stepping in front of her.

"Get out of my way. I need to get back to Hodges. God knows what you three have going on at Sunnyside, or what you've done to Henry and Lee."

"Stop worrying about Henry and Lee. We petitioned for safety. They're safe for now," Girl James shouted.

"So you say, but I don't know what you really petitioned for," Lilly said, pushing Girl James James James out of the way again. She had once seen the oldest James turn a foe into a pincushion and drop him on a table in a seamstress's shop, and it had taken Hodges and Lilly two full days to undo his dirty work. The poor man was full of tiny pinpricks by the time they rescued him. *I hope nothing so terrible has happened to Henry and Lee.*

"You'd better listen to me because I'm not joking," Girl James yelped. "I let you touch me, I let you touch me, I let you touch me," she screamed.

"Why should I trust you?" Lilly yelled back.

"The Mt. Vesuvius thing was an *accident*. How many times do I have to tell you? But if you think that was bad, I'm here to tell you this is worse. We've got major problems, Princess," the pixie-like Girl James said, narrowing her eyes even more. She was as serious and as afraid as Lilly had ever seen her.

Maybe the little devil is telling the truth, Lilly thought. After all, she had let Lilly touch her, and touching Girl James was never allowed. James's skin, according to Hodges, hurt all the time and Lilly had seen firsthand that the human touch, or any touch, caused her excruciating pain. Whatever Girl James had done to be robbed of the ability to be hugged or touched seemed unnecessarily cruel in light of what Lilly knew about humans, but she had never really understood *what* the Jameses were. Were they some kind of mutated version of *Them*, or were they once closer to something such as Hodges and she and had evolved into whatever they were now? Or had they been created by *Them* and were something altogether new? Lilly doubted she'd ever know, but that didn't matter. At this point, she needed to know if James was telling the truth, so she grabbed Girl James by the arm. Girl James twitched, grimaced, and then cried out. It was a stifled cry, but to Lilly's surprise, she didn't pull back or even try to break free from her grip.

"Happy?" Girl James asked, her eyes fluttering and her face growing white, having drained itself of color.

Lilly dropped her hand. Deep red fingers prints remained burned into James's skin. "I'm sorry, James," she said. "I knew touch hurt you, but this — I had no idea."

"Grab me again, if you want," she said, as if having her arm grabbed wasn't painful in the slightest.

Lilly sighed. *What is wrong with me? I'm acting as though I don't believe Hodges. And what am I going to do about Hodges? He will blow a gasket when I tell him we have to work with the Three Jameses, and it's looking as if that's what I'm going to have to do.*

Girl James was still offering her arm for Lilly's grasp. "Look, Li, I am sorry about Hodges and you being cast out of the fold and being sent to Calcutta, too, but just this once, Lilly Beale," Girl James pleaded, "we have to work together. Of course, when this is over ..." she said, smirking.

"That's good, James," Lilly said. "That'll get me on your team." But before she could say another word, she was interrupted by a hissing sound and then a *swish, swish,* as if someone was sweeping the floor. Lilly and Girl James spun in the direction of the hiss and the sound of movement, but there was nothing there. "See anything?" she asked, searching in every direction. *It's one of Them. This is bad — very bad.*

"No," Girl James answered. "*Nada.*"

A disembodied voice cackled, imitating Girl James. "We have to work together." The swish and hiss grew louder and then faded out.

"That's our biggest problem right now," Girl James said, looking up at the ceiling as if she expected a body to appear out of nowhere.

"You don't have to say that again," Lilly said, feeling as if she had awakened unexpectedly and found herself stuck on top of a roller coaster about to make the rush downhill. What else could she do now that one of *Them* had been made known to her? As much as she hated to partner up with the Three Jameses, Girl James was right. "So they've gotten loose?"

"I'm afraid so. Somehow. And I swear, Lilly Beale, the Three Jameses had nothing to do with it. At least not intentionally."

"But how, if you didn't do it?" Lilly was skeptical to say the least. "I mean, that voice. Wasn't that—?"

"Don't know. I think it was, but they could be imitating him. Believe me, we're as afraid of those things as you are," Girl James said. "And if they've got him, then the rest of us are next."

"You don't think they've opened the—" Lilly started to say, but Girl James cut her off.

"They have," she said. "I heard them."

So the portal has been opened and They *are loose again.*

Girl James had a talent her brothers and Lilly and Hodges didn't have. If anything was off in the universe, no matter what time of day or night or no matter where it was, she could tell. She knew when the abnormal was taking place, when the universe tipped slightly off-center and the natural way of things became skewed. She could hear the tiniest and what, to most entities, seemed to be insignificant, shifts in the universe. "It snapped and popped like a dry twig," she said. "It woke me straight out of a dead sleep."

"A dead sleep?" Lilly asked.

"Yep," Girl James said.

This was bad, so bad Lilly found it hard to imagine that the Three Jameses were responsible. It was a known fact among the Protectors, to whom Hodges and Lilly belonged, that Girl James died every night. Call it a bad spell, or call it sticking your nose in the wrong place at the wrong time, but as the result of some unfortunate interaction with those *things*, Girl James died at the end of every day and had to relive the experience of being reborn and growing up the next. By midday she became an adult again, but the whole business was troublesome and painful, at least from what Lilly had heard. Her brothers had been searching for a way to break this scenario for centuries, but so far, no luck. Serves the little monster right, Lilly thought, and then she regretted thinking such an ugly thought so unlike her. *I'm behaving like a human being. What's happening to me? Hodges acts like one, too. That can't be right. Poor James. She can't be touched, and she dies everyday. How cruel the universe can be.* As much as she didn't care for the Jameses, Lilly had to admit that Hodges and she had been together with them for so long that she had come to think of them as family. Of course, the Jameses, when compared to the families who visited Sunnyside, were more like the part of the family you never wanted to invite to Thanksgiving dinner or to family parties because you never knew what they might do or say.

Regardless of the role the Jameses served in her life, if the beasts had gotten loose and the three Jameses weren't responsible, it would take every angel, leprechaun, fairy, and entity of good intent to send them back to where they had come. But then again, the Jameses were dimwits at times, and what they thought was funny usually ended up resulting in a major disaster. This could be one of those times, especially because the voice was so familiar. Of course, there was a slight chance that what was causing the trouble was entirely new, but that was remote.

"I did not, nor did any member of my clan, release those hideous bastards," Girl James said, her voice shaky, "You can't believe I'd release them, even if they promised my skin would stop hurting and I wouldn't have to die every night."

Lilly stared at Girl James without saying a word.

"If I'm lying, I'll bathe in holy water for a month," she said.

"Is that so? Holy water won't do a thing to you and we both know it. You've been watching too many movies."

"We ditched *Them*, remember? James James James and I did not do as ordered. Why would we do what they wanted now, when we didn't do it back then?"

"If it turns out I'm lying, I'll indenture myself to Hodges and his—"

"And confess to all the horrible wicked things in the last three centuries, especially the ones that made Hodges and me look like incompetent twits?" Lilly asked. "And you'll make these confessions to the *proper* authorities?" The powers above them knew what the three Jameses had done anyway, Lilly thought, but she enjoyed making the creepy wisp of trouble jump through hoops.

"Yes," Girl James answered.

"If you aren't telling the truth, I'm going to have Hodges release Tattoo," Lilly said. She had never been right when it had come to trusting a James, but she had always had the sense that something was off prior to agreeing to anything with them. This time she knew James was being truthful—perhaps for the first time, but truthful all the same, because this time the Jameses' safety was on the line. Girl James was a purely selfish creature, as were all the Jameses, so Hodges and she were safe—they had a purely selfish promise from a purely selfish creature. Lilly stuck out her hand.

Girl James snatched Lilly's hand and grimaced. The two shook on their partnership with Lilly squeezing James's hand as hard as she could, but James only gritted her teeth. It was a vigorous shake on both their parts, promising a cooperative and untroubled union.

"You'd better not pull a fast one," Lilly said, trying to appear threatening by raising her eyebrows, scrunching up her nose, and snarling. "I've got a few tricks of my own, thanks to you three."

"Partners?" Girl James asked, unfazed by Lilly's curled upper lip and wrinkled nose.

"Partners," Lilly said, hoping she wouldn't be sorry.

14
Henry

Henry was on something like his tenth "uh huh" when the woman he was staring at finally spoke up.

"What are you boys waiting for?" she asked. "You act like you've seen a ghost." She stood on her tiptoes, her rich brown hair swirling in airy ringlets around her face. Her olive skin was as smooth and velvety and her mouth as pink, plump, and inviting as Henry could remember.

"Isabella?" Henry said. "Is it really you?"

Lee said, "I'm scared, Henry. Something ain't right. It ain't right at all. The dead can't…"

Henry wasn't able to keep listening to Lee. His long-sleeved shirt was overheating him and making him dizzy. Between the heat and finding himself in his current state, he was sure he was imagining what he saw in front of him. *That girl is Isabella all right, or I'm the shoe leather on the bottom of my boot.*

Isabella grabbed Henry by the shoulders, pulled him to her, and gave him a solid wet kiss right on the lips.

This is real. This girl is real. God, please let her be the real thing, Henry thought, trying to decide if he should be worried or whoop it up for joy. Parts he once thought would never tingle again, tingled. "Isabella?" he asked again. If this young woman was Isabella, she hadn't aged a day since he last saw her fifty-two years ago. *Should I be happy or scream for help?*

"Quit your worrying. There's nothing to be afraid of. We've got places to be and things to do, Henry Cole Calhoun," she said with such gusto Henry had to laugh. She wiggled the rusted door handle on the driver's side and tugged open the door, creaking and squealing its only signs of complaint. "Climb on in, Henry. You come around to the other side with me, Lee."

While Henry scrambled onto the drivers' side, Lee and Isabella slid in on the passenger side. Henry settled onto the faded vinyl seat and adjusted the mirror.

Lee fiddled with the radio as if he were fixated on finding a radio station, his eyebrows knit together in one straight line over his youthful eyes and nose, but Henry knew that look well. Lee's frown was one of suspicion and didn't have a thing to do with the radio. It was a look that said, "Doomsday is upon us."

"Just once in your life, Lee," Henry said, "think of the unexpected and unusual as a good thing."

"Sure, Henry, I'll try to do that," Lee said, not changing his expression.

Isabella yanked the door shut, slamming it so loud Lee jumped, jabbing Henry in the ribs with his elbow and causing Henry to groan. Henry and Lee's eyes met for a moment. Lee was obviously worried, but now Henry was, too. There was something unnerving about the way Isabella slammed the door, and between the bang of the door and the click of the lock Henry had snapped back, but he wasn't sure it was reality.

Lee had been on to something when he'd said, "This ain't right." Henry was now gripped by the kind of fear you have at night when you're a kid and you're hanging your bare feet out from under the covers. He had that same sense of dread that told you a monster was under the bed and it was going to tear off your feet and eat them if you were brazen enough to keep them there. By all rights, he told himself, he was, more than likely, dead and had nothing to fear at all. That must be it, he thought. I've died and gone to heaven. But, on second thought, if this were heaven, his daughter would have met him. He probably would have met Maryluz, and probably Lou-Ella, too, being as she had been one of his dearest friends at Sunnyside and had let him ramble on and on from time to time about his life lived ass-backwards. But he had noticed that his family and friends were nowhere to be found, at least not yet, so heaven probably wasn't where he was.

"Welcome back, boys," Isabella said with a grin. "Welcome to Hog Temple, Texas. The new, improved version—of course."

Hog Temple? We are supposed to be on our way to Mexico.

A white SUV drove past them. A bumper sticker with the words "Mexico Can Wait" printed next to a picture of an angel wagging a finger glared back at Henry from the SUV's rear bumper as the vehicle moved into the distance. Henry and Lee looked first at each other, and then at Isabella, whose angelic face, whose tiny feet he knew lay hidden in the lizard skin cowboys boots she was wearing, whose faded blue jeans and whose silver rodeo buckle she had won when she was a teen, were almost too adorable, too precious to be true.

Henry remembered reading that if a thing felt too good to be true, it probably wasn't. He had been alive long enough to know that where you found truth, you wouldn't necessarily find goodness, or where you found goodness, the truth was often hidden. People were a funny lot when it came to truth. Most folks didn't care for the truth and would often be good in the midst of the ugliest goings-on.

"Come on Henry," Isabella said, tapping her slender fingers on the dash. "Don't just sit there. What are you waiting for? Stop your worrying. Let's get moving. Let's get on the road."

Henry put the truck in gear and steered it toward the exit leading to what looked like the highway to Sunnyside. "Where are we off to?" he asked, trying to sound curious rather than nervous, suspecting Isabella wasn't going to tell him but hoping she would.

"You'll figure it out," she said.

Henry gritted his teeth as he swung the pickup onto the highway.

Lee played with the knob on the radio, settled on a country station, and hummed along with a tune Henry hadn't heard in over fifty-five years.

He felt as though he was finally resettling into his younger skin. His mother always said he dwelled on the negative, so maybe that was what he was doing, but there was no denying it—his change in age, the Princess turning into a statue, the empty parking lot at Wal-Mart, Lee talking to a rope, and the sudden appearance of a woman long dead was cause for concern. Henry bobbed his head in time to the radio's beat, but his nerves were unraveling, pinging loose like guitar strings stretched too tight. He had no idea where the three of them were headed and Isabella wasn't spilling the beans or directing him—and that's what worried him the most.

15
Lilly

Lilly and Girl James sat in the cab of Lilly's truck hashing out what they might do.

"I have to be back at my apartment no later than seven," Girl James said. "I have a little problem I have to deal with."

"The dying thing?" Lilly asked.

"That, too," Girl James answered. "Those creeps, whatever they are, are somehow connected to the center. At least that's what James Number One thinks. They're coming through a portal, somehow, somewhere, but he can't put his finger on it. At least that was the last thing I heard."

"But why? And why now, on my watch?" Lilly asked, more to herself than to Girl James. "Even if they're loose, I'm pretty sure they can't get completely free."

"Have you ever had contact with *Them* before now? I mean, besides the time Hodges and you sent them flying to you-know-where?"

"Not recently. Not that I know of. Maybe once—right before Mt. Vesuvius. I thought I heard something from *Them* but honestly, I thought it was you, you, and you playing tricks. I can't say exactly when it was, and it wasn't direct contact, just the hint of something that reminded me of *Them*," Lilly said. "It was minute, really. So brief I thought I was having a memory." *It was probably something you and those wicked brothers of yours did.*

"Baby James swears there's one of them working at the center. He says he can smell it."

"They don't smell," Lilly said.

"He says they do," Girl James said, with a good amount of venom in her voice.

"Is that right?" Lilly said. "First of all, how do you know it's *Them*? Hodges and I did a good job of—"

"You and Hodges? Back then? A good job?" Girl James laughed. "Notify the network news, CNN, Fox Network, MSNBC—"

"Let me tell you a thing or two about being—" Lilly started to say, but before she could work them both into a bigger fit than they were already, her cell phone rang. It was Hodges.

"Lilly, you have to get back here, right now." His voice was riddled with fear. "Something ain't right. It ain't right."

"What's going on?" Lilly asked.

"Every last resident has gone to sleep. And I mean a very deep sleep."

"What?" Lilly shouted into the phone.

"Sweet mother of the Netherworlds," Girl James shouted. "You're yelling into the phone." She gestured to Lilly, indicating she should lower her voice. "Nobody *talks* into those things—that's why I hate cell phones."

"Who was that?" Hodges yelled back.

"Girl James," Lilly answered, without thinking.

"Girl James?" Hodges screamed.

"It's a long story. I'll tell you when I get there, so calm down," Lilly said, trying to control her voice.

"I cannot calm down," Hodges yelled. "First, I got every resident and the night manager conked out in REDS, and then I got Miguel Rodriguez running around the place sassing me like a boy just past puberty— and looking damn near close in age to one, too."

"What?"

"You heard me," Hodges said. "My troubles are multiplying faster than rabbits on holiday."

"But Hodges, why did you put them in REDS?"

"I didn't. That's what I'm trying to tell you."

"I didn't either," Lilly said.

"I know that, Li, but somebody did," Hodges said, his voice shaky.

"What's going on?" Girl James asked.

Things were on the verge of getting completely out of control. The one thing Lilly had always been good at was keeping events in order. Not so much anymore, but she was doing the best she could to set their lives upright again. She hoped Hodges would eventually understand her motivation. "Hodges says everybody is in Reality Earned Dream State. REDS," she said to Girl James.

"What is that?" Girl asked.

"They're in a state where they're dreaming about life as they once wished it to be. It's as real to them as we are to each other, so they're all happy, but if they snap out unexpectedly, they're zapped to who-knows-where. It's something Protectors do when they're trying to make something right that's going drastically wrong, but we're the only Protectors that I know of, and we didn't do it."

"It's *Them*," Girl James answered. "They're chameleons, and they're going to have some *soul food*, if you know what I mean." She snickered.

"I heard that," Hodges whispered. "Don't say a word, because I know you're working with Girl James. You know I've got that special way of knowing."

"Listen, Hodges, I'm not making a mistake," Lilly said, "and I don't have time to explain it to you."

"You best get back here as fast as you can—that is, if you're able, being with James and all. We've got some major figuring out to do because the world done gone to hell in a hand basket," he said. "And I know what I'm talking about."

Lilly could hear someone whooping it up in the background.

"Oh, sweet Jesus," Hodges said, before the line went dead.

"Do you know what they're after?" Lilly asked Girl James.

"The usual," she answered. "To rule the world."

"Is this one of your stupid games, James?" Lilly asked. "Because if it is, I'll—"

"Go ahead. Touch me again. I'll let you."

"I feel like smacking you," Lilly said.

"Swat me, punch me, whatever, but slugging me won't change the fact that they've taken over the center."

Lilly shook her head in disbelief. *This can't be happening.*

"They're all over the center, aren't they?" Girl James said, shaking her head. "And just when I have to go home to die." She blinked her eyes several times, an indication to Lilly that her impending death was more unpleasant than Lilly had suspected.

"I don't know," Lilly answered, looking at the cell phone in her hand. *Whatever those things are up to, it must be big, because their timing is impeccable and they don't just pop loose whenever they feel like it. Maybe James is right.*

"I won't be able to tell you what's going on, James, until after I've been to Sunnyside." Lilly dropped the cell phone on the seat and started up the truck.

"Can't you just use some special power, some special mental thing to find out?" Girl James asked.

"I can try, but the good guys aren't equipped with the latest psychic technologies like the bad guys," Lilly said, not hiding her disgust. *Why does it always have to be like this?*

"Okay, then," James said, sounding surprised.

"Why don't you try?"

"I did already. Nothing. I got nothing. It's like every single resident is suffering from empty brain syndrome. Never seen anything like it."

Lilly stared at a man fumbling with his keys and trying to manage an oversized package at the same time. *The more things change, the more they stay the same. Who said that originally? Whoever it was, was right.*

"Look, if you're going to sit here and ponder the mysteries of the universe, I'll get myself home," James said, as if she had just stumbled on a brilliant idea. "Don't mind me."

Before Lilly could protest, Girl James disappeared. On some level, Lilly thought, it's comforting to see that when you get right down to it, James is still the same old James. Lilly scanned the Wal-Mart parking lot to see if anything else was amiss. *Nothing. Good.* She put the car in gear, her hands slipping against the black plastic knob. She was sweaty, as if she had a fever, but she wasn't ill—she was burning up from worry. *I'm a Protector. I don't worry, but I'm worrying. What's wrong with me?*

Be cool. Be cool, she told herself as she pulled out of her parking space, driving slowly between the rows of parked cars until she reached the exit. She eased her truck onto the roadway and into the Sunday afternoon traffic, moving steadily in the direction of the center. Miguel Rodriguez is lucid, she thought, and I didn't bring him around, so how could that have happened?

Out of this whole drama, Miguel would be the first part she would address. After all, he was the only resident she knew of able to carry on a conversation. Miguel would have to know something—at least, she hoped he did. Yes, Miguel, who was now a teen, should be able to shed some light on how to climb out of this pool of insanity they had fallen into. He just had to. She was depending on it.

16
Katherine

"You're right," James James James said. "You're not old anymore, but you don't want to stay that way, even if right now you think you do."

A sigh sounded from behind Katherine, and then a voice spoke. "I'm not old, either, but I'd like to be older than I am at this minute. James is right. You don't want to stay that age."

Katherine turned around to see a young girl with crazy black hair sticking out every which way. She had blue-green eyes the color of Arctic water and a wild look on her face, as if she were an exotic animal recently captured and ready to defend itself. The combination, to Katherine, was odd, to say the least. "James," the strange child said, seeming to get older as she spoke. "I'm Girl James, James's sister." The garden they were in was suddenly teeming with people, Katherine noted, most of whom were Jameses.

James James James smiled.

Katherine blinked. This new James was aging right before her eyes.

"Sorry," the new James said. "I have a little problem—one I hope to recover from someday."

Katherine pulled back from Girl James, who was now grimacing and groaning as her arms and legs took on greater proportions.

"She does that," James James James said. "No need to be afraid. It's harder on her than it is on us."

Even if what he was saying was true, watching her grow from a child into an adult was disturbing. Katherine turned away when Girl James's childish skin peeled off and left a shell of her former self lying on the ground next to her.

"You can look now," Girl James said.

Katherine turned around.

"I think it's time we went to the tower," Girl James said to her brother. "We have a bigger problem than we initially thought."

"What's that?" James James James asked.

"I was with Lilly in the Wal-Mart when *Them* swept past. *Them* spoke with Baby James's voice. They've got him and he's trapped. He must have been fooling around in Lilly and Hodges's garden with Lou-Ella when *Them* got loose."

"You have a baby brother?" Katherine asked.

"Not really. He's the youngest, so we call him Baby James. Sweet baby." James James James's laugh, Katherine thought, was meant to let her know that Baby wasn't always sweet. Maybe it was in the way in which the elder James's laugh stopped and started, then wobbled and broke. Katherine could recognize nervous, troubled laughter when she heard it, and this laughter hinted at something yet to be told.

"I love babies," Katherine squealed, again in a twelve-year-old child's voice. *Why did I say that? Children have always given me the willies — they're too vulnerable.* Along with her words and thoughts came an unnatural hatred. She let out a deep, husky moan she had never heard from anyone, much less herself, and in a voice clearly not hers. Katherine clutched her throat. She felt as if worms were living under her skin. She wanted to rip out whatever foreign thing inhabited her. "What's inside me?" she screamed, leaping from the bench and backing away from both Jameses. "You fed me something and it's growing inside me, didn't you? Didn't you?"

"You haven't told her about *Them*?" Girl James asked.

"I was getting around to it," James said. "I didn't want to frighten her. I thought we could take care of it before she ... she doesn't remember."

"Doesn't remember? Then you need to refresh her memory. What is wrong with you? Are you going soft?"

What don't I remember?

"Look, I like Katherine, I ..."

"You *like* Katherine? You can't like her. We cannot afford that sort of thing."

"Yes. I care."

"You are not a human being, let me remind you."

He's not? No, of course he isn't. But what is he? Katherine thought.

"James, if you're thinking what I think you're thinking, don't. This is not the time."

"Even if I told her, it wouldn't help. She has to remember on her own." James seemed sad to Katherine, although he was glaring at Girl James, and Girl James looked as if she were going to explode. The way things had been going, Katherine thought she just might. Whatever Girl James and James James James were, there was one thing Katherine knew for sure: In this world, anybody could turn out to be anything, and the most unimaginable of all unimaginable things could happen. She reached out to touch Girl James, to calm her down.

Girl James leapt backwards.

"Don't touch her," James said. "She's funny about being touched."

Katherine wouldn't have called it funny. To tell the truth, she hadn't found much of anything funny lately.

"When? When were you going to tell her, James?" Girl James asked. "Does she at least know what she is?"

"I thought we'd take care of our problem first and then things would unfold naturally."

"But what if they don't?" Girl James sputtered.

"They will. And if there's a problem, I'll take care of it."

Katherine had never seen James in such a state. He was actually defending his defense of her. *How sweet. I knew he was special. What am I doing? I'm trying to make something logical out of something illogical.* She shook her head; she was feeling lightheaded and tired. "I'm sleepy," she said in a little girl's voice, but the two Jameses didn't notice. *But wait, what am I? If I'm something other than who I think I am, am I good or bad? What if I've done horrible things?*

Girl James screamed, flexing and waving what were now her adult fingers. "And how are you going to take care of it? And when? Once they have her lock, stock, and barrel? Because once they've claimed her, the world is going to find itself in a—a world of hurt, as they say. And you know it."

"This world is already a world of hurt," James James James screamed back.

Katherine put her hands over her ears. "Everybody shut up," she said. "Somebody wake me. Wake me right now."

"Katherine, I promise you, James James James will explain all this in a minute," Girl James shouted between Katherine's fingers, "but right now, you need to be sweetness and light. Think loving thoughts. That's the only thing that will keep them from taking complete control of you—and if they get control of you, you'll be twelve for eternity and ... you don't want to know."

"But who are *They*?" Katherine asked.

"James? James?" Girl James said.

"Even if I told her, she wouldn't believe me. I've said this before, unless she remembers on her own, it doesn't matter what we say." James shook his head.

Katherine closed her eyes. *I'm having a nightmare.*

"You're not dreaming," Girl James said. "And whatever you do, fight those ugly feelings you have about Lilly."

Lilly, that sneak, always bringing in illegal gifts to the residents, making them feel as if they had a right to be fancy-free when what they need is to take their medicine and be careful. Lilly, with her special hair dyes and rinses from companies no one has ever heard of. Who in the world uses Orange Soufflé hair conditioner? I'm the one who really cares what happens to the old folks around Sunnyside. Katherine felt a renewed sense of anger. *It was me, me, me who should have been loved the most.*

"What did I just tell you? Stop thinking bad thoughts about Lilly. You both cared about the residents, so stop it. Stop it. It's because of you that *They* found a way into the center in the first place."

"I haven't done anything," Katherine screamed, now all too aware of her circumstances. At least, she didn't *think* she had done anything wrong.

"Leave her alone. She can't be faulted for what she doesn't know," James James James said. "Leave Miss Kitty alone."

"Miss Kitty? Is that what you're calling her now?" Girl James squawked.

"I'll call her whatever I please," James James James said.

"That's his pet name for me," Katherine said, sounding, once again, like a woman.

"Pet names? Miss Kitty? You are way out of line, James," Girl James said. "You have to get a grip on yourself. Picking up a girlfriend is not what you were put here for."

"Is that right? I suppose you'd rather I do exactly as I was put here to do. Is that what you want? Because if you do, I'll be happy to …"

"Listen up, know-it-all," Girl James yelled, her fists flailing the air in front of his face. "If we let her stay on the same track she's on, we're all going to pay."

"Stop," Katherine shouted. "Don't fight. And you leave James alone, Girl," Katherine demanded, still speaking as an adult. "If I did anything, I don't remember, and if I did something I don't remember, I can't be blamed." Again reverting to a child's voice, she shouted, "I'm innocent, innocent—innocent of all charges, and I won't go to my room." *Go to my room? What am I saying? What have I done, anyway? I'm so confused.*

"Calm down, Kat," James said.

But she couldn't calm down. Her present situation was overwhelming. This constant switching between being a grownup and a child was worse than menopause. At least she wasn't having night sweats. Nevertheless, the roller coaster of emotions she was on, coupled with worrying about how she was going to get back to her original self, was too much for a woman of experience, now stuck in the body of a little girl. She burst into tears.

"Don't cry, Katherine," Girl James said, in what seemed to Katherine as a moment of guilt. Guilt, regret, and remorse ... these seemed to be the words of the day.

"I guess it's not entirely your fault," Girl James went on. "It's partly Baby James's doing, too, but he didn't mean to do anything bad. He was just having a little fun with Lou-Ella, but now *They* have the two of them. And those things would like nothing better than to get their hands on you again, and that's what's got us all scared to death."

James James James stood up and grabbed Girl James by the arm. "What do you mean, Baby James didn't mean to do anything bad? What was he doing with Lou-Ella?"

Girl James shook her head, her tightly wound curls reminding Katherine of burnt onion rings.

"You had better tell me this minute what Baby James has done, and you'd better be quick about it," James snarled, squeezing Girl James tighter. "And you'd better do it before Hodges shows up, or I'm going to let him have a go at you."

Girl James shrunk, staring at her feet, bare and small in the shadow of the much larger James. Katherine was stunned by how tiny Girl James was, how small her hands and feet were compared to her own twelve-year-old body. The harder James glared at his sister, the smaller she became. *Is she shrinking? Is she going to eventually disappear?* Katherine moved closer to Girl James to see if she could catch her in the act of shrinking.

"He just wanted to see what would happen if he took one of the residents to the garden, instead of Hodges doing it, and had her eat the rampion. He thought it would be fun," she said.

"And you helped him?"

"Yes," she said.

"And because of Baby and you, an innocent human being, whose only purpose in coming to Sunnyside was to be released from suffering, will be made to suffer even more?"

Girl James nodded her head.

"And we're going to lose Katherine, who has little to do with this?"

Girl James looked up, first at Katherine, and then at James. "You know it was her jealousy that provided the—"

"Not intentionally," he said.

"James, she contacted *Them* in the first place."

"Not intentionally."

What did I do without meaning to?

"She won't stop them. Her kind never does. They're simple and obsessed only with what they want. Their motto should be "Gimme, Gimme, Gimme."

"You're wrong this time. She'll do the right thing."

"We chose Hodges's and Lilly's side. What makes you think she won't choose *Them* once she 'wakes up'? Katherine has the power. I can hear them muttering about it around the clock. *They* are gathering, so when she finally uses it ..."

"Yes, I know."

"*They* are going to fully show themselves—soon."

What? I didn't mean to do anything wrong. I was just concerned for the residents. Katherine felt like crying. So her jealousy had helped unleash something awful on all of them. But wait ... she didn't know what it was that was about to be unleashed. And as far as her kind went, what was her kind? *And what power? I don't have any power. If I had any power, a whole lot of my life would look different from—*

"Petty jealousy isn't a crime," James said.

"You're right," Girl James said, passing her hand over Katherine's head and her own. "But don't tell me you didn't suspect. She's immune to Lilly and you know it...and she's made you...I don't have to say it. If that isn't power, I don't know what is. We chose not do the one thing they created us to do, and now they need her to make us do it. Don't you get it, James? Katherine must be the..."

"Stop," James said.

Stop what? What must I be? How did I end up here? I never wanted to work in an old folks' home, but what did *I want to do? Where did my life go? Once day I was sixteen, the next day I was sixty. Where did the time go?* "What am I?" Katherine asked. "What must I be?"

"Tell her James," Girl James snarled. "Tell her."

All around Katherine were rows of blue, white, and purple flowers, their leaves emitting a sweet odor, begging her to rip them from their stems and eat them. She dropped to her knees, tore away handfuls of leaves, stuffed them into her mouth, and chewed them, savoring the flavor, which was unlike anything she had ever tasted. I could do this all day, she told herself, forgetting everything they had been talking about earlier. "James James James," she said in her child's voice, "this is the yummiest salad I've ever had."

"Stop it, Katherine," James James James said, dragging her to her feet. "If you eat too many of those, you could get stuck being a child, and I don't want that— you don't, either."

Katherine didn't care what he wanted. The only thing she cared about was eating as much of the green stuff as she could get her hands on. Her mouth was bursting with the joy of something so tasty, so heavenly, she couldn't begin to describe it. How could he ask her not to eat the leaves? With each burst of flavor, she experienced the presence of someone she had loved and lost. She reached back in time and relived a moment. Her older sister Mora appeared again, and again, and every cross word she had ever had with her was replaced by a new experience, one filled with love, forgiveness, and renewal. Love, love, love. With each bite, she swelled with a love so great she couldn't imagine life without the succulent leaves. Katherine couldn't eat fast enough. She hadn't realized how hungry she was until after the first bite. It was then that she became ravenous. Were there enough leaves to satisfy her hunger? She doubted it, but she hoped there were. As Katherine stooped for yet another handful of greens, James yanked her back.

James and Girl James stared, first at Katherine, and then at each other. Finally, Girl James spoke. "We don't have time to waste. I'm going through the gate. I can lure them out if you will call for Hodges," she said.

"You'll need help," James said, "But I can't leave Katherine here. She'll eat herself to a permanent infancy, and that's what *They* want."

They *want a baby so* they *can control the baby's every move. Na, na, na. I don't care what they want. I'm hungry.* Katherine picked a leaf off her blouse and popped it into her mouth. She saw herself as a teenager, and James was coming to her door holding flowers. They were both young and in love.

"She's eating another one," Katherine heard Girl James say, but by then she was lost in the dreamy world of teen love.

James James James squatted in front of Katherine, brushed the remaining leaves off her clothes, took her by the shoulders, and said, "Listen to me, Kat, you have to remember you are not a twelve-year-old, but a sixty-six-year-old woman. That is not me you are imagining. If you concentrate, you can control your thoughts. You have the power to make whatever you want happen. Girl James and I have to go to a dark place, and you can't come with us, so you are going to be left here alone."

"Are you crazy? We can't leave her alone," Girl James said. "She's a child with a child's mind and she has been eating the rampion. You know what that does to a person."

"Katherine, call for Lilly and Hodges. If you concentrate hard enough, they'll come."

"We can't leave her alone."

"We have no choice," James said. "Whatever you do, Kat, don't eat any more greens. Do you understand?"

"Yes, sir," Katherine said in the tiniest voice she had ever heard.

"Stay here, James," Girl James said. "Take care of her. I'll go. I know how much she means to you and besides, she's a child and part of *Them* — she's long past the point of trust. Stay."

"Are you sure?"

"What's the worst that can happen? They can't kill me."

Why are they after me? And who are they? I'm a part of Them*? Is she talking about my mama and daddy? I want to go to the fair and buy some cotton candy.* A swirl of cotton candy appeared in her hand. She took a bite and threw it aside. *Did I do that? What am I thinking? I want to go where Girl James is going. What's wrong with me?* It was then that an iron door in the wall surrounding the garden, a door

Katherine had not noticed earlier, burst open with a startling bang and Girl James flew through the entranceway, sucked into the dark hole now staring back at them.

James James James grabbed Katherine, holding her back. "Girl," he shouted, "Girl." But no one answered.

Did I cause that? What did I do? A voice called to Katherine from the blackness. "Baby, it's Mora. Help me, baby. Help me." Her cry for help was mournful and full of terror. Katherine fought to wrench free. With James screaming "No," she threw herself into the darkness, tumbling through black, empty space until she landed with a thud at the bottom of a great, cold, and grey stone tower similar to an old lighthouse, but without an entrance or outside stairs. A golden rope hung from a window in the glow of a shimmering white light. Hands of all shapes and sizes reached toward her through its airy golden sheath. An infinite number of souls bound together pressed their faces against the silky prison, wailing in agony. "Let us help you up to your sister who spins," a chorus of voices cried.

"Yes, let them," she heard Mora whisper over and over. "Yes, let them pass you up to me." Leaning out of the tower's window was a woman with a smile so sweet that Katherine's mouth was flooded with the taste of sugar. This woman was more than her sister, more than her own mother—she was all of them and more. She was the source of all life—of that Katherine was sure—and whatever she really was, she vibrated with such great warmth that all Katherine wanted to do was fling herself into her arms and dissolve in what she was sure would be a pool of pure joy. She could feel self-doubt, insecurity, and sorrow being sucked out of her bones. Her skin rippled and her muscles jerked from the release of all things that could destroy a person. As quickly as the spasms dispersed, they were replaced by an ecstasy she was sure could be experienced only in the presence of the most powerful being in the universe. *Am I standing in front of God? I don't care who this is. I want these feelings to last forever.* How she needed to get to the woman whose arms stretched toward her.

"I have all that you need," the woman said. "I want to love you." She smiled, her eyes giving off a glow brighter than the sun, and Katherine knew the woman spoke the truth. "Come to me. Call out my master's name and all will be yours," she said.

"I'm coming," Katherine whispered. But before Katherine could grab the outstretched hands offering to help her climb to the tower, Girl James stuck her head out of the squirming mass, the sheath stretched over her face like a glittery stocking, and shouted, "Go back, go back." As Katherine stumbled backwards, Girl James ripped open the sheath and shoved, through the small opening, a teenager who tumbled onto the ground in front of her.

"Be quick. Take her with you," Girl James shouted. The teen came to an abrupt stop on the ground at Katherine's feet. The sheath snapped shut, and the wailing of trapped souls increased, as did the woman's cries in the tower.

"Lou-Ella," Katherine shouted, startled by her sudden appearance and newfound youthfulness.

"Help us," the souls cried. "Please help us get out of here."

"Come to me, baby," the woman in the towers said, her face fading in and out. "I'm your sister Mora and I need you."

As Lou-Ella threw her arms around Katherine, a whirlwind of sounds, screams, cries, laughter, and garbled words engulfed them. The girls closed their eyes and clung together, their hands and arms pinching the cloth and skin around each other's waists and shoulders. But just when Katherine was sure they were going to be tossed into the mouths of the loudest howlers, a thick, callused hand came out of nowhere and yanked them through the barrage of sound. James James James had retrieved them from the darkness and Katherine found that Lou-Ella and she were safe in the garden.

"Katherine, call for Lilly and Hodges—do it now, with all your might. Lou-Ella, stay put. I'm going after the others," James said. "Tell Hodges where I've gone. You have to be a grownup now, Kat. You and Lou-Ella stay away from this door. Do not think ill of Lilly or Hodges, and do not eat the greens. I mean it. Do not eat the greens, and do not think ill of Lilly and Hodges."

"Rampion," Lou-Ella said, shuddering. "Baby James calls it rampion."

"Baby James," James James James said, shaking his head, "has been reading too many fairy tales. Trust me, greens—rampion, whatever you call them—are not to be eaten. Understand?"

"Oh, I understand," Lou-Ella said. "Honey, you don't have to tell me twice."

"Yes, sir," Katherine said, nodding.

"Don't forget. Do not eat the greens." James James James said a few words in a language Katherine didn't understand, and then dove through the doorway and into the darkness.

Lou-Ella Whitehead screamed and pounded her head with her fists clenched so tightly they'd taken on the hue of dirty soap.

"Mrs. Whitehead?" Katherine asked, remembering for a moment that she was actually the temporary day manager at Sunnyside and Lou-Ella was one of the residents for whom she was responsible. "Mrs. Whitehead?"

"Yes?" Lou-Ella answered, dropping her hands, appearing to be taken aback by being called Mrs. Whitehead.

"What happened? I thought you were dead," Katherine said, feeling like a grownup.

They sat down in a large patch of flowers and greens.

"I wish I had been," Lou-Ella said. "I hope I am. Tell me I am."

Katherine wanted to say "At least you're not old anymore," but she was wishing she were her old self again, so she thought it better to keep her mouth shut about age, or anything to do with it. "Well, you're not dead. I can you tell that," she said, pulling a handful of leaves off a nearby plant and cramming her mouth full.

"You'd better stop eating that shit," Lou-Ella said. "It's what got me in trouble in the first place. Those leaves and that nasty little sprite named James."

"You mean Baby James?" Katherine asked.

"Whatever his name is. He's in there with Girl James, too. Listen, Katherine, it's one thing to feel warm and loved and to be able to think that all the mistakes you made never happened, but the price you pay for feeling so damned right about your life is—

you don't want to know. Let's just say once *They* have a hold of you, you're going to get to know yourself and the things you don't want to know better than you could have ever imagined." She shook her head. "That heinous bastard tricked me into going through the gate—"

"Baby James tricked you?"

"I don't know for sure, but I think so. Somebody did. And then there I was with millions of other folks, tied up in that thing that looks like a rope, but isn't. Now that I think of it, it's closer to a hair net caught in a dirty sink. At least it smells like that. You have no idea." Lou-Ella looked around as if she were searching for something. "You were lucky that James's sister made you step back. And I was lucky she happened along when she did. She took our places, you know. She did that for you—and what's happening to her now is just too horrible, assuming she's done things she sorely and deeply regrets." Lou-Ella wailed and shook her head.

"Nobody's here but you and me, and pretty soon Miss Lilly and Mr. Hodges will be here." Katherine closed her eyes and sent out what she hoped was a telepathic SOS for Lilly and Hodges. *Come to the garden. Rescue us. It's Katherine and Lou-Ella. James James James told me to call for you. We need you, so please come get us. Help. Help. Katherine and Lou-Ella are calling you for help. Hodges. Hair Princess. Hodges. Hair Princess. It's Katherine and Lou-Ella. We need your help. Honest, we do.* But she couldn't resist one more leaf, so with her eyes still closed, she yanked another handful of leaves from under her knee and stuffed them in her mouth.

"Everybody from Sunnyside is ..." Lou-Ella started, but stopped. She dropped her head into her hands, weeping, shaking, and shuddering. In a matter of seconds, her weeping went from deep sobs to a long, drawn-out yowl, to a whine and then to a low, guttural moan that was so unnerving Katherine had to get up and move. For all she knew, Lou-Ella might have left her good sense, if she had ever had any, back where she had just come from. Frankly, Katherine had had enough of weirdoes and events she couldn't make heads or tails of. Besides, she had greens to pick and greens to eat.

Katherine knew she had been warned not to eat the lush leaves surrounding her, but the urge to eat was overpowering, because they were so tasty, so succulent. The way she felt after one bite was divine. If you hadn't eaten them, you couldn't possibly understand. Imagine having the one lover you loved the most return to you with open arms to give back all he or she had taken. Imagine the warmth of your mother's womb and the safety of your father's arms. Imagine never being afraid or hurt or worried about anything. Imagine having all the money in the world and wanting for nothing. Absolutely nothing. Eating the leaves made Katherine feel all these things and more. They were everything she had read they would be in the fairy tales of her original childhood. Besides, when she ate them she was able to visit her sister, the one person she had loved the most, and she could re-imagine her life the way she wished she had lived it. Oh, no, she wasn't about to stop tearing leaves from their stems and popping them into her mouth. *No way.* Katherine wandered the garden by herself while Lou-Ella cowered in a corner sobbing, her arms wrapped around her knees. In her visionary stupor, she wandered to the gate.

"Get back here," Lou-Ella screamed, leaping to her feet. "Get away from that gate right now." She raced over to Katherine and grabbed her by the hand, dragging her back to the wall, where she had previously cringed and trembled with fear, and sat her down. "You had best listen to me," she said. "You are not thinking clearly. Stop eating, and listen."

Katherine tried to shake her hand loose from Lou-Ella's, but held tight.

"I'm going to tell you what happened to me," Lou-Ella said. "And if what happened to me is what normally goes on over there, I can only guess what's happening to our friends."

Once Lou-Ella was seated, Katherine tilted her head toward her. She was giddy with anticipation for what James might bring back to her from wherever he had gone, and silly from having eaten so much rampion, so she had no interest in listening to Lou-Ella's story. But she had been raised to have manners, so she had to listen. It would have been rude to do otherwise. As Lou-Ella prattled on,

Katherine momentarily drifted off, but Lou-Ella grabbed her by the chin and brought her back around.

"Listen up, Katherine Wilson," Lou-Ella whispered. "This whole business started when that new water delivery boy, Baby James, asked me if I had any regrets, if there was anything I had done I was truly sorry for."

17
Henry

Henry drove as if he knew where he was going, and in an odd way, he did. Something told him he was heading home, but then again, he thought, you probably didn't have to be a genius to make that guess. Maybe he was hoping he was heading home. Maybe he was heading to the funny farm.

"So what have you been doing on the other side?" Lee asked Isabella. "God must have you doing something besides floating around in the sky."

"What in hell is wrong with you?" Henry snapped, clutching the steering wheel as if it were life itself. "Does she look like she's floating? What kind of question is that to ask?"

"Well, what do you want me to ask? How's the weather?" Lee slapped his knee. "How's the weather on this side, Isabella? You got weather over here, do you?"

"How do you know what side we're on?" Henry asked. "She ain't said nothing about us being dead." He searched the highway for other cars or trucks, but there were none. There were houses here and there, but no churches or schools. He felt as if he were traveling through an unfinished canvas, with only the hills and the basic buildings in place. He had the distinct feeling that the artist of this painting he had entered was still busy figuring out what he would paint next—people or things—and where he would put them. *Crazy. These are crazy thoughts I'm having. Maybe I'm plain losing my marbles.*

Isabella laughed. "Weather? Not so you'd recognize it, but I guess you could say we have weather. What kind of weather would you like, Lee?"

"Sunny. I'd like the sky to open up and see the big old sun shining down on me."

"Is that right?" Isabella asked.

"Sure, why not?"

"Why don't you ask for a leprechaun and a pot of gold at the end of the rainbow?" Henry said, feeling annoyed by the conversation, but not knowing why.

"Ain't you the crank with nothing to be cranky about. You spend your old age complaining you ain't never got enough of Isabella, and now here she is and you got nothing to do but worry about what I'm asking. Ain't you ungrateful? Don't you think you might be a bit more agreeable?"

"If I knew what was going on, I might," Henry said.

A car with shamrocks painted on the doors and a rainbow over the words "Pot o' Gold Gifts" appeared on the highway beside them, and then passed by, zipping along until it was a few hundred yards ahead of them.

"Hey, Henry, check that out. There's your leprechaun," Lee said, waving to the driver dressed in a green jacket and wearing a green beret, now watching them from her rearview mirror.

Isabella waved, too, and the driver waved back.

"How about a rainbow, Isabella? I'd like to see a rainbow cross the sky right in front of us," Lee said, and then stuck his tongue out at Henry.

"What is wrong with you?" Henry asked.

"Nothing. Nothing at all."

"Now, boys," Isabella said, "no fighting. This is a happy day."

"On account of Isabella, I'll cut you some slack, Lee, and pretend you didn't do that," Henry said. *Happy day, my ass. I hope it turns out to be a happy day, but Lee has finally started acting the way folks expect a man to act in old age, and there ain't nothing happy about that. It's a damn pathetic sight, is what it is, and Lee ought to know it.* But before Henry could say another word to Lee about how damn dumb a grown man with his tongue hanging out looked, the sky in front of them lit up with the brightest, biggest rainbow Henry had ever seen.

"Woo-wee," Lee shouted. "Ain't that a beaut?"

"Oh, my," Isabella gasped. "Yes, it is."

"What in hell?" Henry said, slowing down.

Isabella put her hand on Henry's arm. "Just keep driving, honey. There's nothing to worry about. We're headed—"

"Where, Isabella? Where are we headed? And what's going on?" Henry asked, his voice getting higher pitched with every word.

"We're almost there," Isabella said.

"I sure as hell hope so," Henry said, trying to keep his focus on the gray river of road stretched out in front of him and not on the rainbow hovering on the horizon. *This is one heck of a hallucination I'm having, if that's what it is. But I guess I'm about to find out.* And he prayed for the first time in a long time, prayed that whatever was happening was a good thing, even if he wasn't sure he deserved anything good.

18
Lilly

Hodges met Lilly at the door. The veins on his forehead writhed with every heartbeat. His eyes held a new clarity, and in them Lilly could see the past and present, but not the future.

"You eyes are popping," Lilly said, easing her way past Hodges.

"Damn right they're popping," Hodges said, rubbing his hands together and cracking his knuckles.

Out of the corner of her eye, Lilly caught Tattoo winking. She glared at it, hoping it would get the hint to stop. Instead, it winked again and blew her a kiss. "Tattoo is animated again," Lilly said. "You'd better take care of it."

"A winking tattoo is the least of our problems," Hodges said, smacking his arm. The tattoo's eyes rolled around like a couple of marbles, and then settled into a blank stare. Lilly smiled at the dazed tattoo and winked back.

"When did everybody blank out?" Lilly asked, remembering Girl James's comment about empty brains. She couldn't shake the feeling that the Jameses had something to do with what was happening, even if their part, against all odds this time, was small.

"Where are Henry and Lee?" Hodges asked back.

"Me first," Lilly said.

"Damn near everybody here slipped into REDS around 4:30."

"Right around the same time I turned into a piece of porcelain, a fire got started in Wal-Mart, Girl James showed up, and Henry and Lee disappeared," Lilly answered. "No coincidence there. And there was the 'rope.' And Baby James spoke through it."

"Oh, good Lord," Hodges moaned.

Miguel Rodriguez stuck his head around the corner. "Princess," he shouted. "How do you like me now?"

Holy smokes, Lilly thought. I may not be of this world, but having been in this world for longer than I can remember, I know a fine piece of work when I see one. And there's a beautiful example of humanity. Miguel's skin was creamy mocha, his chest broad, his face no longer weathered, and his smile compelling. "Hey, Miguel," she said. "You look a lot healthier than the last time I saw you." *You were hooked up to several drips and your parchment-skinned hands and arms were bruised from that nurse trying so hard to find a vein.* "How old are you now?"

"Nineteen," he said, grinning like a brand-new rodeo champion.

"What do you make of what's happened to you, and to the other residents?" Lilly asked. She tried to behave as if this was an everyday occurrence, hoping Miguel would say something of significance.

"Got me," Miguel answered. "I've never done anything I regretted, really, if you don't count having lived my whole life on Henry's ranch working with horses. I never had a girlfriend, never had a wife, never drank, smoked, or did anything except break horses. That's it."

"That's it? Are you sure?" Lilly asked. "Let me check something." She put her hands on his head and absorbed his memories through her fingertips. Sure enough, he was telling the truth. She removed her hands. "All done," she said.

"I'm dreaming," Miguel said, shuddering. "Are you dreaming, too?

"Nope. Neither of us is dreaming," Lilly said.

"Thanks be to Heaven, unless I have to start all over again and end up back in there," he said, pointing down the hall in the direction of his room. "That's the last thing I'd want, Miss Lilly."

"I don't think you're going to have to go back the way you were, Miguel," she said. *Not if I have anything to do with it.*

"I need some help here," Hodges said, sounding panicky. "Folks aren't breathing right, so I've got to keep an eye on every person in this place, including the night manager. They are breathing real shallow, as if they're about to—" Hodges made a slash across his throat with his hand. "Do you hear me, Lilly?"

"I heard you, Hodges." She listened for any messages sent from the comatose, any random thoughts set loose that might give her an idea as to what had happened, but their minds were blank, and there were no extraneous thoughts on the run.

"I need some help here, Lilly. I ain't lying." Hodges's hands flew in every direction for emphasis. As if he were trying to get them under control, he clasped them together, but he couldn't keep them still. In a matter of seconds, they broke loose and began rubbing each other in a hard, rhythmic pattern. They were on their own. The pain of that realization flashed across Hodges's face so fast even he was startled. Lilly was afraid that any second Hodges might get so upset he'd burst into flames—and that was all she needed.

"Hodges, calm down. You've been around ... how long? Use your head."

"Folks will be arriving later this evening to visit family members, and when they do, the shit is going to fly." Hodges made a swirl in the air with his finger and then punched his fist into the palm of his hand. "You know what I mean? And how do you suppose we're going to explain this? Regular folks aren't supposed to know about *us*."

"I know that, Hodges," Lilly said.

"This ain't *anything*, Lilly. This is *something*."

Poor Hodges. He's more human than the humans. "Give me a second," Lilly said. *If the residents are having trouble breathing, Hodges and I are in for a long night.* "Miguel," Lilly said, "please help Mr. Hodges check on everybody."

"Uh huh," Miguel said, walking over to a mirror. He examined his teeth and his eyes. "Let me know when you're ready, Hodges."

"Do something," Hodges wailed.

"I'll suspend time, Hodges, but in this situation, it can only be for a few hours," Lilly said.

"Are you sure you can do that, Li? Because the last time you tried to suspend time, half the folks in this place turned into toddlers and I was running around like a man trying to round up cats in a fish market."

"I was just learning back then, Hodges." Lilly groaned and rolled her eyes. "Trust me. I've mastered the technique."

"Then do it," he said, dropping his hands to his sides. "Before everybody croaks and gets away from us."

Lilly threw up a hand. "Not in front of Miguel," she said.

"I'm using all the strength I've got to keep them breathing and from waking too soon," Hodges said. "But we got a time constraint, Lilly, and it's not related to anything you do. You best not be forgetting I can only do so much."

Lilly nodded, narrowed her eyes, and raised her hands as if to push something in front of her away.

"Go on now," Hodges said. "Hurry."

"You might accidentally freeze, Miguel," Lilly said, watching Miguel pat his hair into place.

"What?" Miguel said, rearranging his now silky black hair.

"I'm going to have to do something dramatic," Lilly said. "You might not be able to move when I'm done, Miguel. At least not for a little while, but you'll be able to see and hear."

"Then don't do it—whatever it is you're planning," he said.

"I have to. Sorry," she answered. "Close your eyes." With a quick snap and clap of her hands, Sunnyside went still. Hodges froze in front of Lilly, but Miguel was still talking.

"I don't want to be stuck in one place," Miguel was saying, just as Lilly noticed Hodges was stone-still.

"Great," Lilly said. "Sorry, Hodges. I swear, I thought I had it right this time. I always forget it's two snaps."

"What's wrong with Hodges?" Miguel asked, leaving the mirror where he had been admiring himself. He wandered over and snapped his fingers in Hodges's face.

"I wouldn't do that if I were you," Lilly said. "He can still hear and see. He's unable to move, that's all."

"Woo-wee," Miguel said, shaking his head. "This is some dream. Are you magic?"

"Something like that," Lilly said. *So Miguel is convinced he's dreaming. Fine with me.* "But not as magic as I'd like to be."

"I'm sorry about that," Miguel said, and Lilly could see from his mournful expression that he truly was sorry. She patted his arm.

"All this funny business started when Lou-Ella passed," Lilly said, turning to Hodges and peering directly into his eyes. "Didn't it?" She could see Hodges, a tiny speck of what he had been, staring back at her from behind his pupils, nodding his head. "Damn it, Hodges, I'm sorry about this. I have to check Lou-Ella's old room. As soon as I'm done, I'll come right back to see what I can do to unfreeze you."

"Miss Lilly," Miguel said, clutching her arm. He was squinting and his lips were yanked so tight they had drained of color. "If I'm dreaming, I don't want to wake up," he whispered. "Seriously, I don't."

"You won't," Lilly said. "I promise." For the first time, she felt like crying. *Things are getting worse by the second,* she wanted to tell Hodges, but there was no point in stating the obvious. *If only Girl James wasn't preoccupied with dying. And worst of all, when she comes back to life, I'm going to have to wait for her to grow up. Now I'm going to have to find James Number One to get Hodges out of this.* Lilly stepped inside the elevator. *But where could he be? And how will I find him before Girl James grows up again? There has to be something among Lou-Ella's belongings that will give me a clue as to what's going on.*

The elevator stopped on the second floor. Lilly stepped into the empty hallway and marched toward what had been Lou-Ella's suite.

19
Katherine

Guilt could be debilitating. Of that, Katherine had no doubt. Listening to Lou-Ella's story and watching her suffer as she told it was enough to convince her of that, so Katherine decided that the only thing left for her to do was to let Lou-Ella work her guilt and grief out on her own. She tried one last time to comfort Lou-Ella, but her efforts were futile, so she wandered the garden by herself, leaving Lou-Ella to ruminate over her misdeeds. Besides, all she really cared about was eating the greens.

The plants were the greenest she had ever seen. When Katherine was feeling like a grownup, she was able to resist the shimmering tender leaves, but just barely, even then. When she was feeling childish, which was most of the time now, she couldn't.

Once seated on the ground next to a large patch of greens—or rampion, as Baby James had called it—Katherine picked the purple flowers, tucking some of them behind her ear. The greens had been the draw, but it was what they offered in the end that Lou-Ella had really been after. Like Katherine, Lou-Ella had first been tempted to feast on the greens and had, after her belly was full almost to the point of bursting, moved through the iron door in the wall until she had reached the foot of the tower where the rope had hung, tittering and writhing in its golden glory. Just as Katherine had done, Lou-Ella had rushed ahead, but Girl James had not been there to prevent Lou-Ella from succumbing to temptation, to put herself between Lou-Ella and *Them*. Even if she had been, Katherine was doubtful that Girl James would have saved Mrs. Whitehead. Perhaps Girl James had saved her, Katherine Wilson, because of her love for James James James. *That's right. I love James James James. Love him, love him, love him. He loves me, he loves me not; he loves me, he loves me not. What am I thinking? I have to snap out of this.*

She thought about the silly rope that wasn't a rope; she wondered what part of the golden rope Girl James had become. She wondered if Girl James was the main strand that held the string of souls together. What Lou-Ella had climbed had not been a rope at all, although she called it that. It had been a monster, one so insidious it had disguised itself, first as a golden rope and then as Lou-Ella's younger self, making her long for a youth not forgotten but unchangeable, once she had been incorporated into the shiny weave. Lou-Ella had sobbed as she recounted how she had been made to relive her biggest mistake, a drunken evening with her lover, during which her toddler found his way to the swimming pool and drowned. She had been forced to relive these events over and over again—and would have had to for eternity had she not been rescued. This was the ultimate price you paid for eating the rampion, unless you had been brought to the garden by Lilly or Hodges. That much she understood, because once trapped inside the slithering mass with Baby James, he was forced to tell her the truth about the garden's purpose.

Lou-Ella had told Katherine that the golden rope was the path to a rip in the universe, disguised as a tower that led to the pit where all souls went to suffer their wrongs over and over again, always repeating the same errors in judgment they had made while alive. As time passed in this other universe, their suffering increased exponentially. This was not Rumplestiltskin's tower, where the girl was kept to spin straw into gold, but an illusion belonging to the masters of pain, the same beings determined to rule heaven and earth. In their quest to do so, they disguised themselves as a girl resembling the spinner of the fairy tale, emanating the one thing that mattered most to those they were trying to seduce. In actuality, they were the kind of girl the spinner would have become, had she chosen to embrace the dark side and taken on the role of humanity's tormentor. "Tell us our names," *They* had whispered, over and over, to Lou-Ella and to the others they had trapped, "and we'll set you free."

"If there was a hell, surely this was it," Lou-Ella had sworn to Katherine.

Katherine reviewed Lou-Ella's story. Girl James had saved Katherine and had put herself in her place, because James James James loved Katherine, and Girl James loved her brothers and would do anything to save them. It was as simple as that, Lou-Ella reassured Katherine.

Well, I'll be. It really is as simple as that.

James James James had tried to rescue his sister and had been grabbed and gone in a flash. Katherine had seen him dive through the door in the garden wall, so she knew Lou-Ella had to be telling the truth. There was no point in trying to figure out whose fault this was, because they were all at fault. Lou-Ella had been tempted, tricked into pulling strands of what she thought was hair hanging from the tower—strands she thought would lead her to the young woman she once was and to a new life when really, the strands were part of the braided rope that led to *Them*. But it wasn't Girl James's fault that Lou-Ella had gotten trapped in the hell she had described to Katherine, not really. So why had Girl James saved Lou-Ella, too? *If Girl James ever gets out of there and back to Sunnyside, I'm going to ask her. Of course, if I hadn't been so full of myself and so concerned with a hairstylist who dressed like she was straight out of a punk rock band, I wouldn't be twelve years old and in danger of never growing up again.*

Growing up. Yes, she wanted to grow up, to be sixty-six again with James, lying next to him in his bedroom. It was this longing that brought her back to the problem at hand: freeing the Jameses and the other residents of Sunnyside trapped in the bowels of *Them*.

Now that Katherine was pretty certain her hatred for and jealousy of Lilly had been partially responsible for guiding *Them* back into the world and creating her present circumstances, her only hope was that Lilly and Hodges would eventually find her, forgive her, and be willing to free the Jameses with everyone else. *I must be the portal through which* Them *is coming into the world. Please, it can't be me, can it?*

"Hodges, Lilly," she called, frantic and humbled by her realization. "Please help me. I need you." But the garden was quiet except for Lou-Ella's blubbering. "Lilly, Hodges," she began again, only this time with a renewed vigor.

20
Lilly

Lou-Ella's room was in disarray. The closets had been emptied into the room, clothes were strewn over the bed, boxes of letters were torn open and old letters had been ripped out of their envelopes and scattered on the floor, and dresser drawers had been pulled out and their contents dumped alongside the letters. Someone had been searching for something—probably searching for a clue, just like Lilly had intended to do. A letter with a large family crest at the top caught Lilly's eye. She bent down, picked it up, and read the words "I will never forgive you. Never." It was a letter from Lou-Ella's ex-husband, written after the death of their child. The letter seethed with guilt and anger. In her hand, the letter pulsated with life. She felt Lou-Ella's presence on the page and could tell that she had read her husband's words over and over until she had the words memorized. Her husband's presence was there, too, loaded with grief and anger so deep it was impossible for Lilly to hold on to the yellow sheets because they burned her fingertips, so she let them fall back into place among the other missives. But there was another presence on the paper, too—and it was the third presence that caused her to bristle.

"Mrs. Gill," Lilly said softly. "Are you here? It's Lilly Beale. You know, the Hair Princess."

"I know who you are," Neely Gill said, creeping out of the bathroom, teary-eyed and wigless. "I'm not dumb. I knew you'd come. I know all about you people."

"Is that right?" Lilly asked.

"You're a secret-keeper, is what you are," she said, sobbing into her hands. "You and Hodges and that other fella."

"What other fella?" Lilly asked.

"The one who delivers the water," she said, dropping her hands and dabbing her eyes with a tissue. "This is his fault—and yours, too."

"Mrs. Gill, you don't really believe Hodges or I would do anything to hurt you or anyone else in Sunnyside, do you? If you did, you wouldn't have come out of the bathroom. Isn't that right?"

"I just want to go to the garden with everybody else," Mrs. Gill wailed. "My whole life I never did anything. Just grew up and took care of my parents and barrel-raced once. I never hurt nobody and for that I get left behind. Lou-Ella left me behind because she hates me."

"Sit down beside me and tell me what you're talking about," Lilly said, patting the bed and sighing. She couldn't stop thinking about how the Jameses had, once again, initiated some horrific trick that had probably gone so far wrong even they couldn't fix it, and now she and Hodges were on their way to being made fools of, yet again. In the meantime, Sunnyside was full of old folks on the verge of dying and if she didn't do something quick, she was going to lose them with their guilt intact. The loss of her current charges in their unsettled state of mind would not bode well for Hodges or her. She also had two residents who had been spared from a coma, and for what she had yet to discover. *There is way too much going on. Watching rocks evolve is starting to look better by the second.*

"I don't want to sit down," Mrs. Gill whined. "I want to go to the garden with everybody else. I want to do something exciting before I die."

"The garden?"

"Lou-Ella hated me. That's why she didn't take me with her."

"I doubt that, Mrs. Gill."

"She did. All because I was the one who introduced her to that fella who made her forget about her baby and now she's left me behind. It's not fair. It's not."

"Lou-Ella was your friend," Lilly said. She couldn't bear to see any of the residents so distraught. The hurt that consumed them cut through her in a cruel and soulful way, but Mrs. Gill was angry, and anger always threw her into a tailspin.

"She blamed me for that baby's death, you know, but everybody knew that baby drowning was her fault and nobody else's.

'All my troubles started the day you brought that no good so-and-so over,' she used to say. Lou-Ella Whitehead was a slut and there wasn't a soul in Hog Temple who didn't know it. Introducing the two of them doesn't make me guilty of anything. I've said so a thousand times if I've said so once. Lou-Ella never liked Miguel, either, because he told her one day after that baby died, when she was out at Henry's ranch, that the whole business was her fault and it was time she took some responsibility. But she blames me because I introduced her to that fella she got stinking snookered with the night that baby passed on."

So why isn't Neely Gill in a coma like the others? It was time to do a sweep of Mrs. Gill's mind, to try and figure out what she knew that Lilly didn't. After all, Mrs. Gill was in Lou-Ella's room, so she had to have been there for a reason.

"Mrs. Gill," Lilly said, putting her hand on the back of the disgruntled woman's head. "What in the world did you do with your new wig? You've lost what few curls you had." Before Neely Gill could speak, Lilly saw her arguing with Lou-Ella. The next thing she saw was Mrs. Gill sitting at home as a child, reading a book. Then there was Neely Gill caring for her aging parents, and then she was in the center talking to the Water Boy, Baby James. Mrs. Gill called Baby James "Water Boy" over and over again in her mind, and Lilly saw that he was the young man who had recently begun delivering water to the center.

The secret-keeper she's talking about is Baby James. So this did *have something to do with the Jameses. Tricked again. Wait until Hodges finds out.*

Then she saw Neely Gill hiding in Lou-Ella's room, watching Lou-Ella tear the room apart and find a gun, and then there was Lou-Ella by the pool fighting with something half human and hideous, and the thing put a mark— *the Mark*— on her neck, and then her skin fell away. Neely Gill's mind slammed shut when she saw Lou-Ella's skin fall away, giving Lilly a start and causing her eyes to fly open. What was even more startling was that Neely Gill was not more than two inches from her face, staring at her.

"What's going on?" Mrs. Gill asked, pulling back.

"I was going to ask you the same thing," Lilly said, gradually recovering from her unexpected expulsion. *Lou-Ella's mark was the real thing.* Them. *They're here.*

"You mean what's going on with me?" Mrs. Gill asked. "What the hell do you think I was doing in here?"

"No offense, Mrs. Gill," Lilly said, "but if I knew, I wouldn't be asking, would I?"

"If you must know, I'm looking for Lou-Ella."

"Lou-Ella? Mrs. Gill, I hate to tell you this, but if you remember, Lou-Ella Whitehead died this morning." If anything, Lilly had to remain calm.

"No, she did not," Mrs. Gill said, leaping up from the bed. "Everybody has been saying that all day, but it's not true."

"Now, Mrs.—" Lilly started to say.

"That's just what you want me to think, and she'd have liked me to think that, too."

"Mrs. Gill, you saw Lou-Ella carried off in the ambulance this morning, didn't you?" Lilly asked.

"Were you there?"

"No," Lilly said. "I was not."

"That was the old Lou-Ella. Not the new, improved Lou-Ella. It's so hard to explain."

The new, improved ... uh-oh. Lou-Ella has been in the garden. So that's the garden Mrs. Gill is talking about. And the door... how could that have happened without Hodges or me? Mrs. Gill was angry, and anger always had a way of interrupting and scattering her thoughts.

"Lou-Ella is alive?" Lilly asked, knowing what this meant. *Of course she is. She's been in the garden, but I saw her fighting one of* Them *is Mrs. Gill's memory. Things are deteriorating faster than I had originally suspected. She must have survived the fight somehow.*

"Of course she's alive—I saw her this morning, right here in this room, ripping through her things, and you know it," Mrs. Gill answered. "Princess, I want to know what is going on and why I wasn't invited to the party—and why that old drunk left me like *this*," she said, sweeping one hand across her face and torso, indicating her aged self.

Wait until I see the Jameses—I am going to give them a piece of my mind if I can remember the correct invocation—for a change—and I am going to send them to a universe from which it will take several lifetimes to return.

Hodges and she were in deep—up past their earlobes in trouble. *Oh, just get it over with. Send us off to the rock pile.* But she knew what Hodges would say if he heard her giving up—"That ain't right, Lilly, giving in like that. That ain't what we were put here for" — so she pulled herself together.

"I'd like to know what's going on myself," Lilly said. "And why Hodges and I weren't invited to the party, either." But she knew, and how she wished she didn't.

"You, that water boy, and Hodges know the truth, don't you?"

"I have an idea, Mrs. Gill, but I can't say yet what's going on." Lilly was confused, and that was the truth.

"Isn't that just like somebody from Hog Temple? Down deep you folks are greedy—greedy as all git-out and wanting to keep your secrets for yourself. My mama, who was not from this place, told me when I was just a kid that one day I was going to find out just how greedy and self-centered the folks in Hog Temple were. That's why they named this place Hog Temple. It's heaven for greedy, whiny pigs only thinking of themselves. Folks live in Hog Temple because they got a big secret they don't want to share. And you know what else she told me? She said that after folks move to Sunnyside they disappear, just like that." She tried snapping her fingers, but she couldn't do more than give them a hard rub. 'You mark my words,' Mama said. And you know something? Mama was right."

Her mother was right to some degree, but not about everything. But maybe the woman had been on to something. Maybe there was something self-centered in having a home for human beings who had earned the right to go to a place where they could focus on regrets, review their lives, and come to terms with their choices before they died. *What is the secret? I used to think it was Hodges and me.*

Maybe helping the people in this little town forgive themselves and having their suffering alleviated was wrong on some level, although Lilly couldn't imagine how that could be. Maybe she and Hodges were running the place all wrong. Maybe they had taken on the characteristics of humanity to a greater degree than they should have, and maybe using their ability to remove guilt to see the residents happy before they moved on had become about making themselves feel good. *Is that the big secret? I don't know. But I do know that whatever the secret is, too many things are happening at once.*

And then there was the option the residents were given on their visit to the garden. Maybe that was wrong, too, but Hodges and she had been taking them to the garden for centuries, so how could it be wrong? Lilly tried to reassure herself that their intentions had been, and still were, honorable, as far as she could tell. And since there had been no complaints from their superiors about their work at Sunnyside, at least not yet, anyway, they must be doing something right. But maybe Hodges and she were simply flexing their free will and getting away with it. *Could we be doing something so...so human? If we are, what does it mean? Does it mean anything?*

Until now, things had run smoothly, but just as in the old Mt. Vesuvius days, when the universe tipped on its side, things were thrown off center and the results were always bad, she couldn't help but feel things here were going to turn out equally horrendous. Hodges and she were going to have their hands full preventing their world from turning sour this time.

"Let's go back to the main floor and see if we can get some answers, Mrs. Gill. Right now we need Mr. Hodges's help."

"And Mr. Winking Tattoo?"

"That, too," Lilly said. *Has every resident in the place seen Hodges's tattoo winking? I am going to have to speak to him.* "I'll do my best to help you. The three of us will—Hodges, Mr. Tattoo, and me—and Miguel. He's awake, just like you."

"Seriously?" Mrs. Gill asked.

"That's what I'm here for," Lilly said. *Now, let me do my job, James, James, and James.* "Haven't I always helped you? Come on, now. I'd like us both to get to where we ought to be." Lilly grabbed Mrs. Gill's hand. "Let's get out of here."

Mrs. Gill hesitated. "Are we going to the garden?"

"Maybe," Lilly said. "But first we have to stop downstairs and you have to stay with Miguel for a while."

"Oh, goody," she said, following Lilly out the door and to the elevator. "This is going to be fun."

Not likely, Lilly thought, her hands quivering. Her hold on time was slipping. She had to get back to Hodges, who was going to have to take action. Hodges and his winking tattoo would have to look in on *Them* and round up the Jameses.

"I can't wait," Mrs. Gill sang, in an off-key tune Lilly was sure she had made up on the spot. "The garden, the garden, the garden, the garden. We'll have fun, fun, fun…"

"Fun is what we'll have, all right," Lilly said, knowing that when she finally got around to the garden, the visit would probably be anything but pleasurable.

Just as they stepped on the elevator, Mrs. Gill said, "I heard somebody crying. Did you?"

"Shh," Lilly said, listening closely. It was then that she heard Katherine's cries for help and Lou-Ella's sobbing.

21
Henry

They pulled into the driveway of what once was Henry's ranch.

"Well, ain't this something else?" Lee shouted, appearing to Henry to be almost silly with enthusiasm.

Henry took a hard look at Lee. "Hey, buddy," he said. "Take a look at yourself. I reckon you must be a hair under twenty-five or twenty-six or so."

"You, too," Lee said.

Isabella laughed. "Welcome home, Mr. Calhoun."

Henry pulled up beside the main barn and turned off the engine.

"Hop on out, Lee," Isabella said. "*Your* wife will be picking you up shortly and taking you home."

"My wife? I ain't got a wife. Never had a wife," he said, his voice shaky. "Somebody is confused—and it ain't me."

"You've got panic written all over your face, Lee," Henry said, jumping out of the truck on the other side, slamming the door shut, and talking through the window. "A wife ain't a bad thing. I can swear to that." *As long as it's the wife you wanted.* But he was worried. If Lee's wife was picking him up, then what did that mean for him? *Is Maryluz going to show up with Angelina? And what's going to happen to Isabella? Is her husband going to roll in for her, too?*

"I know a wife ain't a bad thing, but I'm trying to figure out what the hell is going on here. I'm pretty sure we ain't having the same dream, and if we ain't dead, then what? We eat poisoned food? Did somebody put drugs in those iced drinks we had?" Lee climbed out of the truck, kicked the tires, and then wandered around to where Henry stood, surveying the ranch and the driveway. "Feels real enough."

"What the hell is going on here," Isabella said, "is that you boys asked for something so hard, you finally got it." She slipped out of the truck, slammed the door shut, and came around to the other side, where Henry and Lee were standing.

"How many millions of times did I ask you not to slam the door?" Henry asked, forgetting that he was in an altogether new place and Isabella had been dead for longer than they could say at the moment.

"Any minute now, Maryluz is going to pull up in that ratty hunk of junk she always drove and is going to take her husband home," Isabella said, ignoring Henry's complaint.

"And then what?" Henry asked. "Lee goes home with you? Or is that big ugly fella you were married to showing up ready for a fight?"

"No, honey," Isabella said. "You are my husband. Maryluz is married to Lee."

Henry slapped the side of his head. "Lee, what did I do with my hearing aid?"

"Threw it away," Lee said, shifting from one foot to the other.

"I thought I just heard Isabella say that you were going home with my wife."

"You mean *my* wife," Lee said, backing away from Henry. He stuffed his hands in his pockets.

"I've been eating too much meat because I've been struck with mad-cow disease," Henry said, rolling his eyes.

"No, you ain't," Lee said. "Right, Isabella?"

"No mad cow here," Isabella answered.

"You sure seem confident about what's going on, Lee. Do you know something I don't?" Henry asked.

"No, sir. Things just make sense to me all of a sudden, is all," Lee answered.

"Is that right? Well, don't go telling me Angelina is your daughter, too, or I'm going to have to beat you damn near to death," Henry said. "That's if we ain't already gone."

"Angelina ain't my daughter, Henry," Lee said. "Right, Isabella?"

"Right, Lee. Not yet, anyway."

"Lee Donahue, you mean to tell me you've been sitting around Sunnyside all these years dreaming about being a husband to my wife?"

Lee stepped back another foot. "Are we going to be here forever, Isabella? Because I've got to answer Henry here and I need to know what I'm going to say. Be quick, girl. I don't know how much time I've got."

"You're only here if you want to be. You get to decide whether you stay or go. Maryluz will tell you all about it."

"There's a hitch, ain't there?" Lee said, looking at Henry and then at Isabella.

She nodded.

Henry, Lee, and Isabella stood back from one another and stared for what felt like an hour to Henry.

"Everybody knows your one true love was Isabella," Lee finally sputtered. "You know it, and I know it—and Maryluz knew it. But I swear, Henry, I never acted on my feelings, not once, because I was and still am your best friend. I won't lie to you; I loved Maryluz, and I always thought I could have done right by her if I'd had the chance."

"Is that so?" For the first time in Henry's life, he couldn't look Lee in the eye, so he looked at the hills behind him.

"She knew you didn't love her the way a man should love a wife. She told me as much the day of the big barbecue you threw for Angelina when that child had the baby—the boy you didn't even like much. Hell, everybody could see you didn't have no spark for Maryluz, and after Maryluz and Angelina were gone, you didn't give that little grandson of yours the time of day. But I loved Maryluz, Henry—with my whole heart. And I would have loved the whole kit-and-caboodle if they'd been mine. I always hoped you'd come to your senses and give her up, but I never told a soul what I held in my heart, Henry. I swear it. I never told her or anybody else I loved her. I swear it. I never said a word."

"But she knew, Lee," Isabella said. "And she loved you just as much."

"How do you know?" Henry gasped.

"I've been dead, Henry. Being dead has its privileges, such as knowing things," Isabella said. "Painful as it might be at times."

Henry could hardly breathe. How stupid could he have been? Of course Maryluz had loved Lee. Lee had taken an interest in what she was growing in her indoor garden, he had helped her fix her car, and he had repaired the washing machine when the thing went haywire while he was off on ranch business—which was most of the time. He had paid attention to her and been there for her.

"When you're dead, Henry, it's like hovering over a city watching life go on without you. You see everything, you hear everything, and you can zoom in where you want. But it's lonely at times, Henry, the same as being on earth and having somebody you love not love you back." Isabella turned away. "I've said too much."

Maryluz must have been lonely. She must have felt neglected, unloved. Unloved. Of course she did, because she wasn't loved, not in the way Henry should have loved her, but they had stayed together without sitting down and talking about what they felt. He knew this was a story neglected wives had told lovers throughout the ages, but that was how his daddy had handled his marriage, and his grandparents theirs—but was that a reason to behave the same way? Henry knew better. *So that's my excuse?* Henry shook his head. *Why are my mistakes revealed at the end of my life? Why didn't I see them sooner, so I could have made things right?*

Isabella and Lee stared at Henry as if they were waiting for him to say something, or do something, but he couldn't move. The truth was too horrible. Everything Lee and Isabella had said was true, and Henry knew it. Now, Lee was going to finally be with his one true love and he, Henry Cole Calhoun, at last, had Isabella, the woman he had dreamt about for so many years, the woman he had mourned throughout his long marriage to Maryluz. Isabella was the same woman he had prayed would return to him and here she was, and all he felt was sick. What would he say to Maryluz when he saw her? *Sorry I wasted your life and mine?* And worse, what if Angelina showed up? *What would I say to her? Lee should have been your daddy? I never loved your mother? You're a product of...I can't say.*

Naturally, the girl died at eighteen. She was reckless on account of me, on account of knowing she wasn't born from love. She wanted to disappear as soon as possible. What soul would stick around under those circumstances? It all makes way too much sense. Wake up, man, wake up.

"You can't wake up, Henry," Isabella said. "There's nothing to wake up from. This is real. This is new. This is what you wanted. Everything you see around you, everything that happens from here on out, is what you asked to have happen. And it had to happen, Henry." She headed for the house.

"But Lee is in this with me," Henry shouted after her.

"Lee and everybody else at Sunnyside," Isabella shouted, looking back over her shoulder and smiling.

There was mischief in that smile—and knowing Isabella was up to some mischief made Henry feel better because her mischief had always been something borne of goodness, though he had made an adulterer of her.

"Didn't you read the motto over the door the day you moved into Sunnyside?" she called with her back still to him.

Motto. He thought for a second.

"What's she talking about?" Lee asked.

Well, I'll be a horned toad on a two-way street. If that saying had been a truck, it would have got me coming and going. "We make things right," he said to Lee, laughing.

"I'll be a son-of-a-biscuit-eater," Lee said. "I had plumb forgotten about that old thing. " He shook his head. "Who would have thought?"

"What about your husband?" Henry shouted to Isabella.

"You *are* my husband," she shouted back, opening the door to the house, entering, and letting the door slam shut behind her.

"Me?" Henry said.

"I'm sorry, Henry," Lee stammered. "I don't blame you if you want to whip the tar out of me."

Henry turned to the young cowboy in front of him. He had forgotten how sharp Lee had looked in his youth, how confident and committed Lee had been to being his own version of an upstanding man. The boy could have had any woman in Hog

Temple or elsewhere, but he had waited for his true love and never gotten her—until now. "I gotta live with myself in the long run," Henry remembered Lee saying to him on more than one occasion. This man, his friend, had never asked anything of him or overstepped his bounds, even when he knew he could have. Lee had been a better friend to Henry than Henry had been to him.

"Nope," Henry said. "I couldn't raise a hand to you if I wanted to, Lee—and I don't want to. You go on with Maryluz when she gets here. My only worry is Angelina. I don't know what's become of her in this place, but I loved that child with what little heart I had, Lee. And I don't want to see her hurt because of my selfishness. You've got to believe me."

"I know that to be so, Henry. We all knew you loved that girl the best you could."

"Ain't it a pity a man has to stay a dumbass until he's old?" Henry asked, but before Lee could answer, the clink and clank of Maryluz's rattletrap bumping along the road made the two of them spin in her direction.

Henry's heart thumped in his chest so hard he could almost hear it. What the hell was he going to say to her? He wanted to ask Maryluz about Angelina, once she had gotten used to the idea that they were back in the same world. Or if that didn't work, maybe he'd ask Isabella. He wanted to know—he *had* to know.

Maryluz pulled into the driveway next to Isabella's truck, slammed on the brakes, and, with the engine still running, jumped out, raced straight past Henry into Lee's arms, and kissed and hugged him for all she was worth. She ignored Henry, as if she hadn't noticed he was there. Henry was surprised to find he had to fight the urge to pull Maryluz off Lee and ask her what the hell she thought she was doing. But instead of succumbing to his natural inclination, he turned his back on them and ran to the house, wavering between fear, joy, jealousy, and worry over where Angelina might be, or if she was anywhere at all. He ran, teeming with anxiety over his newly found circumstances, to his precious Isabella, ran to the woman who was now his wife. He raced toward the woman he had wished back to life, the woman who would meet him in the kitchen with a steaming dish of rice, beans, and goat's meat—Henry's favorite—and who would, later that evening, stroke his forehead until he fell asleep in her arms. Life, Henry thought as he sat down to eat, had begun anew, in the improved Hog Temple, Texas, and he hoped with all his might his new life wasn't too good to be true.

22
Katherine

Katherine concentrated first on Lilly and then on Hodges. In doing so, she was bombarded with new knowledge, beginning as a light pelting and then relaxing into a steady, uninterrupted flow.

Girl James had been certain it would be Hodges who would come looking for her because Hodges was the one with the power to grab *Them* without being sucked into the rope. But Lilly was the one who would provide the correct invocation, who would summon the power of those more powerful than she to release those sorry trapped souls. Where this new knowledge was coming from Katherine couldn't say, but as new thoughts and ideas arrived, she opened herself up more and more to receive them. The cries of the captured had gotten under her skin. She could still hear their pitiful pleas for mercy, so she put her hands over her ears to block them, to avoid disrupting the flow of all things new and remarkable. She might need this information to help the souls whose cries threatened to break her concentration.

"Find me, Hodges, find me," she said. *If I have to stay this way forever, okay—but at least free the other folks and James James James, too. My James. Help him.*

When she imagined herself as twelve for the remainder of time, she thought about a vampire novel she had read and one of its famous characters, a little girl who became a vampire and stayed that way for eternity. The thought of being a freak for the remainder of time was so disturbing she repeated her call to Hodges with a renewed vigor.

"Find me, Hodges. Find me, so we can free the others," Katherine chanted until it became a prayer, until she was sure he would understand she was sincere. Finally, there was a fierce whir and a series of violent vibrations, and then a great glowing ball of light appeared. Although what hovered in front of her was only a light, she knew Hodges had arrived.

"I'm here," Hodges whispered.

The light grew brighter as Hodges materialized, and then so bright Katherine had to close her eyes for fear of being blinded. After a few seconds she sensed the light beginning to fade, so she opened her eyes just in time to see the shell of flickering white fall away, leaving Hodges standing in front of her.

"Hurry, Hodges," she howled, jumping to her feet. "I don't think I have much time before I'm permanently a kid and those things you call *Them* own me."

The tattoo on Hodges's forearm winked at Katherine and blew her a kiss.

Hodges thumped the tattoo on the nose with his forefinger. It wrinkled its nose and made an indignant sound that sounded something like "Ouch."

"Wow," Katherine said in her childish voice, "I didn't know he could talk."

"He's just learning," Hodges said, looking sternly at his tattoo. "You have a big job ahead of you. The biggest you've ever had."

The tattoo licked his lips.

"What are you going to do?" Katherine asked.

"As soon as Lilly gets here, we're going to go in after *Them*," Hodges said.

"But *Them* have the Jameses," Katherine groaned. She remembered the Jameses saying that they had created lots of trouble for Lilly and Hodges in the past—they had not made friends of them. Even though what had happened was the youngest James's fault to a large degree, she couldn't let the Jameses take all the blame. "This is my fault," Katherine said. "Honest." Before she could plead further with Hodges to forget any grudge she feared he most likely harbored against the Jameses, Lilly appeared. Katherine watched as Lilly and Hodges looked at each other first and then eyed the closed gate.

"Stay here," Lilly said to Katherine, "and stop eating the greens. You'll end up being a baby—eternally—if you eat much more, and Hodges and I have enough problems as it is."

"Yes, ma'am," Katherine said in a grownup voice, grabbing one last handful of greens and stuffing them in her mouth, chewing rapidly, and then gulping them down as if she actually believed Lilly and Hodges would have no idea what she had just done. She felt silly calling Lilly "ma'am" even if she, Katherine, was really sixty-six—which at this point, she reminded herself, she wasn't—until she remembered that Lilly was hundreds of years older. Well, hell, what makes up reality is in question now, so I might as well stop worrying about everything, she thought.

"Hodges, help me out here," Lilly said. Together, they chanted a few words that sounded to Katherine like a nursery rhyme, clapped their hands, and wiped the air as if they were washing something away. In an instant, Katherine was more interested in what Lilly was doing than in eating the rampion.

Instead of dwelling on what she had no control over, she watched Lilly, now engaged in what Katherine assumed was the invocation necessary to make the world right again, waving her hands and mumbling in a soft, rhythmic foreign language. She imitated the sounds she heard coming from Lilly and as she spoke, her body began to vibrate, increasing in vibratory speed as she was filled with a great truth, the truth about herself that she understood was the very thing James James James and his sister had discussed. Her true self broke through the surface of her skin and her old self fell away. Katherine understood her purpose at Sunnyside, exhilarated by her revelation that she was the apex through which all life flowed and through which goodness gathered strength to hold back being consumed by evil. It was only through Katherine realizing who she was that they could win the battle against *Them*. Instantly, she understood that she had been kept secret from Lilly and Hodges, that she was the portal through which all life flowed, through which goodness and evil could be kept in check. Katherine was the Apex through which all beings in every universe connected, good or evil. Her power was so great that her hate had unleashed *Them*, just as her love would help to overpower *Them*. She wanted to tell Lilly and Hodges, but they were too busy to be bothered with a little girl whose ideas had outgrown her body. So she watched Lilly carefully, knowing that she would have to take charge of this dangerous situation.

As Lilly worked, the sky softened, and the clouds swirled and twirled until they formed wisps of cotton-like clumps that changed from white to pink, and then to deep purple and back again, as if they were part of a giant kaleidoscope. Katherine gasped in awe at the changing sky. The gate flew open and a swirling black tornado swept toward them. Katherine threw one hand over her eyes. The raging twister bore down on her. Her mouth filled with mud and her nostrils and lungs filled with hot ash. She was bombarded with the cries of Sunnyside residents begging for freedom. In her mind's eye, she saw the future: James with a giant pair of knitting needles clicking away as he knit a great net around something that resembled a cross between a hyena and deformed human being. Hodges's tattoo sprang from his arm and stood next to James on two feet, half snake, half man, his jaw snapping around featureless beings whose wails both startled her and elicited sorrow. In one swift snap, the tattoo swallowed the net, and the thing within, and settled back on Hodges's arm, hiccupping, and then burping, but at the same time, keeping his jaw clenched.

Abuse, guilt, self-hatred and depression rose from the damaged, disquieted spirits of those dead and alive, dancing and teasing, touching, groping, and inflicting wound upon wound on the souls now leaping for freedom, until Katherine couldn't stand the suffering that pulsated around her another second. *I have to do something*.

"You were born for this moment," a disembodied voice boomed. In that instant, Katherine ballooned with the knowledge that she was leaving behind a life not fully lived, that her regrets had been few because she hadn't taken any risks, she had hidden from real life, and by doing so she had committed a crime against the gift of life and, thus, herself. She decided that she could give herself power, that if she chose, she could do as much as Hodges, his tattoo, and James. She swelled with strength, knowing that while she could do away with *Them*, the thing that powered the universe could turn on her if it chose and erase her from the memory of time. She stepped forward, afraid but committed. She worked alongside James, participating in actions so brave and unimaginable, she told herself she had to be dreaming. They were fighting the greatest evils of every universe in the past, the present, and the future.

They pushed their way toward the end of one universe after another, casting aside the specter of men in crisp uniforms and black boots burning children alive; they passed by men, women, and children left to die in open fields, withering for lack of food; and they marched past female infants tossed into the Yangtze River to drown. Katherine and James worked their way around women bruised and broken by lovers gone mad and men committing cruel and hideous acts against each other, acts too horrific for Katherine to watch to completion. Together, they waded though the sour smell of decaying flesh, burning bodies, starving children, and bloody, disembodied bowels. As they struggled ahead, Katherine, caught up in the sorrow and sadness of the destruction around her, shuddered and retched.

"What you're seeing is the manifestation of hatred," James said as they plowed through a corner of the universe on the way to the ends of what Katherine somehow understood was her concept of time. "It's hatred made tangible as only humanity can imagine it, with the help of *Them*. Your mind will soon refuse to see what they've caused with their meddling, and will conjure up pain-free visions to hide the insanity. Don't be afraid. We're going to clear away some of this ugliness and drive it back where it belongs. Soon what you see will be just plain silly."

As they advanced, a hand appeared from a partially lighted pocket of a world yet to be fully imagined, holding a silver spinning wheel. James snatched it and, with Katherine's help, gathered up what was left of *Them* and spun them into neat, thin threads. Effortlessly, they rolled the remaining *Them* into balls the size of small boulders and stacked them in the shape of a pyramid, as big,

Katherine thought, as the real pyramids she had seen only in photos.

The hand then reappeared with two pairs of silver knitting needles that stretched and breathed, alive with a vibrant energy the likes of which Katherine had never seen. Am I dreaming? she wondered.

"We are in the illusion of the illusion," James whispered in her ear.

Row, row, row your boat, gently down the stream. Merrily, merrily, merrily, life is but a dream, popped into Katherine's head.

"Life is nothing but a dream," James James James yowled. "Always was, always will be. All you have to do is to dream the right dream and hold on."

The knitting needles pulsated in their hands. "Let's get to work," a disembodied voice shouted. A thread from one of the balls jumped onto one of her needles and stitches were cast on.

Soon what you see will be just plain silly, Katherine remembered James James James saying. She felt the needles expressing joy at doing a job they loved. *So this is what James knits at home.*

Once they started knitting, their hands became a blur and their needles clicked so fast Katherine felt as if the needles, or whatever they really were, were extensions of her fingers. In what seemed like moments, they had knit the wriggling, despicable spirits into tangled nets that writhed and twisted in on each other, their influence on humanity no longer all-encompassing but directed primarily against themselves.

With the nets completed and tossed aside, James and Katherine continued their journey, slashing and cutting through oceans of hatred, greed, and terror-filled silences. They parted the way through grief, sorrow, and love withheld. Together, they plowed through torture, hunger, and neglect, knocking them aside until James raised his hand to indicate that they had come to the end of the world—as they knew it.

On the precipice of time and infinite space, Katherine found that Lilly, Hodges and Mr. Tattoo had beaten them there. Together, they tore apart what appeared to Katherine as the seam in a yet another universe, releasing a flood of souls from across time and setting in motion a universal healing that permeated Katherine's being. The newly freed souls, yowling with the relief of freedom, gathered around Katherine, Lilly, and Hodges for protection, and cried while clutching their arms and legs as if they were children afraid of being abandoned.

Girl James and Baby James arrived, exhausted, behind a group of Sunnyside residents, and flew straight to James James James, asking for instructions as to what to do next. Tattoo belched his net full of *Them* through the sufficiently widened tear, launching *Them* into the world beyond, and the three Jameses, along with Hodges and Lilly, took over, working like busy surgeons to close the universe's wound.

As the hot, fetid air escaped the loosened seams being closed, Katherine gasped and then kicked and whipped her arms, grabbing at whatever and whomever she could, but no one seemed to notice what was happening to her. Her lungs gradually filled with a thick, moist sludge, creating a burning sensation throughout her body. Her vision went from clear to speckled gray, until she could no longer see as well as she once had. She was drowning in the foul, viscous atmosphere. As she gasped for air, she came to understand, and gradually embrace, the physicality of dying. As she gave in to death, her arms and legs relaxed and the sensation of sleep gradually swept over her. *This is what drowning feels like. I'm dying. I've completed my job. Done my work. This is what it feels like to die and it's my time. Dying isn't so bad. I can do this ... but ...but I want to say goodbye: just one goodbye. I need to let somebody know I'm leaving. James James James, I'm dying.*

"Yes, Katherine," she heard a voice, deep and far away, answer.

Is that you, James?

"If you want it to be."

I'm dying, James. I have to leave you.

"You're not leaving, Katherine."

I'm not?

"No. You're shedding your old skin. Here. Now take my hand."

Katherine looked for James but couldn't find him, so instead, she reached for Lilly, who was working within arms reach, and Lilly reached back. As their fingertips touched, the now-burning goop flew from her lungs, and the cries of the newly released and frightened souls ceased. The last thing she remembered was the Jameses and their sewing needles, stitching furiously.

When she opened her eyes, she was sixty-six again and back in her apartment, flat on her bed with James James James stretched out next to her, snoring loudly.

Whatever had just happened, Katherine knew one thing for sure: she had not been dreaming—the bed and floor were covered with greens and tiny bits of thread—and, for the first time in her life, she understood who she was and what she had been born to do.

23
Lilly

Hodges and Lilly had imagined the garden into existence so many eons ago that Lilly had forgotten the exact time and day they brought it into being. But one thing was for sure—until now, none of the residents had been able to get there without being led by Hodges. How could they have lived among the humans for so long and still made so many mistakes? Maybe she wasn't the protector she thought she was. The realization stung her. Because of her propensity for poor judgment, she had probably gotten Hodges and herself in deep trouble again, not to mention the unfortunate residents of Sunnyside—the same pitiable folk Hodges and she were charged with protecting.

Lou-Ella had been in the garden just as Lilly had feared. And worse, she had gotten there with help from Baby James. She should be angry with that impulsive imp, but she was angrier with herself. *How did I let Baby James slip past me unnoticed?*

"Forget about Baby James," Hodges said, reading her mind as she knew he might.

"But how—"

"Katherine. It was Katherine," Hodges said. "She's the Apex. A life unlived, a human who ain't susceptible to you, carrying a part of *Them*, and a part of *Them* not susceptible to *Them*, otherwise known as the three Jameses. The way I see it, the Three Jameses exercised free will and that's where they broke from *Them*. Katherine had no original guilt, not to speak of, but she had no great happiness either. Add a drop of the thing from which we were all imagined, and there you have it. Katherine was still raw, still connected to the original source of life. Like other humans, she couldn't spin away to make her own life here, and it was that connection that connected us all and sent every damn thing into a tailspin. She wasn't fully imagined away from the source of life when she was born, away from the original light, so she called us to her, including *Them*. She hated you and loved James, her first real communion with humanity, and it was all that love and hate bubbling up in one person yet to really take on life that attracted all of us. Those two ingredients were enough to spring the door for *Them*. Makes sense to me."

Lilly stared at Hodges. He had never sounded so poetic.

"Katherine," Hodge's tattoo sputtered, "didn't know what she was doing, didn't know —"

"Shush," Hodges ordered.

"But she wasn't supposed to — I mean, we were …"

"You know what they say," Hodges said, pointing above, "Them folks work in mysterious ways." Hodges's tattoo winked and whistled.

"But I thought it was up to us to lead her." Lilly was frustrated. So much had taken place without their permission. *I thought we were supposed to be in control at Sunnyside. Isn't that why were we put there? To support, guide, reveal, and heal?*

"What happened is what was supposed to happen, Lilly. Stop worrying about what is and what isn't. Hell, how were you going to reach Katherine? She had no great need to be forgiven — she's a lot like Miguel and Neely Gill. Her only wrong was the one she did to herself. She didn't fully live the life she was given because she couldn't."

"No wonder Miguel and Mrs. Gill aren't in a coma — the only thing they did wrong was not to live their lives fully. Why didn't I see that earlier?"

"Stop your worrying and let's get back to work," Hodges said to Lilly and to Tattoo, who was now rolling his eyes and puckering up.

"Yes, sir," Lilly answered, humbled by his ability to move on. She was in Hodges's area of expertise now. She looked back on the events as they had unfolded. As Hodges and she approached the foot of the tower, which was throbbing with energy provided by the mounting number of troubled souls held captive within it, darkness, old souls, the past, the present, and future had whipped around them in a threatening frenzy. "Do something," disembodied voices had demanded, and so they had flown into action.

Hodges's tattoo had roared to life and leapt from his arm, grabbing the golden rope with its teeth, tearing it open and snacking on as many of *Them* as he could, and burping loudly afterward.

James James James had sprung forth and, with a great gnashing of teeth and clicking of what might have appeared to the average human to be long knitting needles but were, in actuality, claws, proceeded to weave the heavens into a great net-like container enclosing as many of *Them* as he could, but not all of *Them*.

The heavens raged with *Them's* fury. Hate, fear, and the things most likely to tempt their foes to set them free, swirled and twirled through the universe, spinning around Katherine, James, Lilly, and Hodges. But Lilly and Hodges fought hard, stunning the entities over and over, struggling against the great power thrust outward by *Them,* that battled for the freedom to inflict greater pain and suffering than they already had. And just as Lilly was about to summon the Protectors' collective power to help in the brawl, Katherine flew into the foray, compelled to do one extraordinary thing—the thing she was destined to do. With a violent crash, she spun *Them* into great wisps of what would have looked to the human eye like cotton candy, and clapped her hands until *Them* burst into a billion pieces and could be finally swept into a pile and into James's net.

Finally separated from their prey, thanks to Katherine and James James James, and remanded to darkness, and a universe as yet not fully imagined, *Them* roared in anguish, reminding her as they were cast into the outer world that a piece of *Them* lived in every human being. As the great gash at the end of time was sewn shut to keep *Them* from returning for as long as possible, the tower, the rope, and the garden vanished. Katherine and James vanished and Lilly, Hodges, Baby James, Lou-Ella, and Girl James, who was now an old woman of about ninety, found themselves back at Sunnyside. Lilly, as were the others, was ready for a nap.

"Good boy," Hodges said to Tattoo, who was now looking bloated but satisfied, back in place on Hodges's arm. "You made a snack of a few of *Them* bad boys, didn't you?"

Tattoo nodded sleepily.

"Where are James James James and Katherine?" Girl James asked.

"Resting," Lilly said. "As they should be."

"What time is it?" Girl James asked Hodges in a shaky voice.

"11:58 p.m.," he said, glancing at a nearby clock that told the day and time and then patting her on the shoulder. "We've been gone all day. Look at the clock — it says it's Sunday evening, almost midnight. In a few minutes, it will be Monday."

"Oh," Girl James said, her voice cracking. "I'll be dying soon." Her now white curls straightened themselves, sticking straight out from her head as if deliberately spiked.

"That's right," Lilly said, frowning and touching the ends of Girl James's hair. "You know, this hair of yours could use a little work." She absentmindedly worked her fingers through Girl James's hair and over her head.

"Hair? Who cares about hair? You touched me," she shouted. "Hodges touched me. Didn't you notice? It didn't hurt."

"No, didn't feel pain," Tattoo said from Hodges's arm. "That's all over now. No good deed goes unpunished."

"What are you talking about?" Lilly asked Tattoo, who gave her a weak wink just before falling asleep.

"He's learning how to talk," Hodges apologized. "You can't pay attention to him. He's got no idea what he's saying. I think what he means is because of your good deed, you don't need to be punished anymore."

"Oh, I see," Girl James said, looking closely at Mr. Tattoo, who opened one eye and nodded a sloppy nod. "He looks drunk."

"He must have digested a few too many *Them*," Hodges said, chuckling and then looking over at Baby James.

"This place is awfully quiet," Baby James said, ducking into a nearby room.

"Keep an eye on him, would you, Hodges?" Lilly asked. Girl James may have been redeemed somewhat, but in Lilly's eyes, Baby James had some explaining to do.

There was a loud thud as Girl James hit the floor, an old woman dead from a heart attack, or something equally fatal, but she was smiling. In a few minutes, she would be born again. After an hour, she'd be toddling and talking. Lilly sat down and cradled the body of Girl James in her arms.

Baby James raced into the room. "No one's here. They're all gone. Where'd everybody go?"

"To make room for the next crew," Lilly, Hodges, and Tattoo answered in unison, though Tattoo was talking in his sleep .

"Waa, waa," Girl James cried as a newborn lying in Lilly's lap.

Hodges picked her up and cradled her in his arms.

"Girl baby," Tattoo said, waking, stretching, and then going back to sleep.

"Go foo mimi?" Girl James said, bursting with life, waving her arms and kicking her tiny feet.

"Yes," Lilly answered.

"That's exactly what she means," Hodges said, putting Girl James on the floor and watching her crawl around in circles. He looked across the room. "How about giving me a hand here, Baby James, seeing as how you are the main man, the one damn near solely responsible for creating this mess. You might as well put yourself to work doing something useful."

That's not exactly true, Hodges, Lilly thought. She twisted the earring in her eyebrow, then the one in her lip, and finally, the one in her cheek.

I don't care, Hodges answered telepathically. *The boy has caused us plenty of trouble in the past. He ain't seen nothing yet, anyway. He's got some making up to do for this and more, so don't begrudge me giving him an order or two. Besides, if Baby James ain't careful, he'll find himself with some big lessons to learn, and he'll have to learn 'em the same way as Mr. Tattoo.*

"Yes, sir," Baby James said, heading down the hall after Hodges.

Lilly was tired. She looked at Girl James, now admiring her hair in a nearby mirror.

"No more pain when you touch me, Lilly Beale," Girl James said.

"I hear you," Lilly answered.

"I had one chance to right my wrong," Girl James said still staring at into the mirror. "And am I glad I took it."

You and everybody else, Lilly almost said. So, Girl James had taken the opportunity to do one right thing out of love without knowing the consequences and she had been duly rewarded. No more suffering when touched. *Good for her.*

"Why did it take so long?"

"I don't know," Lilly answered. "Probably because what you had to do didn't require figuring out. You had to do something selfless, without thinking about it. That *is* what you did, didn't you?"

"Yep, I suppose it is," she said.

Yes, Hodges and I are almost done here, Lilly thought, nodding to Girl James, but we have to get back to Katherine.

24
Henry

"Where am I?" Henry asked as he finished off his jalapeño omelet. Everything around him had an unnatural golden glow and every time Isabella or he moved, the movement was followed by a golden trail. *This house and everything in it makes me jumpy.* Henry shoved his plate full of uneaten fried potatoes and tortillas aside.

Isabella smiled and poured him another cup of coffee.

"Where am I? Exactly?" he asked.

"Where are you? Exactly?" Isabella said.

"Exactly," he answered, noticing her voice had a new high to it. She was bursting with energy, and that was unnatural, too.

"Let me think a second. That's a tough question to answer. Where do you think you are?" she asked, dropping onto a chair next to Henry with the coffee pot still in her hand.

"I'm not stupid and I'm certainly not deserving, so I ain't in Heaven. Maybe I'm between worlds."

"Maybe," Isabella said, it seemed to Henry, as if there were nothing on earth to worry about. "More coffee?"

It was only seven in the morning and as far as Henry could tell, she was already dressed and rushing around as if she were ready to head out for a full day of cattle wrangling. "No, thanks," Henry said, lifting his cup. "Got a full one." He was still in his t-shirt and boxers, having been told to relax, to enjoy his life in the new, improved version of Hog Temple, but he wasn't comfortable or relaxed by a long shot. "I want some answers," he snarled.

Isabella got up and put the coffee pot back on the stove. "I'd like to help you, Henry, but I can't because I don't really know myself. All I know is that I've been here a long time and I've seen a lot of folks come and go."

Henry stared at Isabella. He wouldn't have been surprised if monsters appeared, and if pressed for the truth, he'd have said that was exactly what he expected. Any minute now, he thought, this whole business is going to turn in on me. "What's the catch, Bella?"

"You're not angry about Maryluz and Lee, are you?" Isabella asked. "Because you have what you wanted and Lee, well, he has—"

"No. No, I'm not angry, but I'd be a liar if I said I wasn't surprised at old Lee keeping that to himself all these years. You want to know something? I'm a bit ashamed of myself. I saw the way Maryluz damn near jumped from the car into his arms. Why, that girl was kissing him so hard a man couldn't have gotten a breath between them. Nobody, not even you, loved me that much and I never loved anybody, even you, that hard. Makes me wonder what else I missed when I was living in—you know?" Henry was afraid to say the words. He was afraid saying the words "Hog Temple" would land him back at Sunnyside. Better to keep his mouth shut and just think them.

"Does seeing Maryluz with Lee really shame you?" Isabella asked.

"It does, Isabella. I'm sorry to have to say so, but it does."

"But I thought you'd be happy we were finally together," Isabella said, the pep gone from her voice.

"I am happy being here with you, but seeing Maryluz, not seeing Angelina, seeing Lee act like a boy with a new saddle, and with my wife, no less—it's damned disturbing, Isabella, but not the way you'd think. It gives a man pause to think."

Isabella's face twisted in a way Henry had never seen, as if she had drifted off to a foreign land.

"But now I've gone and hurt your feelings and for that, I am sorry."

"Don't be sorry for being honest, Henry," Isabella said, snapping back into the moment. "If there's one place to tell the truth, it's here."

"You think it might be true that the love you get in a lifetime is in proportion to the love you dish out?" Henry asked.

"Don't know," Isabella said.

"Where's Angelina?" Henry asked.

"Waiting, I suspect," Isabella said.

"For what?"

"It's hard to say."

"Seeing as how we're youngsters again, my guess is she's still a twinkle in somebody's eye, right?"

"Could be."

"But when she's born, she won't be mine, will she?" Henry was afraid of the answer to this question; after all, he had loved his daughter as best he could, but now that his daughter was on his mind, he had to admit he hadn't done a good job of loving her, either. She had grown up wild and reckless, probably to get his attention, and her wildness had taken her life. *Oh, God, I'm responsible for my daughter getting killed.* Guilt ripped through him and he thumped his chest with one fist to keep from sobbing.

"I don't know if she'll be yours," Isabella said. "That depends on a few things."

"On what?"

"Can't say for sure. Your job is to figure out what it depends on."

"Is my grandson Samuel going to be born?" Henry asked. He wondered what Samuel was doing today back in the original Hog Temple. He wondered if Samuel wondered what he was doing, or if he even knew Henry had escaped Sunnyside. *That old tub of lard.* Probably Samuel didn't give two shits and a holler what Henry was doing, but for some reason, he missed Sam. "You think folks mourned you when you died?" Henry asked.

"I hope so," Isabella said. "Didn't you?"

"Hell, Bella, I hadn't seen you in years. My heart ached for you the second you sent me packing," Henry said. "I am, once again, ashamed to have to say so, but it's true. I never stopped missing you."

"What's so shameful?" Isabella asked.

"Seeing Maryluz so crazy over Lee and knowing I never loved her, not the way a man should love his wife. I have to ask myself so many things. You know, I never noticed how truly pretty she was until she came flying out of that old piece of junk I gave her to drive." Henry was sweating now, and on top of sweating, he was embarrassed—embarrassed that he had been a fool for a woman he couldn't have back, embarrassed that he punished his wife for not being Isabella. *That is what I did, didn't I? I didn't love her with my heart—not my whole heart. Loving a woman with half a heart is the same as lying to her, isn't it?*

"Henry? Henry?"

Henry looked up. He had drifted off. How long he had been caught up in self-flagellation he couldn't say, but from the look on Isabella's face, he had been gone for some time.

"What's wrong, Henry?"

"Haven't you seen any of your family or your friends here in this place?" he asked, hoping she'd be distracted and not ask him what he had been thinking.

"This is your world, Henry, not mine," Isabella answered. "You called me into your world. Things here in the new, improved Hog Temple are the way you and your friends at Sunnyside wanted them. You got your wish—you'll all eventually get what you want, if you really want what you say you want. That is the whole point of Sunnyside, believe it or not."

"Getting my wish—it ain't permanent, though, is it?" Henry asked. He couldn't say why he felt this way, but he did.

"Only if you don't want it to be," Isabella said. "You've got a nice ranch here, Henry. Why don't you get outside and enjoy it?"

"Why am I here?" Henry asked.

"You tell me. Why *are* you here? I'm the one who should be asking that question."

"Did we want the same things, Isabella? Did we, once upon a time?"

"I think we did, sweetheart," Isabella answered. "But I don't remember. I was dead for a long time, Henry. I'm not sure it's a good idea for me to have been awakened after all this time. But you woke me, Henry Calhoun—you and Lee and the others and I've been waiting, waiting, and waiting. It seems I've been waiting several lifetimes for you to show up."

Her eyes were sad, as if she were waiting for something that was never going to happen, and this made Henry feel worse. *Have I made everyone in my old life unhappy? Why am I here? Would somebody tell me why I'm here? Please?* A neighing horse interrupted Henry's thoughts. He rose from the table and looked out the kitchen window. There was a small spotted pony in a corral and a large chocolate brown stallion prancing in circles in another corral nearby.

"The Petition of Protection is why you're here."

"What are you talking about?" Henry asked, still staring out the window.

"I guess you'd call it a spell. Or a prayer, or an invocation," Isabella said.

"Who would do such a thing? Lee? He's been hiding every other damn thing. Maybe he's some kind of wizard, too."

"Lilly did this for you. Your Hair Princess. She's keeping you safe."

"The Hair Princess? She has something to do with this?"

Isabella laughed, appearing genuinely happy for the moment. "You think she's ... what? A plain old dyed-in-the-wool hairstylist?" Isabella asked.

"Ain't no such thing, Missy," Henry said. "Those girls got a gift that shoots right out of their fingers." He laughed.

"If you only knew," Isabella said, sounding glum again.

"You let the Hair Princess get her hands on your head and then you'll know what I'm talking about," he said, laughing loudly.

"Don't joke about her, Henry. She gave you what you wanted and it's that wanting that's blocking the ugly out. You do believe me, don't you, Henry, when I say she petitioned for you to be cared for and that's one of the reasons you're here?"

"Don't know. From the looks of things around here, anything is possible. Bless the Princess if she's protecting Lee and me, though. Bless her."

A horse whinnied.

"That stallion looks just like Miguel's old horse, the one he called Burrito. And that pony looks just like the one I brought for

Samuel." He turned back to Isabella. "You know that kid never saddled him up? Not once. Didn't get near the thing."

"Why was that, Henry?" Isabella asked, slipping one arm around him.

"Don't know," Henry answered. "I hired Miguel to teach him to ride. I even got the cook to take him out to the corral to pet the damn thing, but he wouldn't go near it."

"You sent the cook out to the corral to help that little child bond with a horse?"

"So? What was wrong with that? I had the ranch to run. Sam could have let Miguel put him on that pony and given him a once-around the corral but he wouldn't, so I sent him back out with the cook. Miguel was the best horseman in Texas and, if you asked me, the best damn horseman on the whole damn continent."

"That doesn't sound like you, Henry. You wouldn't have done that with Angelina."

"Angelina never needed me to coax her onto a pony. She wanted to do everything by herself," Henry said. "She wouldn't have wanted me to hang over her."

"I guess it's tough to figure out what a child wants," Isabella said.

"I never did know what that boy wanted," Henry said, agitated. The memory of Samuel and that pony irritated him, stuck him like a burr caught between the cotton knit of your sock and the soft underside of your foot. "That kid was stubborn from day one, and he turned into a lump of a middle-aged man with nothing on the brain. I mean, *nothing*."

"You sound as if you blame him for what he became," Isabella said.

"A man is responsible for himself," Henry said. "That's all there is to it. A man who doesn't like the way things are going has to get off his rear end and change them. Simple as that."

"Is that right?" Isabella asked.

"That is right," Henry answered. "Right as rain."

"And a little boy, Henry? What if things aren't going his way? What if there's something he doesn't like? How does he change the things he wants changed so he can become the man he wants to become?"

"Oh, hell, Isabella, you know a child can't control what goes on around him." This conversation was getting on his nerves. He and Isabella were about to have their first fight in this new life if they kept talking about Samuel. "It's best we stop talking about the boy," he said, "before we have a spat."

"Come on then, Henry," Isabella said. "Let's go for a ride."

Henry caught his reflection in the window. He had gotten even younger overnight. He was in his early twenties now. "How young am I going to get?" he asked.

"How young do you want to be?" Isabella asked.

"Not as young as Samuel was when I brought him that pony. You know, I took that boy out to the corral, handed him over to Miguel, and watched him have a fit. On my way out, I could hear him screaming after me, 'No, I want *you* to teach me to ride the pony. I want *you*.' I had a ranch to run. I gave him the best I could and that wasn't enough. He was always fussing about something."

"You didn't answer my question, Henry," Isabella said.

"However old I am right this minute will be just fine," Henry said. He looked around the kitchen. The floors were a fine polished wood, the counters were made of a rich blue Mexican tile with a delicate floral print, and the walls were a warm dark orange, the color of a cantaloupe's inside, only darker. A fireplace sat at one end of the room where, Henry imagined, later in the year Isabella and he would sit sipping hot cider and watching the flames light up the dark winters. This kitchen was similar to his old kitchen, only fresher and more sophisticated than his had been.

"You're right, Bella. We should get outside," he said. Sitting at the table in his t-shirt and boxers suddenly made him feel cheesy, unworthy, and stupid. His mother had always said that a decent man never came to the table half-dressed, and he never had, so Henry rose and headed back to the bedroom to get dressed. How about that, Henry thought, even in this Hog Temple, I can still hear my mother's voice. He chuckled, relieved to have the barrage of guilt lifted, even if it turned out to be only for a moment.

"Hurry up, Henry," Isabella called after him. "The horses are waiting."

Horses? What about people? Where are all the people? And Isabella? Is she really Isabella? So far, she hasn't mentioned anyone from her old life except Maryluz, Lee, Samuel, and Miguel, but they're all from my life, too. Now that I think about it, they're all folks close to me, from my inner circle. Henry tried to hide his troubles, but he was sure she'd be able to tell something was gnawing at him slow and steady, the same as mice working their way through a bag of horse feed. There was something slightly off kilter about this Isabella—she was sweet, all right, just as he remembered her—but something about her made him feel as if she were somebody else trying to tell him something. Just what was it she was getting at, though? Maybe she was only being the woman he wanted her to be. After all, she had said that this was all his doing. But if that was the case, why hadn't she come back to him in his youth? Henry sighed. Maybe he would never know the answer. Then again, maybe the answer didn't matter, because they were together now. Maybe he should just go with the flow, as he had heard his grandson Samuel say so many times. Maybe.

Isabella and Henry walked hand-in-hand to the corral where Miguel's old stallion and Samuel's small brown pony waited. The air had a freshness to it that made Henry feel alive in a way he had never experienced. He turned to say something to Isabella but she was crying.

"Something is wrong, Henry," she said, pulling her hand away, becoming translucent. "I'm being called away."

"But where?" Henry tried to grab her, but his hands passed right through her.

"I don't know."

He could see she was frightened and he, in turn, was frightened by her fear.

"Henry, you have to decide something right away," a strange voice said. "I'm afraid by dusk you'll be gone, or Isabella will. You have to decide whether you want to stay or go." As the voice spoke, Isabella became whole again.

"Ordinarily, you wouldn't be told this," the voice said, "but your time is coming to an end sooner than it normally would, so I'm telling you. You can stay here with Isabella or you can go back and make something right—but only one thing. Or you can go back and finish out your life as it stood. But you'll have to take Lee with you. You have to make a decision, and soon."

Take Lee with me? I don't know. Can I do that? Jesus, what am I supposed to do? Ruin Lee's happiness again? "What just happened?" Henry demanded. *To hell with the horses and being outside. The other shoe has dropped. The monsters are on their way.*

"I don't know," Isabella said, shaking.

"Ordinarily, this wouldn't be happening now," the voice said again.

"Do you hear that?" Henry yelled at Isabella.

"Hear what?"

"This is the craziest place I've ever been," Henry shouted, shaking Isabella. "And what are you talking about when you say 'ordinarily'? There's nothing ordinary about this place."

"What are you talking about, Henry?"

"Don't lie to me, Bella. I hear you. Now you hear me. I'm doing what I need to do, whatever it is, and Lee's happiness is not to be fooled with. I was worried you weren't real, and now this. What are you, really? Who are you, really?"

"Isabella. Honest. I'm Isabella, Henry. I swear," she said, wringing her hands.

"But she's not going to be for long," the voice said.

There was a rushing sound. Isabella faded away, and Henry staggered, falling into someone's arms. He felt small and helpless and when he looked up, he was staring into Miguel's troubled face. Henry was no longer himself but Samuel, and in Samuel's body he felt a longing for his grandfather, a wanting so great he burst into tears. As three-year-old Samuel, he needed his grandfather to hold him, to teach him to ride. He was afraid of Miguel's horse and the spotted brown pony with the red saddle that snorted and stomped.

"Your grandfather is doing the best he can for you," Miguel said, giving him a hug and setting him on the ground. "He'll be back soon. Try not to be afraid of the pony. He will be gentle."

But what Henry as Samuel felt was lonely, empty, and abandoned—the kind of sorrow he had felt when as Henry, Isabella had left him to go back to her husband—only this sorrow he felt as Samuel was greater, with no end in sight. His sorrow turned inward. He buried his face in Miguel's shirt and sobbed until Miguel scooped him up in his thick brown arms and carried him back inside, where he deposited Henry on the couch, on which, in Samuel's body, in Samuel's grief, he cried until he fell asleep. Henry, as Sam, slept until Isabella woke him, whereupon he found himself grown and Henry once again.

"Henry," she said in a somber tone, "Get up, honey. Dinner will be ready before long—and dusk is almost here."

"That it is," Henry answered, sitting up, noticing the darkness of the room and the absence of light in the window. He was exhausted and confused. *Was I really Sam? I must have been inside Sam's head. Poor boy. How selfish of me. How cruel I was to him.* He gazed at the rapidly fading daylight.

"Henry," the voice out of nowhere said, "We don't have much time."

"You are right about that," Henry said, running his hand through his hair. "You are sure right about that."

~MONDAY~

25
Katherine

James James James and Katherine sat together on her couch watching TV and knitting. The center was going to be shut down for a few days while it was getting a new coat of paint and Katherine was determined to enjoy her days off and her time with James.

Sunnyside was under new management—James and she were the new owners and Katherine was inundated with delight over their new roles.

"How's that sweater coming? Katherine asked.

"Good, good," he answered, looping a cable holder through a bundle of stitches, clipping it closed, and letting it dangle from the center of the sweater.

"I think mine is going to turn out pretty darn sharp," she said, knitting two and then purling two. "I think I'll keep this one at work so I can throw it on when the AC gets cranked up to chill." She fumbled with her needles for a second and then morphed herself into a twenty-year-old.

"Don't do that," James said, resting his knitting in his lap. "You don't need to change. Really, you don't."

"Young hands help me knit faster," Katherine said, the click of her needles increasing in speed.

"I suppose, but you don't need to be so girlish," he said. "Besides, there's no hurry anyway to finish, if you know what I mean."

"But sometimes it's fun to be twenty," she said, laughing. "And now that I can do the same things as you, it's hard not to have a little fun."

"I love you best the way you were when I first got to know you."

"You mean when I was twelve and stuck in the garden?" She laughed the laugh of a woman of experience. "When I was silly and only wanted to stuff myself with greens?"

"No."

James seemed so serious since they had returned. "Just teasing, James," Katherine answered, morphing back into her sixties. *But why did it take so long for me to recognize that I had wronged myself?*

"You always knew in your heart of hearts," James said. "That's why you decided to come to work here. No accidents, Miss Kitty."

Katherine leaned over a pile of yarn resting between them and gave him a kiss. "Do you think we should rebuild the garden, or come up with something of our own once the new residents get here?" she asked, clicking her needles together a bit more slowly than before.

"Let's do something more creative," James said. "More artistic, more colorful, and more contemporary. We should come up with our own plan of action. Something less prone to the wiles of restless spirits."

"Spirits such as you, Baby, and Girl?"

"Exactly," he said, smirking.

"Good idea," Katherine answered. "Yes, let's." She could now appreciate the way Lilly and Hodges had run the center before James and she were given charge, but things this time would have to be different.

"If there's one thing I understand, it is pesky little devils," James said, returning to his knitting.

None of them, not the Jameses, not Lilly, and not Hodges, could afford for *Them* to regain the kind of foothold they had just had in the universe, although Katherine was sure it was hardly possible for *Them* to finagle their way out of the dark hole in which they had been remanded.

Hodges's tattoo had done some serious work on those vile and slippery entities whose decayed flesh she could still smell. Tattoo had swallowed as many of *Them* whole as he could, and had held them in place until James and she could carve a path through the deepest regions of the other worlds, where only the most dangerous and darkest thoughts resided. Once at their destination, Lilly and Hodges had held any loose dark forces in place while the Three Jameses had torn open the universe so Tattoo could deposit *Them* on the other side. As soon as *Them* had been properly disposed of, the Jameses had whip-stitched the universe shut with such speed that at first Katherine thought she had imagined it, but she soon realized she hadn't. Of course, she was also pretty sure Tattoo hadn't spit all of *Them* out and had snacked on plenty of *Them*, too, though no one had said anything.

The hours with Lilly, Hodges, and the Jameses had been the most exciting time of Katherine's life and she told James as much afterward. Dale Evans, Amelia Earhart, and those karate girls from the movies haven't got a thing on me, Katherine bragged to herself. *I am the goddess of the swift kick in the esoteric ass. That's what I am.* And she was renewed and full of energy, though she had every right to be exhausted. Katherine was living life now, for sure, even if it was from the other side.

Yes, Katherine told herself, coming up with a unique way of assisting the guilt-ridden, the old, and infirm with righting their wrongs and getting a second chance at living the life they had regretted not having lived was an opportunity—a necessity—James and she could not afford to pass up. "Contemporary sounds good, as long as it we don't go off the deep end," Katherine said. James was so creative, too. She was certain that together they could devise a more up-to-date and efficient way of attending to their duties. They could out-do Lilly and Hodges any day. *After all, I am smarter than Lilly.*

"Aht, aht," James scolded her.

"Sorry," she said. "Old habits are hard to break."

"How about some coffee?" Katherine's older sister Mora yelled from the kitchen. "Girl James is almost done making the forgiveness cookies."

"Forgiveness cookies?" James yelled back.

"Yes, it's something totally new. One bite and a person can forgive anything," Mora said from the doorway, as if such a thing was as normal as breathing.

"Is that right, Girl James?" James James James asked.

"Yeah," Girl James replied, standing next to Mora with a cookie in her hand. "I made them from Baby James's recipe. Baby is going to give a test batch to Lilly and Hodges to try out on the folks at the recreation center."

Oh, I get it—that's the way it's supposed to work, but it probably won't with Baby James involved, Katherine thought.

"Uh huh," Girl James agreed.

If those cookies do make a person forgive and forget, folks wanting to suit themselves will be scrambling like flies to a cow pie to get their grubby, greedy hands on those things. I hate thinking ill of folks, but that's the nature of humanity. Bad idea if you ask me, Katherine thought.

"I have a question for you, Girl," Katherine said. "Why did you push Lou-Ella out of the 'rope' with me when you did?"

"Because I was there the night her baby died, but I was dying myself and couldn't save him. By the time I was a grownup again, he was long gone to the other side. When I was trapped with her, I did the only thing I could think of to make up for not saving her baby."

So, you're not the wicked little devil I once thought you were.

"That's between you and me, Kat," Girl said, smacking her lips.

"I asked if anybody wanted coffee," Mora said again before Katherine could respond. "It's freshly brewed."

"Goodness and mercy," Girl James said.

What?

"Goodness and mercy. They're a choice," Girl answered Katherine's thought.

"I'll have some wine," Katherine said to Mora, looking up at Girl James. "A big tall glass of red out of that box of wine on the second shelf in the fridge."

"Whatever you like," Mora said, scooting away.

Katherine watched her sister slip into the kitchen feeling much the same way she had felt as a child when Mora would carry her from one room to another. She felt airy and light, as if she had balloons tied to her arms and legs and might float away any second. The memory of it made her feel safe. *When I was in the garden, James promised me I'd see Mora one more time, but having her here, to help with the center…well, it's…it's…*

"A reward," James said. "Think of it as a reward for a job well done—a job we all trusted you to do as well as you did."

The world is a miraculous place.

"Sometimes it is," James said. "You have no idea."

"Cookies, anyone?" Girl James asked, shoving a tray of chocolate chip cookies under Katherine's nose. "Homemade."

"No cookies, if you don't mind. Thanks, anyway," she answered. *There is no way I am eating anything that little bugger cooked up.*

Girl James made a "humph" sound and sauntered off to the kitchen, her cookies bouncing slightly on the plate. Maybe they really were chocolate chip, but Katherine knew enough now about Girl and Baby James to know better than to trust them, especially when there was no need for them to cook anything—all that was required of any of the Jameses was a quick snap and a flash, and they could have whatever they wanted.

"They swore they'd lay off the fancy tricks," James James James reminded Katherine. "Hodges made them promise."

No, that nasty jaw-snapping tattoo of Hodges's made them.

"That, too," James said, clicking away.

Mora disappeared into the kitchen behind Girl James and returned with a glass of wine, setting it down on an end table next to Katherine, and then retreated to the laundry room where Katherine was sure, from the sound of things, her sister was loading the washer. "I'm going to take care of you the way I should have when you were little," she told Katherine when she burst back to life in Kat's living room

If Katherine had had to swear to it, she would have sworn she saw a mischievous glint in Girl James's eyes when she had said "Uh huh"—the kind that could land a spirit in big trouble. She wondered how Lilly and Hodges would enjoy their latest assignment after they had tested Girl James's cookies—if they were dumb enough to take them. "You have Baby take those test cookies on up to Lilly and Hodges," Katherine said, more suspect than ever that the two of them were up to some old tricks. "You just go on and do that and see where those cookies land you."

"You two had better not be up to any funny business," James James James said, finishing up the front of the sweater he was knitting.

"We're not," Girl James said.

"Lilly and Hodges have been through enough," James said, holding up the now completed front of the sweater he had been working on and showing off the two finely knit cables racing up the front. "We promised them we'd behave."

Katherine nodded and smiled. She ran her fingers over the soft pale blue alpaca, but just as she was about to compliment James on his fine work, a low cackle and the word "cookie" edged their way into her thoughts from somewhere off in the universe. She could have sworn she heard Baby James out there chuckling; she was sure of it. She listened closely. *Yep, that's Baby laughing all right. That confirms it. This forgiveness cookie business is so, so wrong.*

There was more laughter, only now it seemed to come from farther away.

Katherine titled her head and listened, straining to hear.

This time the sound of weak laughter, bordering on hysteria, slipped across the universe, as if Baby had found something so funny he was laughing himself sick.

Katherine rested her knitting on her lap. She looked at James James James, who looked back.

"Baby James," James shouted. "You get back here right now."

There was more explosive laughter from someplace in the heavens.

"Baby just dropped off a batch of cookies with Hodges," Mora shouted from the laundry room, her voice full of happiness, as if there was nothing at all to worry about. "He'll be back shortly."

Oh, no, he won't, thought Katherine.

James James James shook his head. "Not again," he groaned.

A thunderous laugh shook the walls and then there was an ominous silence.

James threw down his knitting and stood up.

Oh, boy, we are in for it now.

26
Lilly

"How long do you plan on keeping him there?" Lilly asked, running a finger over the new tattoo on Hodges's forearm, just under the Jesus-looking tattoo Katherine had long ago named Tattoo.

"As long as it takes, I reckon," Hodges said. "Tattoo is about done with his time and I was needing a replacement. This old boy will do just fine." He ran his finger over the recently applied ink.

Tattoo reached down and thumped the head of a tattoo of a baby in a bonnet sitting in a highchair. The baby scowled and kicked his feet.

"However long it takes him to learn his place," Hodges said.

"He does look cute," Lilly said, tickling the baby under the chin. "You think they'll miss him?"

"I can't see why they would. He's done nothing but cause trouble since day one. With Katherine part of the crew, they're a threesome without him. Truth be known, I do believe James James James, in his heart, will be grateful for the discipline Baby James will get from Tattoo and from taking his place later on." Hodges held his arm up to the light so he could get a good look at Baby James, now transformed into a tattoo, squirming in his tattooed highchair and trying to stand up.

"Oh, look," Lilly said. "He's trying to punch Tattoo."

Tattoo leaned over the words "Jesus ain't Santa Claus" and gave Baby another thump on the forehead.

"He's lucky I don't let Tattoo have a real go at him. I didn't appreciate being turned into a toad with flies for eyes and then having to hop in circles for three hours. I almost got stepped on out there on the lawn. He had me blindly hopping to nowhere."

"It was an accident," a squeaky little voice shouted from Hodges's arm. "I swear it."

"It always is," Hodges shouted back. "That's the trouble with you …you …whatever you are."

"Help, help. Somebody get me out of these diapers—get this bonnet off my head and take me off this hairy arm. Help me, somebody, please," Baby squealed.

"You best behave," Hodges snarled, putting his hand over Baby's mouth, but Lilly could still hear his muffled screams, unintelligible as they were. "It's about time you learned a thing or two about how to act decent," Hodges said firmly. "Human beings behave better than you."

It had taken Lilly over four hours to undo the effect of the so-called forgiveness cookies, but she had done so with no help from anyone. "You know what, Hodges?" she said, "I think my invocation skills are improving."

"Yes, they are," Tattoo said, winking.

"I wasn't talking to you," Lilly said.

Tattoo frowned.

"He's full of himself now that he can talk. Ain't you, Tattoo?" Hodges asked.

Tattoo nodded and returned to tormenting Baby by tying his bonnet tighter and putting a knot in the bow. While the two of them wrestled, Hodges began arranging chairs around the tables set up in the recreation center for Monday night bingo.

"Looks as if this is the place to be," Lilly said, pointing to the eclectic mix of old and young people already lined up at the door. Hodges and she were still twenty minutes from opening, so she guessed they'd have a packed house. Lilly took a skinny pink hair tie out of her pocket and pulled her long blonde hair up into a ponytail.

This time around, Lilly was no longer the young girl with the spiked hair, but a willowy thirty-five, dressed in clean, pressed jeans and a pink blouse dotted with miniature white roses, wearing a tiny gold chain around her throat and a pair of pointy-toed boots with sharp narrow heels. She no longer had her cheek, eyebrow, and lip pierced, but was wearing pale peach lipstick and a matching shade of peach blush on an otherwise unencumbered face. Hodges, on the other hand, still looked like the Hodges he was when he lived in Hog Temple—except that he was no longer dressed as an aide, but was wearing blue jeans, work boots, and an emerald green shirt reading *Ireland Rocks My World*.

"I liked your spiked red hair," Hodges said as they set up the tables, "and your pieced cheek. You seemed more natural back in Hog Temple. For the life of me, I don't understand why you changed it."

"Oh, Hodges, Shakespeare once said, 'All the world's a stage,' and I think he was right. I'm just having a little fun. Besides, the folks in this place need me to look more like somebody they can sit down and have a cup of coffee with. The old folks at Sunnyside were always more understanding of the young, and more patient. Lilly with the red-spiked hair and piercings entertained them, gave them something to chatter about. These folks here, well, they're going to be a tougher crowd than the last one we had."

"Is that right?" Hodges asked, frowning.

"I'm afraid it is."

"Lots of regret?" Hodges asked, slapping his arm.

"Oh, yes," Lilly said.

"Guilt, too?"

"Plenty."

"Opinions on the way things should have been?" he asked.

"Absolutely. Strong ones. The strongest we've seen so far."

Hodges groaned. A yip and yell rose from his arm.

Tattoo and Baby, tangled in a brawl, were beating each other with a renewed fury. Baby had Tattoo by one ear, biting it as hard as he could. Hodges gave his arm a hard whack. The two tattoos parted, having been knocked senseless. They toppled on their sides, hanging onto Hodges's arm in a confused stupor. "How many times do I have to tell you two to stop?" Hodges snarled.

"Heard you," Tattoo said, retreating to his place above the words *Jesus ain't Santa Claus*.

Baby James squirmed in his highchair that hung precariously upside down, threatening to fall off Hodges's forearm. Hodges righted it and went back to talking to Lilly. "How many for bingo tonight, do you think?"

"Two-hundred, give or take twenty," Lilly said.

"You know, Lilly, we haven't lived in a place with this many folks needing to correct themselves in a long, long time. Don't know how easy it'll be to get used to. Too many politicians—they're the toughest to help get right, if you ask me."

"We'll adjust, Hodges, and we'll do a good job."

"But it snows here a lot. Snow ain't my thing. You know I hate the cold."

"Albany is like that, Hodges. All of upstate New York is like that. You'll get used to it," she said. "Besides, I know where you can get twelve coats." Lilly laughed.

"No, thank you," Hodges said. "You can leave those coats right where I left them."

"Who knows, Hodges, you might learn to love the snow. You can go skiing, learn to snowboard, and sit by a fire afterward sipping hot cider. I hear they even have a winter carnival where people ski right down to the bottom of Main Street from in front of the capital." But before she could finish, she noticed that Hodges's knit eyebrows were frozen in place, so she stopped.

Poor Hodges. He must be exhausted from all he's had to deal with over the last few days, she thought. Lilly slid an arm around his waist and together they watched as the bingo staff wheeled in the equipment for the night's game.

A young man in his early twenties passed by, partially hunched over, his scraggly auburn hair sticking out all over his head like a patch of wild grass, his sagging face sprinkled with freckles, his green eyes filled with grief, and his young heart full of sorrow.

"Time to go to work," Hodges said, shaking his head, catching the boy's eye and then smiling.

"Right you are," Lilly answered. "Hey there, young man," she called. "Can I see you for a minute?"

"Yes, ma'am," he said, in a rich Irish accent. He lumbered over to where Hodges and she stood. He was tall and lanky, his arms sinewy, his hands callused, marking him, in Lilly's opinion, as a carpenter.

"I'd like to introduce myself. My name is Lilly Beale. I'm the new hairstylist over on State Street, near the jewelry store. This is my assistant, Hodges. He's a barber."

"A barber?" Hodges said. "So now I'm a barber?"

"That's right," Lilly said, giving Hodges one of her "I'll tell you later" looks. "Here's my card," she said to the boy, handing him a card with "Hair Princess" and her contact information written in deep green letters on a soft crème-colored background.

"Hair Princess?" he asked. "No offense to you, but I never heard of such a thing. Are you really a princess?"

"No offense taken," Lilly said, smiling. "And I am, kind of."

"That's right smart of you," he said, looking at her card a second time. "Nobody's going to forget a girl called the Hair Princess."

"I hope not," Lilly said. "In addition to Monday night bingo, Hodges and I also run the recreation center on the weekends. You know, the basketball games, special events—everything that goes on around here on Saturday and Sunday."

"I'll be seeing you around, then, for sure. Me grandpa does the carpentry work for the church and I help him when I can." He looked around the gym and waved to a couple of elderly men putting bingo cards on a table and then turned back to Lilly and Hodges. "Nice meeting you, ma'am. You, too, Mr. Hodges," the boy said, stuffing the card in his pocket with one hand and sticking out his other hand for Hodges and Lilly to shake. They took turns shaking the boy's hand and as they did, some of the sorrow lifted from his eyes.

"My name is Wiley O'Rourke," he said. "Me and my grandpa just moved here from Ireland."

A tiny disembodied voice squeaked, "Wiley? As in coyote?" and laughed. Hodges and Tattoo thumped Baby on the head.

"Excuse me?" the boy said. "I didn't understand what you just said. I'm not good with these American accents. Not yet, anyways."

"Sorry," Hodges said. "I was wondering if you had any suggestions as to where I might find a good Mexican food place later tonight. We're new in the area, too."

"There's a place over in Troy. Can't remember the name, but it's a good one," he said.

"Listen," Lilly said. "Hodges and I are offering free shampoos and haircuts tomorrow as a way to get to know folks in the neighborhood. Would you like to come by and let me give your hair a going-over? I even brought a hard-to-get shampoo with me for washing my guests' hair, special-made from a little place called Hog Temple, Texas—Betty's Orange Soufflé shampoo. It's guaranteed to change your outlook on life after only one washing. And it won't cost you a dime."

"That would be great," Wiley said, running his hand through his hair.

"How about a forgiveness cookie?" the baby on Hodges's forearm shouted, but his squeaky voice was barely audible.

"What?" Wiley asked.

"Hodges said we'll be serving cookies," Lilly said, glaring at Baby with a look that said if he spoke one more time, she was going to take away his tongue. Baby pressed his lips together so that they formed a straight line across his face.

"Cookies would be nice, but I'm not too big on sweets," Wiley said. "But that's nice of you, just the same."

"Pizza, then?" Lilly asked.

"That would be good," Wiley answered. A large man in overalls shouted to Wiley to get going and to stop talking. "That's me grandpa," he said. "I need to help him set up the spinning bucket—where they put the number balls. Nice meeting you." Wiley trudged off across the gym toward his grandfather, who was now smiling and chatting with another man.

"Think he'll show up tomorrow?" Hodges asked.

"Did you give him a dose?" Lilly asked.

"Sure did."

"So did I."

They looked at each other and smirked. "Then he'll be there," they said at the same time.

"You know, I think I like being a blonde this time, Hodges," Lilly said as they made way their around some tables over to the door, where a group of men and women in their late seventies were lining up.

"You do look nice," Hodges said. "Just takes some getting used to."

"Tell me something. How do you think Katherine and James will do with Sunnyside?" Lilly asked. "It took Katherine a long while to get to the point where she was ready to find out who she was. I'm still a little worried about her."

"She's strong-willed is all, Lilly. You don't need to worry. Katherine and James were made for each other. Look what they did with *Them*. Nope, I don't think we need to worry about any more Hog Temple incidents, Princess. I really don't."

Lilly nodded. Katherine had risen up when she was needed, surprising Hodges and her, even though they knew what she had done was what she had been born to do.

"They'll do all right by us, they will. And don't be worrying; worry is a human trait anyway, though I've always said we're getting more human by the day. Rubs off, you know."

"I think you might have something, Hodges," Lilly said.

"Besides, we've got Mr. Trouble under control, don't we, now?" Hodges said to his forearm, winking at Tattoo and pointing to Baby.

Lilly looked over at Tattoo and gave him a quick wink. "Is that right, Mr. Tattoo? We've got Mr. Trouble under control?"

Baby James pouted in his highchair.

Mr. Tattoo winked back.

The door to the gym opened and bingo players scurried by, trying to beat each other to the best seats, the ones located nearest the callers, the food, and the bathrooms.

A short, stout man with a thick gray beard, accompanying a tiny, round woman with rosy, flushed cheeks, both in their middle seventies, were arguing over where they were going to sit. In a flash, the two were barking at each other as if they were two starving dogs going after the same piece of meat.

"Oh, great heavens," Hodges said, heading towards them.

"I told you we had our work cut out for us here," Lilly called after him.

Hodges waved back at her, shaking his head and walking steadily in the direction of the two, now tugging on the same bingo card. As Hodges got closer, the man tore up the card and hurled pieces across the table.

The woman grabbed another card off the table, ripped it into four large pieces, and tossed them in the air screaming in an Americanized Irish accent, "I should have left ya when I was twenty," and then stomped her feet and kicked her chair.

"Hey, now, folks," Wiley called from across the room.

The couple stopped and turned in the direction of the scraggly carpenter now holding a fiddle and standing next to his grandfather. The old man snatched up a guitar from a case resting at his feet and a man next to him yelled, "Hey, now," rested a fiddle against his shoulder, and the three struck up an old Irish tune, "Take Her in Your Arms," and played as enthusiastically as any group of musicians Lilly had ever heard. The fighting couple's attention was diverted from each other and they turned toward Wiley, from whose mouth flowed a song so lovely, and a voice so warm and deep, that everyone in the room was stunned into silence, even Lilly.

Hodges reached the couple and bowed. He then took the angry chubby woman into his arms and waltzed her out to a clear space, where together they danced as Wiley's grandfather fiddled with increasing enthusiasm. Wiley sang and the would-be bingo players stomped their feet and clapped. After a few minutes, a boy with a banjo joined the fray and the ragged bunch progressed to a lively version of "Eileen Curran."

After a few minutes, the woman's husband cut in and Hodges moved on to a gawky woman in her early thirties, sitting quietly on a bench by herself. Hodges lifted the long-limbed girl to her feet and twirled her out onto the floor to the center of the room. The music grew wilder and wilder, moving rapidly from one traditional Irish foot- stomping tune to another. Wiley's hair shone under the lights and sweat rolled down his face as the intensity of his playing increased. Together Hodges and his new partner danced as if they had no audience, crossing back and forth over the wooden floor as gracefully as if they had been born with music in their bones and their feet already in motion. Strands of the girl's hair, tied back in a messy ponytail, fell loose and bounced against her shoulders as they leapt and tapped and spun toward each other. Soon the two of them were alone in the center of a crowd no longer concerned with who was going to announce numbers or where they were going to sit, but who instead urged them on, calling out in Irish for a jig or a tune they remembered from their childhoods.

Yes, we do have our work cut out for us, Lilly thought, smiling and clapping, and some mighty good work it is. As Henry would say, some mighty good work it is.

27
Henry

Henry sat at the table staring at Isabella. He had never seen such a beautiful girl in his entire life. It would be hard to give her up again, but this was the thing he had to do—wanted to do. Henry knew his decision wouldn't make sense—hell, it didn't make sense on a number of levels—but there was something satisfying, something rewarding in having made the decision he had. He couldn't change the fact that he had never been in love with Maryluz or that he had not been the father he could have been to Angelina, though he had loved her as best he could in his own way. He had one choice, one chance to make something right in the world, and his choice was to go back and raise his grandson, to give the boy the love he had needed, the love Henry had withheld during his preoccupation with horses, cattle, and his obsession with money. He understood now that it was not money that drew him so much as it was his aversion to pain, and so he had driven himself and passed his pain on to a child whose only need was to feel cared for, to be held, to know that his grandfather loved him above all else. He could not, in good conscience, go back and claim Maryluz for himself because of Maryluz and Lee. He had no right to take that away from them, now that they were where they had longed to be. He would go back to the original Hog Temple and do the right thing by his grandson. Henry had committed his share of wrongdoings. Who hadn't? But this was one thing he could make right in the world, and if his grandson sent him off to an assisted-living center in his old age, then so be it. Henry would take his chances. If he wasn't dreaming, if he really had only one choice to make and the opportunity to make things right, then this was his choice, as crazy as he knew it would sound to the woman he was about to leave again.

Isabella smiled sweetly.

"You're going back, aren't you?" the voice said.

Henry nodded his head and sipped his coffee.

"But why? You could stay here with Isabella. You'd be forever young, Henry, and you could finally have the life you wanted," the voice said.

"Oh, it's tempting to stay here, honey," Henry said. "Tempting in so many ways. I know you think me a fool, and perhaps I am, but I can't stay, baby. Don't take it personally."

"Who are you talking to, Henry?"

"Don't you recognize paradise when you see it?" the voice asked.

"To myself, baby."

Isabella nodded and stirred her coffee.

"I'm going back and I'm doing what's right by Samuel," he said to the voice.

"You sure about that?" the voice asked.

"I'm not sure of anything anymore, but I know it's the right thing to do. A man has to live with his conscience. And I don't think I could go on as a young man in this life knowing I had done so much wrong in the last one."

Isabella nodded her head as if Henry were talking to her. Her agreement wasn't wasted on him, either.

She's a smart girl, Henry thought. She'll eventually understand. It's going to be a terrible shame to leave her behind again, but my mind is made up.

"I have to go back to Samuel, Isabella," Henry said, this time talking to her and not the voice. "I can't leave the boy on his own."

"It's the right thing to do, Henry, if you say it is," she said. "But you can change your mind at the last second and stay here with me. The boy is grown, and he has his own life."

"If that's what you call it, Bella. I caused him to choose that life and I have to make it right."

"Are you sure you want to go back?" Isabella asked.

"If you go back, you're going to have to grow old and die because that's the way it is back there. If you stay here with Isabella, you can be young forever," the voice whispered in his ear.

"Forever?" Henry asked. "With Isabella? Forever? Eternity?"

"That's right," the voice said. "Eternity."

"It's mighty tempting to stay here with you, Bella, honey. It surely is," Henry said, trying to ignore the voice, but he knew if he thought about it too long he might succumb to the easy route. No, he couldn't do that. He had made a decision and he knew it was the right one. "Nope, Isabella. I'd be a liar if I said your offer wasn't my dream come true, but I have to say no. I made up my mind to go back and do what I ought to have done, and that's that."

Isabella frowned. "Oh, Henry," she said.

She wasn't happy, but it didn't matter now. Henry couldn't be swayed from his decision. Hers was nothing more than a pinprick of hurt, but his grandson's suffering, if measured, was as wide and deep as the Grand Canyon. He knew that for sure. Why else would the boy have grown into a man obsessed with cats, computers, and numbers? When he died, he wanted Samuel to be able to say, "My grandfather loved me more than anything else." He wanted Samuel to live with someone he loved and who loved him back, instead of surrounding himself with a houseful of animals and computer games designed solely to give him something to do until he died. It didn't take a psychologist to tell him that the boy, grown into a sad, lonely man, was counting the minutes until death finally put him the hell out of his misery.

"I have to do this, Isabella," Henry said. "I have a chance to do the thing that's in my heart to do." He thumped his breastbone with his fist. "And since I only have one choice of wrongs to make right, I'm choosing this one."

"I understand, Henry," she said. "It's just that I had hoped you and me could…well, never mind. My life was what it was back in the old Hog Temple, and it will be fine here. I made my decision and you've made yours. Be well, Henry." She blew him a kiss.

There was a rushing sound and Henry felt as if he were flying backwards. All kinds of people swirled around him—gladiators, soldiers, peasants, old women, young women, men and women aging, being born, dying, cowboys, teachers, Egyptians, Arabs, children, Native Americans, a Chinese princess—and then there was darkness and then the sound of a child saying, "Daddy, Daddy, wake up. It's time to get up."

Henry opened his eyes. He was back on his ranch, or so he thought, but the room seemed unfamiliar. There were paintings on the wall, paintings he had never seen before but paintings he instinctively recognized as his. Even he, no matter how out of it he might be, could recognize his own handiwork. Henry looked at the calendar-clock on the bedside table. It was still the same year, but the boy beside the bed he remembered as his grandson was only around three. "Sam, hop in here with me," Henry heard himself say.

Sam scrambled onto the bed, over Henry, and plopped on the pillow next to him.

Okay, so I'm dreaming, or in a coma. Or maybe Samuel has been made a child again, but if that's so, what good is it for him to be a child if I'm an old man, close to death?

After a few minutes he decided he'd make the best of his situation, whatever it was. "How about if I take you with me today? You can sit on my saddle right in front of me. What do you think?" *What am I saying? I don't even know where I am.*

Samuel threw his chubby brown arms around Henry's neck and gave him a hug. "Okay, Daddy," he said.

Daddy? Is he talking to me? What's going on? "Come on, son, let's get dressed." Henry's body was on automatic. He picked Sam up, got out of bed, and placed him on a chair next to his dresser. He looked in the mirror. Henry was in his twenties, not his eighties. And he was wearing boxers. Boxers with red lips all over them, the kind of boxers a woman gives a man, but he never wears. He looked around the room. There were photos on a nearby wall of what appeared to be family and friends.

"Let's go, Daddy," Samuel shouted, kicking the chair and clapping his hands.

"In a second, son," Henry said, looking closely at the photos. There was one of Lee with his arm around a woman who looked just like Maryluz. Lee was holding a little girl who looked just like Angelina—except for her hair. It was a burnt orange color closer to the color of Lee's hair than that of Maryluz's. There was a photo of what looked like Sam's first birthday party. Standing across the table watching Sam play in his cake was Lou-Ella, without the red face of a drunk, holding her child who once had drowned but who, in this time and place, had not. Hanging right next to the birthday photo was a picture of Miguel and Neely Gill dressed in scuba diving gear on the deck of a boat somewhere off the coast of Mexico, with the words "Feliz Navidad" scrawled across one corner in Miguel's handwriting. As far as Henry could remember, Miguel never went anywhere outside of Hog Temple if he didn't have to, and he sure as hell had never been scuba diving. He didn't even know how to swim. "Well, I'll be damned," Henry said.

"You'll be damned over what?" a woman asked from the doorway.

Henry turned. "Isabella?" he said, dumbfounded.

"What's the matter, Henry? You don't recognize your own wife?" she asked. "Don't tell me you've forgotten my name."

"Your name?"

"Tell Daddy Mommy's name," she said to Samuel. "Daddy must not be feeling well."

"Rosalina," Samuel said, jumping off the chair and running into his mother's arms.

"But..." Henry said.

"Sometimes, Henry Cole Calhoun, a man gets rewarded for doing the right thing, and by doing the right thing he sets the record straight all the way around. " Rosalina, still Isabella in Henry's mind, winked. "And things change. Now, let's go get some breakfast. Your mama has cooked up some grits and cornbread, and I believe your poppa is out at the chicken coop collecting eggs for some omelets. Oh, and don't forget: Lee, Maria, and Angelica are coming over for dinner later."

"Maria? Angelica?"

"Lee's wife and daughter."

Does she mean Maryluz and Angelina? Their names are different, too? At least Lee and Sam's names are the same. There was some relief in knowing Sam was still Sam and Lee was still Lee, although he couldn't have explained why he felt that if asked. Even so, there was almost too much going on for him to get a handle on himself, so there was no way he was going to bother inquiring as to why their names hadn't changed. Maybe what they were called didn't matter, but running the ranch did because it was what kept them housed, clothed, and fed. "But what about the horses? The cattle? The ranch? I can't just up and do nothing."

"Honey, don't you remember anything?" Isabella, who was now Rosalina, asked. "Miguel runs the ranch ever since the two of you became partners—you said you wanted to spend more time painting and more time with Sam and me, and Miguel said he wanted a bigger part in running the operations. He's doing just what you two agreed on. Now, come along, we've got a birthday party to get ready for."

This must be how Rip Van Winkle felt after his long sleep, he thought. "I ..." Henry couldn't remember becoming partners with Miguel, but if anybody had needed a good horseman and honest man for a partner, Miguel was the man. *Whoever I am now, at least I made one good decision.*

"Everything will come back to you soon enough. Just relax," she said, smiling and adjusting Sam on her hip.

There was so much he wanted to know. *Am I dreaming? Am I? What if I am? So what?*

"Did you hear me?" Rosalina asked.

Henry nodded.

"Then come on in the kitchen when you're ready," she said. An excited Sam squirmed against her hip, swung his legs, and sang a nursery school rhyme Henry hadn't heard before.

Henry looked first at his hands and then his feet; he examined his bedroom, and then looked out the window. It was sunny and the sky was an exaggerated turquoise blue; it was the bluest he had ever seen it—so blue it seemed to vibrate with a life of its own. He thought about the activities Isabella, who now called herself Rosalina, had scheduled. He could hardly believe what was happening but whatever it was, it filled him with joy. Henry Calhoun had a new life — a new life, mind you — and this time he wasn't going to be a fool; he could see what was happening for what it was — an opportunity. Henry filled with excitement; he was going to enjoy the afternoon. He was going to get a kick out of seeing Lee, Maryluz, now called Maria, and the child who had once been his daughter. He was going to see them happy. This time around, Henry was going to love with all his heart, and he was going to give Sam and Rosalina what they were due. He would be a better friend to Lee, a real friend to the woman who had once been his wife, and a kind uncle to her child; he would enjoy the rest of his life and appreciate the little things, every last one of them. This time he would do all that he should have done before. He would be as good a person as was humanly possible — at least, he hoped he would. And this, he thought, was all any one human being could wish for, all a person could aspire to. At the end of this life, Henry Cole Calhoun would die with no regrets — of that he was certain — and the same would be true for all the former residents of the Sunnyside Assisted-Living Center — of that he was certain, too.

Epilogue

When I had started reading the novel to James, she had been around eight years old. Now she was an old woman asleep in my lap.

"Let's go, Girl James," I said, waking her.

"Let's go, Angelica Donahue," she answered in a tinny voice, imitating me.

I got her to her feet and helped her to the couch. "You need to lie down someplace comfortable."

"Don't leave me alone," she squawked. "I'm going to die soon and turn into a baby."

"Yes, I know," I said. "Don't worry. I won't leave you." Once she was comfortable on my couch, I pulled my chair over to her side and sat, waiting. We had been through this before.